Perfectly Parvin

Perfectly Parvin

Olivia Abtahi

putnam

G. P. PUTNAM'S SONS

G. P. PUTNAM'S SONS
An imprint of Penguin Random House LLC, New York

Copyright © 2021 by Olivia Abtahi

Visit us online at penguinrandomhouse.com

Library of Congress Cataloging-in-Publication Data
Names: Abtahi, Olivia, author.
Title: Perfectly Parvin / Olivia Abtahi.
Description: New York: G. P. Putnam's Sons, [2021] | Summary: "After being
dumped at the beginning of freshman year, Iranian American Parvin Mohammadi
sets out to win the ultimate date to Homecoming"—Provided by publisher.
Identifiers: LCCN 2020058461 (print) | LCCN 2020058462 (ebook) |
ISBN 9780593109427 (hardcover) | ISBN 9780593109434 (ebook)
Subjects: CYAC: Dating (Social customs)—Fiction. | Individuality—Fiction. |
Friendship—Fiction. | Iranian Americans—Fiction. | Racially mixed people—
Fiction. | High schools—Fiction. | Schools—Fiction.
Classification: LCC PZ7.1.A186 Pe 2021 (print) | LCC PZ7.1.A186 (ebook) |
DDC [Fic]—dc23
LC record available at https://lccn.loc.gov/2020058461
LC ebook record available at https://lccn.loc.gov/2020058462

Manufactured in Canada
ISBN 9780593109427

1 3 5 7 9 10 8 6 4 2

Design by Suki Boynton
Text set in Imprint MT Std

For all the daughters who look
nothing like their mothers.

AUGUST

. . .

THINGS I HAVE GOING FOR ME:

- My BFFs, Ruth and Fabián
- Summer vacation at the beach
- Parents who let me order pizza last night
- An awesome aunt who teaches me how to do my makeup over video chat
- ~~Good grades~~ Decent grades

BUT MOST IMPORTANT:

- A boy who I like . . . and who I think might like me back

Tuesday

THE BEACH
1:00 P.M.

"Wesley!" I ran toward the dunes. The beach was packed with families and rogue sun umbrellas that threatened to hit someone in the wind. Seagulls circled overhead, waiting for someone to drop a stray French fry from their lunch onto the sand. Was it the most romantic spot? Not exactly. But who cared? I'd made friends with a cute boy, and he was waving back at me. "Come on, Wesley—they found it!"

He smiled that shy smile that made his braces sparkle, and I swooned.

"Let's go," he said from across the beach. Wesley was tall and gangly, and he wore cool board shorts with elephants on them. Obviously, I had a massive, massive crush on him.

I ran toward him in my pink bikini. Mom had helped me wax just about every part of my body to be able to wear this thing, and I was abnormally proud of it. If only Wesley knew how much I'd done to look like the rest of the girls here at the beach—the ones who definitely didn't need to worry about shaving their toes. All Iranians came with their own carpets, and half Iranians like me were no exception.

I caught up with him, and we hurried over to one of those guys with a metal detector, the kind they waved around the beach looking for lost wedding rings. He was digging frantically toward something, and more people gathered to see what it was. He kept saying things like "It's a big one!" or "Definitely from a shipwreck!" and swatting away kids who tried to help, saying it was "his discovery."

Too bad he was digging for the fake treasure Wesley had helped me plant last night. The metal he was searching for would barely buy him a soda if he scrapped it for parts, and it was hard to not laugh and potentially spoil the whole thing. Wesley clenched my arm, willing me to be quiet, but I could tell he was struggling to be silent, too. My skin prickled where he touched it.

"I see it," the man cried. "There's gold in there, for sure!" He had on a bucket hat and a big stripe of zinc oxide on his nose. He looked like a demented camp counselor.

Wesley grabbed my hand, his whole body vibrating with quiet chuckles. I'd never held a boy's hand before. It felt nice, though a bit sweaty. Maybe all boys' hands were sweaty?

We watched as the gold digger unearthed a metal box and threw it back up onto the sand. He clambered out of the hole he'd dug. A hush fell over the whole beach, waiting to see what was inside.

The lid creaked open.

"AHHHH!" he screamed. He slammed the lid shut and turned to the huge audience now waiting around the hole. Only, his face was completely blue.

"It sprayed me!" he spluttered. "It's booby-trapped!"

"BA-HA-HA-HA-HA!" I cackled along with the rest of the crowd. I'd rigged the box to squirt ink the second it opened and filled it with rusty tools to set off the metal detector. Wesley and I'd both agreed that since this was our last week at the beach, we had to leave with a spectacular prank. But this was better than anything I could have imagined.

"I can't . . . breathe . . . ," Wesley wheezed next to me, tears streaming down his pale face. His eyelashes were so blond I could barely see them.

The metal detector man tried to wipe the ink away with a beach towel and got sand in his eyes instead. "Whatever's inside must be even more valuable to be protected!" He blinked rapidly as he addressed the group. "We'll need to get the authorities involved!"

I couldn't take it anymore. "THAR SHE BLOWS!" I screamed in a bad pirate accent, bursting into laughter. The man with the metal detector flinched and stumbled, almost tripping over his "treasure." A mother next to us gasped, yanking her child away from me. Clearly, we looked deranged.

I turned to Wesley. "Let's go." We'd be long gone before "the authorities" got here. "Race you!"

We ran toward the ocean, shouting "Yarrr!" and "Avast, mateys!" Wesley held my hand the whole time.

Wednesday

THE BOARDWALK
8:00 P.M.

The next night I led us to the shops by the beach. "Do you want to get some ice cream?"

Wesley nodded. It was our last day together, and I was weirdly quiet, even though I'd spent the whole summer talking his ear off. Wesley was a good listener like that.

We'd met that summer on the beach. I'd spied Wesley

watching me play backgammon a few weeks ago, when Dad had gotten all the other Middle Eastern people vacationing here in on his game. I'd noticed how Wesley's parents were the kind of people who were absurdly proud of their fancy cooler, and how his dad wore a gold college ring on his finger. All their beach towels were monogrammed.

I finally asked Wesley if he wanted to play, and when he said yes, his mom and dad looked terrified and moved their umbrella farther away. Who doesn't like backgammon? Still, he hung out with us anyway.

Wesley was cute and skinny with sandy hair bleached blond by the sun, and his lips seemed permanently chapped from the salt. He didn't talk much, but he was always interested in what I had to say. Whatever I suggested, from ice cream to boogie boarding, he usually said yes. For once, I had a friend at the beach while my BFFs, Ruth and Fabián, were stuck in the DC suburbs.

Though I was secretly hoping Wesley and I could be more than friends.

We got our ice cream cones, walked to the water, and sat down on the cool sand. I shivered in my dress. Wesley wore a nice sweater that brought out the blue in his eyes, and I wondered if he thought my brown eyes were just as beautiful.

"Are you cold?" he asked.

"A little." I took a bite of my freezing cold ice cream.

"Here," he said, putting his arm around me. Whoa. He didn't even pretend to yawn or anything! Friends didn't just sling their arms over each other, did they? Oh, wait. I did that with Ruth and Fabián all the time. Either way, I hoped Wesley would break out of his shy shell and make a move.

After all, starting high school with a boyfriend would be

amazing. Everyone in middle school had already coupled up by the end of spring, and Ruth and Fabián had even turned people down. It was time for me to get a boyfriend of my own, even though nobody from middle school had been interested.

Wesley didn't even have to be my soul mate or anything, just someone who would laugh at my jokes and hold my hand. Knowing someone thought I was cute would probably be the best feeling in the world. But I had no idea. It hadn't happened to me before.

"Are you nervous about school?" I asked, inhaling his sweater's salty, soapy smell. Wesley was from my part of town back near DC and was starting at the same high school as me. He didn't know anyone going to James K. Polk High, since everyone else from his private school would be going on to Sacred Heart High. He said his parents were switching him because it made more "economic sense," but I think that just meant that James K. Polk was cheaper, as in, free. I would have been freaking out about the change, but Wesley didn't talk about it much.

"I'm a little nervous," he admitted. I could feel his arm shaking as he rested it on my shoulder. He leaned into me.

"Yeah?" I breathed. We were really close together now. *C'mon, Wesley!* I signaled with my eyes. *Make a move!*

He gulped. "Yeah."

Just then, my phone buzzed in my pocket. Mom and Dad were probably texting me to come home soon since we had an early drive back to Northern Virginia in the morning. Not now, parents! Couldn't they tell Something was about to happen? I had no idea what that Something was, of course, but it felt important.

"Listen, Parvin," Wesley said suddenly. He pronounced

my name the way it was spelled, even though the proper pronunciation in Farsi was PAR-veen. I'd never bothered correcting him.

"Mm?" I replied. Was he going to ask me to be his girlfriend? Or even better, his date to the fancy Homecoming that Polk High threw every year? Or what if he was just going to tell me his arm had fallen asleep, and yank it back?

But instead of saying anything, he leaned toward me. I realized what was happening just in time and shut my eyes.

His face crashed into mine, the imprint of his braces digging in. I'd never been kissed on the lips before. It felt like eating a melted Popsicle, only with more teeth.

It's happening! my brain kept shouting. *THIS IS REALLY HAPPENING!* Thank god I had gotten my braces off before coming to the beach, otherwise they would have tangled with Wesley's. This was a dream come true.

He pulled away. I wiped my lips. Kissing was messier than I thought.

"I think you're really cool, Parvin," he said.

Finally! A boy liked me! I didn't want to leave the beach and drive home tomorrow. I wanted to stay in this moment forever.

"Thanks, Wesley," I said, not sure what else to say. My bright orange lip gloss was all over his face, and somehow by his right ear. "Er, you're pretty cool, too."

He wrapped a thin arm around me again.

"Will you be my girlfriend?" he asked, his face super serious. Which was hard, considering all the lip glitter shimmering on it.

YES! I fist-pumped in my mind. This night was going

better than I could have imagined. *YOU'RE GONNA START HIGH SCHOOL WITH A BOYFRIEND! HA-HA-HA-HAAA!*

"Sure," I said casually, as if my head wasn't filled with exploding fireworks. "That would be cool."

Wesley grinned. "So, is this our first date?" he asked, inching so close I could see the freckles on his face. I felt like I was seeing a different side of Wesley—someone who was more confident than the boy I'd dragged around the beach all summer.

I laughed. "Is this a normal first date? Is this what people usually do?"

But Wesley just smiled even wider. "Normal is overrated, Parvin." And then he kissed me again, lip gloss and all.

Friday

JAMES K. POLK HIGH ORIENTATION
5:00 P.M.

To say I had anxiety about starting high school was an understatement, but freshman orientation night was supposed to help with that. Right when it felt like we'd gotten the hang of middle school, we were punted off to a building five times its size and made to start all over again.

At least Fabián and Ruth were starting with me, and I'd get to see Wesley after being apart for a couple of days. Just the thought of starting high school with a boyfriend made me giddy. I was a girl with a boy who liked her. That fact alone was enough to get me through tonight.

My phone buzzed with a WhatsApp message from my

aunt in Iran, followed by a picture of flowers. Why did Iranians always message each other bouquets of flowers?

5:05 PM SARA MOHAMMADI:
Good luck at orientation, azizam!
You're gonna be great!

My whole body vibrated with happiness. *Everything was coming up Parvin.*

"So, where's this boyfriend of yours?" Fabián asked, grabbing a seat next to mine in the auditorium. I scanned the crowded theater for Wesley but didn't see him yet. I'd worn my favorite floral T-shirt, and Ameh Sara had helped me with a special silver eyeshadow tutorial earlier today. My outfit was perfect for my Wesley reunion.

"He'll be here."

I'd told Fabián and Ruth everything the second I came home that night from the beach, my lips still tingling. Fabián had kissed plenty of boys and was not impressed. Ruth, however, was in shock that I had somehow landed a kiss at all.

Fabián just chuckled, his brown skin more tanned since the last time I'd seen him. "Remember when you told everyone you had a boyfriend in fifth grade? And it turned out he was a cartoon?"

"He was very lifelike!" I elbowed him, mussing up his perfectly styled outfit. Fabián put a lot of effort into looking sophisticated but also liked to pretend he didn't care.

"Go easy, Fabián," Ruth piped up, her straight black hair in two high buns for her "special occasion" hairdo. Thank you, Ruth. At least someone was a true friend around here. "Let her be delusional if she wants to be."

"Yeah!" I said, sticking my chin out defensively. "Wait . . ."

"Parvin, can you blame us for thinking this guy sounds too good to be true? You do tend to exaggerate." Fabián patted my arm kindly.

"I never exaggerate!" I cried.

Just then, the lights in the auditorium dimmed, and the whole theater fell silent.

"Welcome, freshman class!" a voice called out. Electronic music blasted from the speakers and lights flashed. We watched as a bunch of teachers entered from stage left and began to dance very, *very* badly.

"I think I'm gonna have a seizure." Fabián shuddered as our eyes were massacred by the faculty's terrible (but enthusiastic) dance moves. Then he began streaming it on his phone, for posterity. Teachers waved their arms, inviting us to dance with them as Ruth sank lower into her chair. Nobody joined them.

"WHOOOO!" I shouted, just because I felt a little bad for the grown-ups who were dancing so hard up there. One of them gave a pained smile, like she knew how embarrassing this whole thing was.

"GET IT!" Fabián shouted, still filming from his phone.

The music suddenly stopped, and microphone feedback echoed throughout the auditorium.

"Generation Z? Meet Generation WE!" a man shouted. He wore a brown suit that looked two sizes too small, and had the kind of expression that can only be described as "desperate." He stepped into the spotlight, clutching his chest as he tried to catch his breath, his round baby face so red it looked like a cherry.

"Let's give it up for our amazing teachers!" He gestured toward the staff who'd been awkwardly swaying around him. A teacher took a puff of his inhaler.

"My name's Principal Saulk, and welcome to James K. Polk High School freshman orientation!" he shouted, spittle flying from the patchy beard he was trying to grow. "And here are your student ambassadors who came to share their high school experiences!"

Principal Saulk gestured to a group of students standing on the side of the stage, and one of them quickly grabbed the mic. She wore head-to-toe black and had pale skin and dark purple hair. She looked cool, in a terrifying way.

"High school," she whispered into the microphone, "is a prison."

"Becca!" Principal Saulk shouted. "You're not supposed to be here!" He chased Becca offstage, but not before she bowed to the rest of us.

"That was amazing," Fabián said into his phone. He had shared the performance with his followers, and I could see comments like "BECCA4EVA" and "We love you Fabián!!111" fill his livestream feed as he pointed the camera at the stage. Being a dancing sensation on Instagram meant Fabián had thousands of fans. But I could barely get him to be a fan of believing I had a real, flesh-and-blood boyfriend.

"High school's not *actually* a prison, though, right?" Ruth twitched, looking upset despite her sunny-yellow K-pop T-shirt. "Making high school a prison would be *illegal*, right?"

I shrugged. Middle school hadn't been a prison, per se, but it hadn't been a walk in the park, either. Who knew what high school would be like? My dad had gone to James

K. Polk High decades ago, back when he was fresh off the boat from Iran. His advice was zero percent helpful.

My heart sank as every student ambassador following Becca gushed about high school, almost as if to make up for Becca's warning. I got the feeling Principal Saulk had chosen a very select social group to speak at orientation, full of good-looking seniors who were thriving. He had completely stacked the deck.

Where was the student ambassador who talked about how it was okay to be nervous and sweat too much and accidentally walk into the boys' bathroom like I had before assembly? Because that was the ambassador for me.

Ruth was so excited for orientation she'd drafted a list of questions and kept squirming in her seat, waiting for some kind of Q&A. She'd even brought her own name tag, with custom gold foil that glinted in the auditorium lights, while everyone else used the stickers provided by the school. Meanwhile, Fabián ignored all the speakers and answered questions from his zillion social media fans. I don't think he looked up from his phone once.

"Being a high school freshman can be intimidating, for sure," a guy on the football team was now saying. "But it's, like, so much more chill than middle school, you know?"

No! I wanted to scream. *I don't know! So tell me what I don't know!*

"It's, like, way harder, but also, more relaxed?" he went on. Oh my god. Of all the students they could have chosen for orientation, they went with the vaguest person ever. When were we going to go over the important stuff? Like, when did we have to take the PSATs (and were they optional)? Was showering/being naked in front of my classmates after gym class mandatory? And did the vending machines have Hot Cheetos (and where were the vending machines)?

But most important, where was Wesley? We needed to start plotting our next prank, like swapping all the ketchup dispensers in the cafeteria with hot sauce or something equally romantic. I glanced around at the auditorium full of five hundred kids, hoping to find him.

James K. Polk was so big I wished it showed up on Google Maps. Ruth, Fabián, and I got lost just trying to find the auditorium. I honestly wished my parents were here for once so they could ask embarrassing questions that were secretly helpful. All of Ruth's questions in her binder were about the arts and crafts closet and whether you could use the industrial-size paper shredder in the front office. Her obsession with crafting was out of control, and I hoped she'd keep it together so everyone could assume we were just as popular and cool as the ambassadors onstage. If only for a couple hours, at least.

"And, like, there's a new squat rack in the gym? So. There's that."

"Thank you, Kyle!" Principal Saulk started clapping enthusiastically. I didn't think Kyle was actually done speaking, but then again, Kyle was clearly useless.

Fabián unglued himself from his phone. "Do you think he's why our football team is so bad?"

"All right, everyone, we're going to go ahead and break out into tour groups. Outside the auditorium are student ambassadors in blue and red shirts—please line up next to one. No more than ten people per group, please!" Principal Saulk shouted before shimmying offstage.

"Finally," I groaned.

Ruth whined, clutching her binder. "I didn't get to ask any of my questions!"

"Come on, Parvin," Fabián said, holding out a hand adorned with rings in the shape of snakes and skulls.

And then, out of the corner of my eye, I saw Wesley. His sandy-colored hair had been chopped off in favor of a buzz cut, but he still looked cute, despite his white polo and khakis. That was strange, since he usually wore a T-shirt and jeans. But at least I could finally introduce him to my friends.

"Wesley!" I waved. "Hey!"

Wesley turned around, and I almost swooned then and there. His braces were off (gasp!), and he looked like a completely new person. He gave me a small wave from where he was sitting next to some students I'd never seen before, and I dragged Ruth and Fabián over.

"Hey, Parvin," he stuttered, getting up quickly. He herded me away from the people he'd been hanging with, clearly wanting to have me all to himself.

Gosh, it had only been a couple days since we'd last seen each other, but I'd missed the shy, nervous way Wesley talked. I couldn't stop staring at his braces-free teeth. Just smelling his brand of soap again made my lips tingle from that night at the beach.

"Wesley, these are my friends," I exclaimed proudly. Hah! Now I had proof that Wesley wasn't made up! "Meet *the* Fabián Castor," I began.

"Charmed," Fabián purred, sticking his hand out, palm down, like he was a duke or something. Fabián had high standards for boys, and he didn't hold his hand out to be kissed by just anyone. I could tell he thought Wesley was handsome, too.

Instead of taking Fabián's hand, though, Wesley just stared at the black nail polish and rings Fabián wore. I watched as his eyes tracked up Fabián's frame, noting the motorcycle boots, the frayed black jeans, and the smoky eyeliner. I thought Fabián looked amazing today, but from the way Wesley cringed, maybe I'd been wrong.

"Hi," Wesley squeaked, keeping his hands in his pockets.

"And I'm Ruth Song." She gave a quick wave, trying to gloss over that awkward moment, but Wesley took a step back. Ruth dropped her hand, self-conscious.

What was going on? Why was Wesley acting so weird?

"Wes? Are you feeling okay?"

"These are your friends?" he asked. Then he glanced back to the group he'd been sitting with. They all wore the same kind of Polite Youths outfit Wesley had on and were just as pale as his white polo. I followed his gaze and was met with a wall of frosty looks.

"Do you know her?" one of them called, gesturing to me. He wore a button-down shirt and something my dad called "slacks." He looked like he was preparing to run for senate—or at least student-body president—both of which could be possible here in Northern Virginia. His name tag said **HUDSON**.

"A little bit," Wesley replied. *A little bit?* Hello! You just asked me to be your girlfriend! For some reason this Hudson guy thought Wesley's response was hilarious, because he started laughing coldly at me as he walked over.

"What kind of name is Parvin, anyway?" Hudson read my name tag, pronouncing it Par-vin, and not PAR-veen, like Ruth and Fabián did. What was going on? Why wasn't Wesley sticking up for me? I felt my friends bristle beside me, ready to step in.

Too late. "Don't you have some used cars to sell?" Fabián sneered, gesturing to Hudson's outfit.

"Yeah!" Ruth added, a bit unhelpfully.

But in that moment, I could have kissed them both. Fabián and Ruth were my ride-or-die BFFs. They weren't going to let just anyone make fun of me. After all, making fun of me was *their* job.

Wesley stared uneasily at the floor. Why was he friends with this jerk? And why wasn't he saying anything? I was starting to get annoyed now.

"Let's go over here," he said finally, leading me alone to an empty hallway away from Hudson and his crew. Gone was the happy twinkle in Wesley's eye from whenever he saw me. Now he looked as nervous about high school as I felt, and he kept running his tongue over his braces-free teeth.

"How do you know those guys?" I asked. *And why won't you look at me?* It felt like the second I'd introduced my friends, Wesley had clammed up. Was he intimidated by how awesome they were? Being BFFs with an influencer could be nerve-racking, sure, but Fabián had been on his best behavior just now.

"They go to my church, actually. I didn't know they'd be here until yesterday."

I nodded. I was glad he was starting school with some friends, even if they seemed dumb.

He still wouldn't meet my eye.

"Wes?" I took a step closer, reaching for his hand. But he shoved them both into his pockets.

Fabián and Ruth gave me a sympathetic look from where they waited over by Wesley's church friends. They were probably wondering where the hysterical boyfriend I'd bragged so much about had gone. I'd told them how funny Wesley was, but he was completely different from the boy in front of me.

For someone who had asked me to be his girlfriend a couple days ago, Wesley sure wasn't acting like my boyfriend.

"Listen, Parvin," Wesley started, finally making eye contact. "I've thought about it a lot, and I think it's better if we just stay friends. You're just . . . a little . . ."

My heart stopped. I held my breath, waiting for Wesley to explain the punch line. This had to be a joke, right? Who dumped someone two days after asking them to be their girlfriend?

"Loud," he said finally. He gestured to all of me, as if I could read his mind and understand what that meant.

I gasped. *Loud? Moi?* This had to be another one of Wesley's jokes, like the time we covered the lifeguard chair in body glitter.

"Shiver me timbers, Wes," I snorted, remembering how much he liked my pirate-speak earlier this week. "Good one, Captain!"

But Wesley just shook his head. "It was fine at the beach and all. But things are different now. You're just really . . . um . . ."

He looked at the ceiling tiles, as if he'd find the right word up there. "Too much."

This couldn't be happening. This had to be a prank.

"What does that even mean?" I chuckled, but it was a strained, shaky sound.

He remained silent. I reached for his hand again, but he kept it in his pocket. "We're still on for hanging out after orientation, right?" I pressed. I had already scoped out the school's parking lot, and if I moved each assigned parking space over by one, Principal Saulk wouldn't have a spot to slide his Prius into tomorrow. It was the perfect trick, and I needed Wesley's help since Fabián and Ruth refused to help with my little schemes anymore.

"Ummm," he said uncomfortably.

The laugh I'd been holding back for when he yelled "Just kidding!" died in my throat. Was this really happening? Wesley had never mentioned before that I was "too loud" or "too much" all summer. He had seemed happy enough listening to me explain why mint chocolate chip was the best ice cream flavor, or why I still wore bronzer even though my skin was already pretty bronze.

Wesley just shook his head. "Sorry, Parvin. I don't think you should be my girlfriend anymore."

He walked away, back to his church friends.

And then I died.

• • •

FIVE SECONDS LATER

Oh, look, a comfortable patch of linoleum.

I think I will lie down for a bit.

• • •

HALLWAY
10 MINUTES LATER

Fabián had emptied a bag of Hot Cheetos, and Ruth was using it to resuscitate me.

"Breathe in, breathe out, breathe in . . ."

I tried to make the bag expand and collapse with my breath, but it felt too hard, and the Cheeto dust kept making me cough. Why bother with breathing? Or existing?

I was so upset I was shaking. Tears of fury pricked at the corners of my eyes. How dare he dump me at orientation? How dare he dump me at all?

"Parvin, do you feel any better?" Ruth rubbed my back. "You look like you're going to cry."

"I'm not sad," I insisted. "Just mad."

"I can't believe him." Fabián shook his head. "That guy is a total loser."

He was forming a human shield in front of me and Ruth so I could hyperventilate in peace under the water fountain by the lockers.

"Exactly." I huffed. "I'm way too cool for him. If anything, *I* should have dumped *him*!"

The truth was, I was still in shock. I didn't understand why this was happening or how I could have misread my relationship with Wesley so badly. My head hurt from all the thoughts spiraling around inside it, wondering what I'd done to make him think I was too much for him, and why being loud was such a bad thing in the first place.

Ruth bit her lip. "Maybe he was just nervous about his first day? It's scary starting over."

"So? You can't dump someone for no real reason!" Fabián pointed out.

I nodded mutely. If I opened my mouth, I'd cry. For better or worse, Fabián and Ruth had seen the whole thing. And Hudson and his group probably had, too. Not only had I been dumped, I'd been dumped with an audience.

I moaned, the shame too much to bear.

Fabián exhaled angrily through his nose and whipped out his smartphone. "I'm tempted to sic my Faby-fans on him."

"Just forget about him, P." Ruth gently plucked the smartphone out of Fabián's hands. "He's not worth ruining orientation. Not when you could be asking questions about the school's sewing machine."

I gulped down hot tears in the back of my throat. Today was a disaster.

Just then, a student ambassador came over. He had light brown hair, green eyes, and wore a T-shirt with the Polk "Partisans" mascot on the front, which was a donkey/elephant hybrid. He looked older than us and was even taller than Fabián.

"Do y'all have a group already? Want to join ours?" he asked.

Ruth shoved the Cheeto bag into her skirt pocket before he could see it—a true friend.

"Yessss." Fabián sparkled, fluttering his eyelashes at the student guide, who was, admittedly, pretty cute.

"Hey, are you okay?" the guide asked me. "What's your name?" He held out his hand, helping me up from the sticky floor.

"Um—" I swallowed, not answering the first question. "Parvin Mohammadi. Or Párveen, if you're fancy," I added. Most people pronounced my name with a soft *A* sound, but it was actually a hard *A*, like in *patio*.

He shook my hand. "Cool. My name's Matías, but my friends call me Matty."

"¿Hablas español?" Fabián shot back in Spanish.

"Pues claro, mi cuate." Matty smiled, revealing a row of even white teeth that nearly blinded me.

"Ooof," Fabián breathed next to me, equally stunned. "Please tell me he's gay."

Matty had a nice smile, I guess. I didn't know. Wesley had a nice smile, too. Where was he now? I craned my neck, wondering whether I could see him in another tour group with his stupid friends.

What was it about me that wasn't girlfriend material? Was I really so dreadful to be with? I didn't have much experience with boys. Wesley had been my first kiss, after all. Maybe I was missing something?

Whatever excitement I'd had for this tour had turned into a heavy block of dread in the middle of my stomach. How could Wesley just shrug and walk away from me like that? How could the world still spin on its axis and continue as normal when a boy who'd spent a whole summer with me had cut out my heart?

Was nothing sacred?

"All right," Matty said. "Let's get this tour started!"

We followed him to a couple other freshmen, none of whom had gone to the same middle school as we had, and crowded around our guide. I tried not to sink into a pit of despair. I really just wanted to go home, blast the AC, and grab ten different blankets to wallow in.

Matty clapped his hands. "If you have any questions, just hold them until the end, okay?"

Ruth put her hand down, devastated.

We followed Matty through the halls as he showed us the arts wing, science labs, language arts center, and library. I could feel Ruth practically vibrating with even more questions, but she restrained herself.

As Matty went over stuff like how our classes were scheduled, how lunch period worked, and how to open our lockers, I could feel some of my first-day-of-school jitters shrink a tiny bit. Finally, someone who knew what they were talking about! Fabián had even pulled his nose out of his phone to hear what Matty had to say, and I could see Ruth smile when Matty made a joke about the cafeteria food.

"That's everything!" Matty said after he showed us both gymnasiums and the band room. We were on the football field's bleachers now, all of us sitting below him on the metal slats in the fading light. "Time for questions."

Ruth's hand shot up like a rocket. I prayed she'd ask a cool question.

"Can everyone use the laminator machine in the library? Even freshmen?"

Oh my god.

Instead of cringing like me, Matty laughed.

"Wow, okay, yeah, let's start with that. I've never actually seen the laminator. But I bet if you asked the librarians, they'd let you use it."

Ruth nodded, satisfied. I could feel her gearing up for another question, but Fabián swooped in.

"Is there a Gay-Straight Alliance?" he asked, looking up from the Polk extracurriculars brochure. "I don't see one in here."

Finally, a cool question. Ruth inhaled sharply. She hadn't come out to her family yet, but Fabián had.

"Great question," Matty replied. "I'm actually in GSA myself—we meet twice a month, and it's sponsored by Ms. Kaiser, the band teacher."

"See you there." Fabián winked, fanning himself with the brochure. Ruth made another note in her notebook. Matty looked at me just then, his grin so sincere I felt myself beaming back.

"Did you have a question?" Gosh, his eyes were so bright. And he smiled at everyone, even if they asked a stupid question like Ruth's. Were all sophomores this nice?

I blinked. "I—sorry?" What were we talking about?

Matty laughed, his dimples catching sunlight at just the right angle, reminding me of Wesley's dimples and how they popped up when he smiled. I felt my pulse accelerate. What was I going to do?

"It's okay. If you have any questions, you can always find me in the sophomore hallway, all right?"

I didn't remember what other questions were asked. By now I could feel my heartbeat in my forehead, the beginnings of a headache coming on. Wesley's words rang in my mind, and the phrases *You're too much* and *You're too loud* echoed painfully. I felt ugly and gross, the shame spreading through me despite Fabián assuring me that Wesley was a loser. *You just got rejected by your first boyfriend, Parvin Mohammadi.*

The truth was, I thought Wesley liked me *because* I was loud and too much. Sure, there were older girls who would rather tan themselves on the beach and read magazines, but that didn't look like a lot of fun. The beach was where you dug for sand crabs and ate enough saltwater taffy to get a cavity. Was tanning and silently reading magazines what he wanted all along? If so, he never said anything to me. What changed? And why didn't I get the memo?

The group started breaking up. I hadn't noticed the tour end. Fabián leaned over and whispered kindly, "You look devastated."

"It was nice meeting you, Parvin," Matty said, shaking my hand. Fabián opted to say goodbye with a hug, and Matty just laughed as he squeezed Fabián back.

"Parvin, come on," Ruth whined from below the bleachers. "My mom's driving us home."

I walked down the empty steps in a daze, still remembering how Wesley could barely look me in the eye when he made it clear he didn't want to hang out, much less have anything to do with me.

"You gonna be okay?" Ruth bit her lip.

I wished she hadn't asked. I could feel my throat spasm from holding back a sob. I clenched my jaw and tossed the hair I'd styled perfectly for orientation behind my shoulder.

"I'm fine, Ruth. Dwen jang-a," I repeated in Korean, having picked up the phrase from Ruth and her mom. Being half Iranian meant languages came easily to me.

Ruth frowned. "You just called yourself a soybean."

. . .

HOME
8:00 P.M.

By the time Mrs. Song dropped me off at home, the sun had set, just like my love life.

"How was orientation?" Dad asked. He was putting together dinner at the kitchen counter. By "dinner" I mean a bunch of sliced cheese, lavash, and olives. He made his cheese boards whenever he and Mom had a long day and were too tired to make anything else. It was best if Mom didn't cook at all.

Dad turned around just as tears began to stream down my face. They felt hot and itchy and paired perfectly with my overwhelming sense of humiliation.

"Parvin joonam, what's wrong?" Dad hugged me tight, his bristly mustache tickling my forehead. He smelled like black tea and pumpkin seeds: classic Dad smell. "Daph?" he shouted. "Could you come here?"

Mom raced up from the office in our basement, her blond bun filled with markers and pens. She and Dad owned an advertising studio in the lower floor of the house, where Mom did most of the visuals and Dad wrote the words and copy for each advertisement. Now that we were back from the beach, they were working longer hours.

"I . . . got . . . dumped!" I wailed into Dad's button-down shirt.

"Oh, sweetie," Mom said, embracing us both. "I didn't realize you were dating someone?"

"I mean, we were only together a couple of days . . ." I trailed off. Explaining how you got dumped to your parents was almost as embarrassing as having the Sex Talk.

"Wait, was it that boy you were playing with at the beach? Winston?" Dad asked, his thick eyebrows bunching in concern.

"Wesley." I nodded. Oh no. I could feel more sobs coming on.

"But . . . you're too young to date! How did I not know

you had a boyfriend?" Dad seethed, looking at Mom. "Daphne, did you know?"

Mom threw her hands into the air, shaking her head in response. She peered down at me, her blue eyes turning serious. "Did you go on any dates? Like to the movies and stuff?"

"No, we just hung out at the beach." I looked between the two of them. Oh, crap. They'd never specifically said I couldn't date. But I didn't exactly ask them for permission, either. Was I about to get in trouble? Another drop of shame slid into my belly. I was boyfriendless and probably grounded.

But instead of getting mad, Mom stroked my hair. "Do you want to talk about it?"

"H-he said that I was too loud!"

Dad's face went from seething to bewildered. "He said *what*?" His eyebrows were so big and bushy that he could never have a poker face. Meanwhile, Mom had to fill hers in with something called brow pencil every day.

"That's what he said? And that's why he dumped you?" She asked this at a normal, less ear-splitting volume than Dad.

I remembered the way Wesley had gestured to all of me, as if I were one big problem.

"He said I was 'too much' in general!" I sobbed. "What does that even mean?"

"I'm going to kill him," Dad growled, taking off his nice watch like he was getting ready to punch someone.

Mom put a pale hand over his. "Mahmoud, leave it."

She turned toward me, resting a cool palm against my warm face. "Listen to me. Sometimes people—mostly men—call women 'too loud' when they have a lot of opinions, or they have a lot to say. Guys at work used to call me 'bossy' for the same reasons."

Dad nodded furiously. "Besides, who wants some boring girl who never speaks up?"

This day felt like a bad dream. Freshman orientation was supposed to prepare me for the first day of school. Instead, it had just made me feel a zillion times worse. How could I start high school now? I could barely wrap my head around what Wesley said to me, much less remember my locker combination. I'd gone from angry to sad to confused in the span of two hours. All I felt now was leg-meltingly tired.

"Is it too early to call Ameh Sara?" I asked.

Dad looked at his watch. "She should be up in a few hours. You can call her then."

Mom must have noticed me fading fast. "It's all right, sweetie. Just go upstairs and I'll bring you some food later."

Dad kissed my forehead, brushing my curly baby hairs back. "It's gonna be okay, baba jaan. Go rest."

I nodded and trudged up the stairs to my room, but I could already hear their argument begin.

"Mahmoud, it wasn't like he was taking her out and driving her anywhere, they were just horsing around on the beach!" Mom said.

"Still," Dad growled. "I am going to gut that boy like a fish. Pedar-sag!"

Oh no. He busted out the Farsi. He basically called Wesley a son of a dog, but not in a nice way.

I scurried the rest of the way up the stairs, away from Dad's wrath.

MY ROOM
10:15 P.M.

I staggered onto my bed and checked my phone. Wesley still hadn't called or texted me, which meant this breakup was cemented now. No "just kidding!" could ever take us back to the way things were before.

Being with Wesley had made me feel so good, as if I were this fun, interesting girl because he wanted to be around me. Not only that, but we'd swapped saliva. Like, actual germs! How could you look at someone you traded lip gloss with and dump them only two days later? It had seemed pretty personal and special, but maybe he didn't feel the same way anymore.

I had a lot of things going for me, but getting a boyfriend had seemed like the ultimate triumph. Now that he wasn't mine, it was hard to think about anything else.

I opened my laptop and double-clicked the video chat, dialing my aunt. Ameh Sara's face instantly filled my computer screen, her brown eyes looking a lot like mine, although she had a different nose that looked like her own mom's. Ameh Sara was my dad's half sister, from when Baba Bozorg (aka my grandpa) had decided to move back to Iran after my grandma died, while Dad stayed in the US for college. I hadn't seen Ameh Sara in person since Baba Bozorg's funeral in Iran, almost eight years ago. She'd tried to visit us for my tenth birthday, but she couldn't get a visa. She was going to try to get a visa to see us again this fall.

"What is it, ameh? Is everything okay?" Sara asked.

In Farsi, the language of Iran, *ameh* means "father's sister," like an aunt. Sara was my only ameh, though. You repeated your title back to someone as a sign of affection.

"Ameh," I wailed, "Wesley broke up with me!"

"WHAT?" Ameh Sara cried.

I'd told Ameh Sara everything about me and Wesley this summer, even more than I'd told Ruth and Fabián. She looked as shocked as I felt.

"I know!" I replied. It felt good to see her look as flabbergasted as I was, like I wasn't crazy for being confused.

"I don't understand," Sara began. She spoke with a slight accent, the word *understand* sounding like "under-eh-stand." "But he kissed you! He asked you to be his girlfriend!"

I hung my head. "I know. He dumped me during freshman orientation."

"Did he say why?"

"Yeah," I replied, my voice small. "He said it was because I was too loud."

Ameh gasped. "He tried to silence you?"

Living in Iran meant that Ameh Sara couldn't sing, dance, or be loud in public, or the modesty police would give her a ticket or—worse—drag her off to jail. I forgot she'd probably have a lot of thoughts on me being called too loud.

"I mean, he didn't try to *silence* me," I replied quickly, worried I'd make Sara go on a political rant against people trying to keep women quiet. Our Skype call was, after all, potentially being monitored by the Iranian government on Sara's end, and I didn't want her getting arrested.

"Cheh olaghi!" Sara fumed. *What a donkey*. I could practically see smoke coming through the computer screen. "How many girls in America are as cultured as you? Or wear such interesting makeup and clothing? Many people would die to have your confidence and be . . . what was it again?"

"Loud," I finished for her.

"Yes, loud!" Sara flapped her arms passionately.

My thoughts stuck on what she said earlier. "You think I'm confident?" Nobody had ever called me that before. Obnoxious? Yes. Confident? Not so much.

"Yes, ameh! You're so funny, and you always take initiative. And it was your idea to video chat me, remember? You were six when you set up Skype for us in Iran."

"Yeah?" I swelled with pride. "I forgot about that . . ."

"See? Whatever is going on is Wesley's problem, not yours. When I come visit you at the end of September, we can take your mind off this boy."

I knew talking to Ameh Sara would help. "Thanks, Ameh," I replied, feeling a bit better. "I'm sorry I called you so early."

She waved me away. "It's okay, Parvin joonam. But I need to get ready for class. I'll talk to you later, okay?"

Ameh Sara was in her last year at the University of Tehran, where she was studying graphic design, just like Mom had. Job prospects in Iran weren't great, though. She was going to visit us in the fall, and Mom was going to teach her how to make 3D designs to hopefully give her a leg up for the job hunt. I couldn't wait until she was here.

"I love you, Ameh," I said.

"Love you, too, ameh. It'll be okay." Sara blew me a kiss and hung up, the now-empty computer screen reflecting my puffy eyes.

I inhaled deeply. Yeah, whatever happened, I'd be all right. Who was Wesley to make me doubt myself? I *was* pretty great, after all. Not just anyone could cover themselves in seaweed and scare an entire section of the beach into running away.

Or mentally calculate the seven-and-a-half-hour time difference to Iran every time I wanted to call my aunt.

Ameh Sara was right. Whatever had just happened, it was Wesley's problem, not mine. I was going to be totally fine.

Saturday

FABIÁN'S HOUSE/MANSION
10:00 A.M.-ISH

Who was I fooling? Everything was not fine. If I was so great, then why didn't I have a boyfriend? Why weren't there boys kicking down my door, demanding to be within five feet of me? I thought I felt okay last night, but today I just felt worse, with puffier eyes and the same number of boyfriends I had since Sara's empowering Friday-night Skype call: zero.

We scheduled an emergency BFF meeting. Well, Ruth did. I spent all this morning scrolling through photos of me and Wesley from the beach, wondering where I went wrong. The picture of the two of us buried in the sand as busty mermaids was not helping me feel better. I still wasn't sure what "too loud/much" meant, but I had a feeling sand mermaids were included in its definition.

"Parvin!" Ruth clapped, snapping me out of my downward spiral. "Don't go to the dark place in your head again, okay? We're worried about you."

Fabián handed me a peanut butter cup. "Eat," he demanded.

Fabián's basement was the best meeting spot because his parents were never home. His mom and dad worked fancy jobs at the Mexican embassy, which kept them super busy and meant they got to live in this amazing house. They'd even converted this entire floor into a dance studio for him. That's how Fabián had gotten so many followers: He uploaded videos of the different dance routines he choreographed and performed. He was almost up to a hundred thousand and had been verified on multiple platforms and everything.

My parents, meanwhile, never seemed to leave our house. Having their design studio in the basement meant they were steps away from making sure we didn't eat junk food, even though they rarely remembered to make dinner. Ruth's mom was the best cook, though she was the most terrifying adult I knew. She worked at Georgetown as a professor of data science or something like that. Who gets their eggs frozen before their PhD studies and only considers sperm donors who went to Harvard? Mrs. Song, that's who.

Fabián and Ruth had tried calling last night, but I'd gone straight to bed after talking to Ameh Sara. Only to wake up and realize I was still dumped and dateless.

I didn't just hurt because Wesley had broken up with me—I hurt because I'd lost a friend. Over the summer, Wesley and I had spent every waking moment together, and losing my accomplice stung, too.

"Want to open some of my PR mail?" Fabián suggested, like he was asking a little kid if she wanted to play.

I nodded pitifully. He handed me a sleek black box.

"Oooh, luxury packaging," Ruth noted. She squirreled away the black ribbon from the box to use for one of her crafting projects.

Inside was a pair of sneakers in shiny, metallic fabric. They looked like an oil slick, with a faint rainbow running throughout. I picked up the card.

"'Dear Fabián—Hope this helps with your next routine!'" I read out loud.

Fabián rolled his eyes. "They just want me to wear those sneakers in my next video."

"Tough life." I handed him the shoes.

"Can I keep the box?" Ruth asked. Doubtless she would turn it into another project, like an oven mitt holder or a paper-clip organizer.

"Sure," Fabián said, handing me another box. I opened that one, too, and it was filled with workout clothing. I helped Fabián stack them into a pile.

"Do you want to talk about Wesley?" he asked.

"Fabián!" Ruth scolded him. "She'll talk when she's ready."

Fabián shook his head. "I know, I know. I just wanted to put the offer out there. In case you did."

I folded a pair of purple sweatpants from the box. I was done crying. And not talking about it somehow gave Wesley even more power.

I cleared my throat. "Am I loud?"

Fabián shrugged. "I mean, yeah. But that's why we like you."

"WHAT?" I cried.

"But in a good way," Ruth quickly added. "You make us laugh. And we have fun with you. Why does being loud have to be a bad thing?"

Why *was* it such a bad thing? "Is that what being loud means, though? Having fun and making people laugh?"

"I think it's when you're not afraid to be yourself. You stick up for what you believe in, and you let everyone know it." Ruth chewed a peanut butter cup thoughtfully.

"I just thought being loud meant you had too many opinions and stuff. Like you were obnoxious, or immature," I said, remembering what my mom had told me last night.

"Then that means *all* boys are loud." Fabián put another box in my lap.

"According to the dictionary, *loud* means 'strongly audible; blatant, or noisy; conspicuous, ostentatious, or garish,'" Ruth read from her phone. "'Antonyms: quiet, shy, restrained.'"

"Garish?" I spat. "As in . . . 'to gare'?" I wasn't totally sure what the word meant, but it couldn't be good. Nobody said anything.

I opened Fabián's other PR box. Inside was a Mexican flag, a bottle of tamarind Jarritos, a pack of Abuelita hot chocolate, and a single flip-flop. I checked the note—it seemed to be fan mail.

"Do you think they know I'm Mexican?" Fabián asked sarcastically.

Ruth silently dragged the flip-flop over to her pile. Lord knows what she was planning to do with it.

"But don't you think it's strange?" I pressed on. "I've never had a boyfriend until Wesley. Fabián—you've had, like, twelve. And Ruth gets valentines every year from random emo boys who are obsessed with her!"

"That's just because I make valentines for the whole school," Ruth insisted.

"What are you saying?" Fabián looked up.

"That maybe there's some truth to what Wesley told me. Maybe I *am* too noisy or too much when it comes to getting a boyfriend. Otherwise I would have had a million dates by now, right?"

Fabián went quiet. He and Ruth exchanged a nervous glance. What weren't they telling me?

"The thing is, Parvin"—Ruth fiddled with the black ribbon—"some people at school *do* think you can be a little . . . um . . . passionate."

I gasped. *Passionate?* How dare they! Passionate hadn't seemed to be a bad thing, but now, knowing people thought it behind my back, it definitely was.

"But that just means you need to wait for someone who sees how great that is. You can't be upset because one person can't handle your amazingness."

"So, let me get this straight: The whole school thinks I'm this passionate person who doesn't shut up and is probably really annoying and obnoxious? And nobody thought to tell me?"

"Parvin, that's not what we're saying," Fabián objected.

But I barely heard him. Who cared if my friends and family liked my "amazingness"? If potential boyfriends didn't, then what was the point? What Wesley told me yesterday was right: I *was* too much. I was noisy, definitely "blatant," and (I checked my leopard-print jumpsuit) 100 percent ostentatious. I was Parvin "Loud" Mohammadi. It seemed like everyone knew it but me.

Someone's phone buzzed, but I was too busy having my realization to care.

"Oh my gosh," Ruth wheezed as she checked her phone. She stared at it like she'd seen a ghost.

"What is it?" Fabián asked.

"Gah!" Suddenly, she threw her phone to the other side of the room, as if she'd seen a big spider on it. It bounced away in its giant glitter case. I jerked out of my shame spiral.

"Ruth, what is wrong with you?" Fabián demanded.

"N-nothing," Ruth stuttered. "Absolutely nothing is wrong."

Fabián narrowed his eyes, staring between Ruth and her far-flung phone. He scurried toward it, flipped it over, and gasped even louder than Ruth did.

"What? What?" I exclaimed.

The blood had drained out of Fabián's face. "Just a white person wearing a sombrero. It was offensive, so I gasped," he replied too quickly to be believable.

"Fabián," I growled. "Show me the phone."

"Fabián, don't—!" Ruth shouted.

With a sigh, Fabián handed it over. And there, at the top of the #JamesKPolkHigh photo feed, was Wesley holding hands with a girl who looked vaguely familiar. **HOMECOMING DATE!** the caption read, followed by a bunch of heart emojis.

"WHAT?" I screamed, throwing Fabián's new shoes across the room. "We're broken up for less than twenty-four hours and he gets a new girlfriend?" Ever since that kiss, I'd been hoping I would be his Homecoming date, even if yesterday had quickly deflated that dream. Besides, Homecoming wasn't until the beginning of October. Who had dates lined up already?

"I told you," Ruth shot at Fabián. "She's in a fragile state."

I zoomed in on the photo and realized the girl was one of Wesley's church friends from orientation who'd been completely quiet as Hudson made fun of my name. To top it off, she had the smallest, daintiest nose I'd ever seen—the complete opposite of the massive one I'd inherited from my dad.

"She's so pale they look related," Ruth said in awe, staring at the photo of her and Wesley in matching polos.

"They're definitely having a plantation wedding," Fabián said.

I clicked into her account, "Teighan_23," and instantly wished I hadn't. Her entire feed was perfectly curated, from photos of her with her friends to staged shots of her notebook and sunglasses collection.

"At least her brand is consistent," Fabián observed.

"Oooh, look at her flower arrangements!" Ruth squealed.

"HELLO?" I howled, hurling Ruth's phone into a PR box. "Whose side are you on?"

I thought I'd been done with the crying portion of this breakup, but it felt like a new pipe had burst. How could Wesley get over me so quickly? Was I that forgettable? Or had Wesley been so repulsed by me that he'd gone running into the arms of this other girl?

"Want to open another box, P?" Fabián asked, handing me a sparkly one with Fabián's name embossed on top. "I think this one has Hot Cheetos in it," he added, trying make me feel better.

This was an actual nightmare. I'd been dumped for a girl who was tall and hairless and knew how to take the perfect selfie. Basically, she was everything I was not.

I guess this was the kind of quiet, non-loud girl Wesley wanted in the end.

"I just want to go home." *And sob into my pillow.*

"Want me to walk you?" Ruth asked. I shook my head, half-heartedly eating a Cheeto. We were supposed to help Fabián film a new dance routine so he'd have better camera angles than what he could get by just sticking his phone on a tripod. Ruth needed to stay and help, seeing as how I was useless. I'd swing by tomorrow when I felt better. Now that I was in high school, I didn't have to go to the Farsi school my parents used to force me to attend anymore, which meant my Sundays were wide open.

"I just need to be by myself for a little bit." I tried hard to smile but failed.

Ruth put a couple peanut butter cups into my pocket. "Just in case," she whispered.

. . .

KICKED OUT OF MY OWN HOUSE
5:00 P.M.

My phone buzzed as I sulked around my neighborhood.

5:32 PM FABIÁN: parvin, how long are you going to mope for? it was just one kiss. it wasn't like . . . a real relationship

5:33 PM RUTH: Let her mourn, Fabián! Remember how sad you were when the dance team lost nationals last year?

5:33 PM FABIÁN: ok, fine—you get one more day of mourning parvin!

5:40 PM PARVIN: So generous, Fabián. So kind.

I put my phone away in the blinding afternoon sunlight and put on my headphones. Mom had forced me out of the house, saying she needed to fumigate my room for cockroaches because of all the food I had left in my bed. She could be so dramatic sometimes.

I walked past the old church in our neighborhood and through the park where the vines were so thick you couldn't tell where one tree ended and another began. I'd been holed up with my air conditioner all day after Fabián's and had forgotten how humidity made going for a walk feel like swimming in warm soup. My curly hair had probably frizzed out into oblivion, but who cared? Nobody was going to see me, and nobody was ever going to think of me as pretty or worth dating again. Better to begin my life as an old crone now.

There was nothing to do about the Wesley situation that could make me feel better. I had Fabián and Ruth, didn't I? As long as I had my friends, I would be okay. Fabián was spending the rest of today editing the dance routine they'd filmed this morning, while Ruth finished prepping her freshman-year memory book. Life was moving on without Wesley. I guess it was time for me to move on, too.

I kicked a rock and turned onto a street where everyone was barbecuing for Labor Day weekend. I smelled burgers and hot dogs cooking from almost every house on the block, and some of them even had slip-and-slides out front. Dad loved to grill Iranian kabobs but had been too busy this year to go to the halal grocer and get the ingredients. We were just going to order in again tonight.

"Parvin?" a voice called out. I took my headphones off and turned around. When I saw who was talking to me, I almost passed out.

There, in the middle of the sidewalk, was Wesley. And he wasn't alone.

"Oh . . . um . . . hi," I squeaked. What was he doing here? He lived on the other side of the beltway, in one of those neighborhoods that had been randomly glommed onto our school district. His cute dimples were out in full force, but he wore another boring polo/khaki combination. Worse, his new girlfriend, Teighan, was with him. How could this be happening?

"I didn't know you lived around here," Wesley said. No *Hi, Parvin, how are you doing since I broke your heart yesterday?*

"Yep," I replied, trying not to cry. "I'm a couple blocks over."

"Wesley, my parents said lunch is ready." Teighan tugged Wesley toward a house with a bunch of SUVs and the old DC football flag. She completely ignored me.

"Oh, sorry, Parvin, this is Teighan. My . . . uh . . . ," Wesley started, trying to introduce us—as if I hadn't stalked her online all night.

"Girlfriend," Teighan announced.

Welp. Time to leave before my soul exits my body. I started to retreat, ready to flop back onto my fumigated bed and live there from now on. Running into an ex-boyfriend was mortifying. But running into him with his new girl-friend was an entirely different circle of the underworld.

Then, a man came out of Teighan's house, clicking bar-becue tongs. It looked like they were having a big party.

"Hey, Wes—who's that?" he asked.

"Hey, Dad, this is my friend Parvin." Did his dad not recognize me from the beach? His parents had spent enough time avoiding eye contact with me; you'd think he'd recognize me. This was a new low. I could see a flush start to creep up Wesley's face. It made me glad that he was just as uncomfort-able as I was.

"Huh," his dad said, frowning at me. "Just making sure you knew each other."

He walked back inside. Well, that was bizarre. Most parents would have insisted I join them for burgers or something, not make sure I wasn't selling their children drugs in a cul-de-sac.

"Sorry about that," Wesley said, looking practically sunburned he was blushing so hard. "My dad can be overprotective sometimes."

"Overprotective?" I asked. I was a fourteen-year-old girl. Why did he feel the need to protect his son from me?

"Our parents go to church together," Teighan said, giving me a fake smile that didn't reach her eyes. "When Wesley asked me to Homecoming, they were sooo excited."

Why was I standing here? Why couldn't I make up some excuse to leave this conversation?

"Are *you* going to Homecoming?" she asked, smiling that horrible smile. Was she grinning because she knew Wesley and I had kissed, and she was trying to make me feel terrible? Or did she not even know Wesley and I had gone out? Was this what non-loud people did—ask embarrassing questions with a smile pasted to their face? For someone who had just been dumped for being too much, I couldn't help but notice that Teighan was definitely too much in her own way.

Wesley waited for my answer, though he knew I didn't have a Homecoming date and probably wouldn't go. But I couldn't tell them that, could I? Then I would melt into a puddle of shame and slip into a storm sewer.

Before I knew what was happening, my mouth opened without my permission.

"Yeah, actually," I replied. "My date and I are sooo excited." What was I saying? If I looked into my date jar there would be zero dates inside it.

Wesley balked. "Really?" he asked. "You already found someone?"

"What do you mean 'already'?" Teighan turned toward him, her long blond hair flying into my face. "Wait, how do you two know each other again?"

Busted. Wesley clearly hadn't told her anything about us. That coward. Still, that meant Teighan hadn't heard me get dumped yesterday, and for that I was grateful.

"Oh, um, from around. Does he go to Polk?" Wesley deflected, trying to sound casual as his voice cracked. I hated how he assumed I was taking a boy to the dance. What if I wanted to take a friend, since I probably wouldn't get asked? Or maybe I was pansexual, like Ruth, and planned on taking a girl or nonbinary person? How dare he define me! Even though I was, unfortunately, straight.

"You'll see them soon enough." I shrugged, ignoring Wesley's shocked face. I got out my phone, even though no one had texted me. "Well, looks like I gotta go help my mom with a social media campaign for one of her clients." I sighed, as if it was a huge imposition.

That was also a lie—Mom worked on social media campaigns, but there was no way she'd let me crash into her Photoshop files and help her with one. But after combing through Teighan's feeds, I knew it was just the thing to say to impress her.

"Oh, wow." Her frosty smile momentarily melted. "That's, like, my dream job."

Wesley didn't say anything. He just stared right at me, clearly hurt. And guess what? It felt really, really good to be the one causing pain for once.

"Wesley! Teighan! Your burgers are ready," a voice called out from Teighan's house.

"See ya later." I smiled back. This conversation wasn't a competition, but I'd definitely won.

Wesley just grunted. "I guess I'll see you at school, Parvin."

"I guess so, Wesley," I said right back. *Nice one, Parvin.*

And then I walked away, noticing how all the cars parked in Teighan's driveway had square red stickers on them, telling us to Make America Great Again.

"Who's your friend?" I overheard someone ask as I walked away from the barbecue.

"No one," Wesley replied.

. . .

HASTY RETREAT
6:05 P.M.

EMERGENCY! I texted Ruth and Fabián. CODE RED. 911.

6:07 PM FABIÁN: what? what is it?

6:08 PM RUTH: Did you eat too much dairy again?

6:08 PM PARVIN: I just ran into Wesley and his new girlfriend! And . . . I told them I already had a date to Homecoming!

6:08 PM FABIÁN: yOU WhAT?

6:08 PM RUTH: ☹ Why would you do that?

6:09 PM PARVIN: I don't know! I panicked!

6:09 PM FABIÁN: now you have to get a date, you fool!

6:10 PM RUTH: But who'll go with her?

Why did I say I had a date to Homecoming? Could Wesley tell I was lying? He seemed pretty upset, though.

Homecoming at Polk was a real step up from the sad Fall Ball we had in middle school, where the gym was decorated with a maximum of two streamers and there were no slow songs so as to discourage any "close proximity." I'd spent most of our middle school functions next to the soda table, watching Fabián dance so well that circles formed around him while shy boys asked Ruth if she wanted to dance.

But still—this lie would seriously backfire if I didn't show up to Homecoming with someone impressive. Someone cool, who would make Wesley feel like dumping me was a mistake. I needed a date to prove I was different from Middle School Parvin, and that I could wake up in the morning and have that amazing feeling again—the feeling of knowing someone liked me.

I walked home in a daze. How could I find someone like that? And even more important, how could I con them into being my date? Because chances were someone that awesome would want nothing to do with me. I thought I had lucked out with Wesley because he liked me just the way I was, but the second he got to school, it was like he was embarrassed to be seen with me. Something about me was just too much for public consumption. If I wanted a date who didn't dump me the second we were in front of his friends, I'd need to have a serious personality change.

But what should I change it to?

By the time I got home, I still had no clue.

Clearly, I needed a plan.

MY HOUSE
8:00 P.M.

Emergency sleepover. Tonight, Ruth and I were going to paint our nails and basically apply everything from my bathroom onto our bodies at the same time while hopefully brainstorming ways to get me a Homecoming date.

Ruth also suggested we watch some of our favorite movies to cheer me up. I'll try anything at this point. She queued up *The Little Mermaid*, *The Princess Bride*, and *My Big Fat Greek Wedding*. She even brought over sheet masks for us to swap out between films, and Mom and Dad actually provided sustenance in the form of takeout kabob, complete with crunchy rice and Iranian desserts. We were getting our Labor Day BBQ after all.

Before I started the first movie, I called Fabián, just to see if he was still busy.

"Parvin, just because I'm gay doesn't mean I want to come to girls' night. I'm still a dude," he explained patiently to me.

"It's not girls' night, Fabián. It's just a movie night to help me feel better, because I am in the throes of heartbreak. So, you don't want to watch films and eat kabob with us?"

"Yes," Fabián explained. "Exactly."

"Or do face masks," I confirmed.

"Wait." He paused.

"Yes?"

"Are they Korean face masks? The fancy ones?"

"Yep."

"Give me ten minutes."

I knew it.

· · ·

MY ROOM
10:00 P.M.

We have consumed three orders of chelo kabob, a Styrofoam thingie of baklava, and an entire packet of Swedish Fish. Fabián nursed a cup of black tea my dad made him, sipping it with his pinkie up like an adult. Who *was* he even?

Ruth moaned, clutching her stomach. She didn't know that the secret to eating kabob was not to fill up too much on rice, but now her stomach was stuffed beyond reason. I couldn't blame her, though—it was sneaky rice, filled with sour cherries and pistachios, and too delicious not to eat. Meanwhile, Fabián inhaled a handful of peanut butter cups and reached for more. Where did it go? He was thin as a rail and could probably win one of those eating competitions and then grab a milkshake on the way home.

I adjusted my sheet mask, my first one of the night. It was already drying out. "Should I use a peach one afterward? Or one that smells like coconut?"

"You should use the peach one," Fabián explained. "It promotes elasticity." Whatever that was. I put on the new mask and cuddled up next to him.

"Get your own blanket," he said, snatching it back.

I cuddled up next to Ruth instead. "Ruthie, are you okay?"

She nodded meekly, taking a sip of water.

I tried rubbing her tummy but she batted my arm away. She must have hit a food coma.

We were getting near the end of *The Little Mermaid*, one of Ruth's favorite animated movies. She used to dress up as Ariel every year for Halloween and comb her hair with a fork and everything.

When the movie finished, I pressed play on *The Princess Bride*. We watched as Buttercup ordered Farm Boy around in what was the weirdest kind of flirting ever.

"Hey, isn't Farm Boy's name Wesley?" Ruth asked.

"It's *Westley*," Fabián corrected.

My body froze up. Just the mention of Wesley's name made me clammy all over again. I could feel the memory of him from that night at the beach dragging me under like dark waves. The glint of his braces loomed closer, leaning in for a kiss. I could practically taste the orange lip gloss I'd worn.

"Parvin? Parvin?" Ruth was shaking me. I resurfaced, blinking back through my sheet mask.

"Are you okay?" she asked, looking worried.

I had almost forgotten where I was. Fabián was staring at me, equally concerned.

She handed me a peanut butter cup. "I'm sorry I brought him up."

"He really did a number on you, didn't he?" Fabián asked, giving me some of his blanket.

"He was my first kiss," I whimpered.

Fabián rubbed my shoulder. "I'm sorry, P. Boys suck." He sighed, taking another dignified sip of tea.

"Let's just watch the movie," I said, and smiled, trying hard not to dissolve into tears.

I swallowed the lump in my throat as Ruth pressed play, ready to get sucked back into the story of pirates, deadly eels, and adventure. Like *The Little Mermaid*, the leading lady in *The Princess Bride* rarely had proper conversations with her true love. Neither of the women actually *did* anything. They simply stared longingly and smiled as they waltzed away into the sunset.

"THAT'S IT!" I shouted, upsetting a bowl of popcorn as I stood up. Fabián yelled. Ruth groaned and rolled away from me, her stomach still too full for her to flinch.

"What is it?" Fabián asked, picking popcorn out of his slicked-back hair.

"All of the women in these movies, they're all the same!" I exclaimed, getting excited.

"You mean they're white?" Fabián asked.

"No, yes, no, I mean—they all act the same. They're all really coy and quiet, and they let guys make the first move and end up with them," I said, like, *duh*. "They are the exact opposite of loud."

Ruth sat up with some effort. "How do you mean?"

"Check it out." I pointed to the different streaming thumbnails from the queue we'd made on my laptop.

"*The Little Mermaid* signs away her voice in exchange for legs, so she doesn't talk *at all*. *My Big Fat Greek Wedding*? Doesn't he just see her through a travel agent window after her makeover, where she got an eyebrow wax and a blowout? And then *The Princess Bride* . . . I mean . . ."

Ruth nods. "All Buttercup does is act pretty. She doesn't really say anything."

"Like *Aladdin*!" Fabián shouts. "Remember how worthless Jasmine was in the original?"

"Exactly! Thank you." I jumped onto my bed. I had finally cracked the code for why I'd never had a boyfriend before, and why the one I did have had dumped me so quickly. How could I become one of those mysterious, alluring female protagonists while talking all the time? Clearly, I was too chatty for a love story of my own.

"I need to speak less," I diagnosed. "I have to become one of those mousey, quiet girls who only laughs and smiles." After flailing around for hours, I had finally figured out what "loud" meant, and it was the reverse of these leading ladies.

"Straight people are so weird," Fabián whispered, clearly in awe of my brilliance.

"Agreed." Ruth shook her head. "But, Parvin, even if that is how girls get the guy, would you want to date someone who's into that?"

I flopped back onto my bed. "Yeah," I said out loud to my ceiling. "I would."

"How could you even pull it off?" Fabián asked. "You gasp every time you get a text message. And yesterday you screamed like a fangirl for the entire faculty at their orientation dance."

"They needed encouragement."

Fabián pursed his lips and said nothing. Ruth continued holding her belly and grimacing in the corner.

"Clearly I am undateable in my current form. So how do I change that?"

"Umm, you don't?" he replied.

"Easy for you to say!" I pointed accusingly. "You get asked out all the time. You've already had half a dozen boyfriends."

Fabián shrugged. "Because I don't try to be someone I'm not. They like me the way I am."

"Yeah, because you're a cool and interesting person," I huffed. "I'm just a walking kick-me sign."

"Who cares if you even go to Homecoming or not?" Fabián popped another chocolate into his mouth. That kid had a hollow leg.

"Have you never had a revenge fantasy before? I need to make Wesley jealous *and* feel bad that he dumped me."

"This is stupid. Why don't I go to Homecoming with you?" Ruth shuffled over. "That way you won't have to worry about finding someone."

"Or you could go with me," Fabián added. He tucked a carved radish garnish from our takeout behind his ear and blew me a kiss.

Having Ruth or Fabián go with me to Homecoming would definitely solve my date issues, but Wesley already knew they were my friends. I needed someone who would make him look like the idiot who let me go and help me save face in front of Teighan.

"Thanks, y'all. But you should go with whoever asks you. Which I'm sure will happen." Fabián had probably been asked already by some online fan.

Ruth gave a happy sigh. "Someone *could* ask me to Homecoming. Like a Promposal, but with autumnal colors. And then we could go get dinner somewhere romantic where they have real candles on the table. I could even wear a pink dress while we slow-danced." Ruth's eyes went misty as she imagined her perfect night. It looked like I wasn't the only one fantasizing about a Homecoming date.

"I just need to tone myself down a little bit, and I'll have a boyfriend in no time."

Fabián snorted, grabbing a Swedish Fish. "I won't even bother talking you out of this stupid idea because there's no way you can pull off not running your mouth all day."

I chewed my lip. I had no idea how I was going to be one of the quiet women from these films. After all, I could barely keep myself from speaking like a pirate while being dumped.

"I'm just gonna have to remind myself," I said firmly.

"But you won't act like that with us, right?" Ruth asked.

"Don't worry, Ruth, I'll never shut up for you." I grinned.

Ruth rolled her eyes.

But I'm pretty sure she smiled.

· · ·

MY ROOM
LATER

Ruth and Fabián were asleep, but my brain was still whirring from the things I'd learned from our movie night. I decided to make a list of all the tips I'd picked up:

THINGS ALL SUCCESSFUL LEADING LADIES HAVE IN COMMON:

- They don't cackle; they giggle and cover their mouths with their hands.
- They are somehow completely hairless from the eyelashes down.
- None of them eat Hot Cheetos.
- Instead of blurting out what they're thinking, they wait until the guy in the movie asks "What are you thinking?"
- They smile 80 percent of the time instead of talking.
- All of the men in the movie lead the conversation (key observation).

I stared at the page, trying to turn the list into a plan that would get me a date. All the women in these movies were so normal. They didn't snort or shout or gasp or prank people like I did. How could I be like them and, instead of being too much, become just right?

HOW TO BE LESS "LOUD":

- Talk at a minimum around people you have to impress (maybe limit to two comments each interaction, just to be safe).
- No more crazy outfits or garish makeup looks.
- Same for my wild hair (and body hair).
- Don't snort or cackle—even if it's really funny.
- Keep Cheeto consumption limited to emergencies.
- Instead of replying to questions, smile, but in a mysterious and alluring way.
- Stop gasping so much (tough, but necessary).
- No more pranks. Full stop.

I looked at the list, feeling proud. I had finally done it: I had pinpointed all the things that were wrong with me, which meant I was on the path to fixing them. It felt good putting them all in this one place, and it made the feat of becoming Quiet Parvin for high school seem way less intimidating.

If only I'd made this list earlier, I'd probably still have a boyfriend.

I settled back into my bed, feeling in control for the first time since being dumped.

And then I put Fabián's hand in a cup of warm water, because it was a sleepover, and he'd eaten all our candy.

SEPTEMBER

· · ·

THINGS I HAVE GOING FOR ME:

- A plan to get a boy to like me
- The single-minded determination
  to make it happen
- Hours of research via movies,
  TV shows, and books
- Friends, family, good health, etc., etc.
- Surprisingly moisturized skin
  that smells like peaches

Sunday

MOHAMMADI ADVERTISING STUDIO
10:00 A.M.

Sunday, the first day of September, which meant I had less than five weeks to find a Homecoming date. The second Ruth and Fabián left, I began making lists and researching *How to get a guy to ask you out* in my room.

Unfortunately, none of the articles had any advice on how to find someone to have a crush on. I had no idea who would be a good Homecoming date, much less one who would make Wesley feel bad. "The heart wants what the heart wants," one of the articles quoted wisely. But it seemed that nobody had the decency to tell me what my heart wanted in the first place.

"Knock-knock," I said, going downstairs. Technically, I was supposed to use the separate entrance to the basement, but Mom and Dad usually didn't have clients over on Sundays. My parents were in the middle of a big campaign for an ad agency and had a tight deadline. They must have been so busy they'd forgotten I was even home. Or to feed me.

"Come on down," Mom shouted from her computer. Her desk was a mess, with printouts, storyboards, and her giant tablet taking up the entire thing. Dad sat across from her, emailing someone at light speed from his pristine work-station. He was typing so fast his mustache was quivering.

The whole studio was painted white, with triangles of color that Mom had added when they refinished the basement, back when they decided to start their own company. A huge bookshelf covered the entire back wall and was chock-full of design books. I used to spend a lot of time down here, picking books at random and looking at the pictures.

"How you feeling?" Mom asked, her eyes not leaving her tablet. She was drawing a tree, and the roots spelled out the name of a company. She tweaked one of the letters.

"Meh," I said, plopping down into one of the swivel chairs.

Only Mom and Dad worked here, but sometimes they had freelancers come in when they were really busy. I sidled up to Mom's desk, flipping through one of her design books. She put her tablet pencil down and finally looked up, running her hands through her pale hair. I hoped they would hire another freelancer soon.

"Just okay?" she asked, scooting over.

"Why aren't you dressed, baba jaan?" Dad finally came out from behind his huge monitor. "I'm supposed to take you to Farsi school in half an hour."

"Dad!" I recoiled. "Farsi school? Really? I thought I was done with Farsi school." Farsi school was a two-hour class held every Sunday in the basement of a Lutheran church in downtown DC. It smelled funny, and the teachers always forgot where we were in our workbooks. Farsi is a super confusing language, not to mention the class was a major time suck since it met on the weekend. Besides—Farsi school was closed all summer, and my parents had never mentioned me starting it back up in the fall. This was the first I was hearing about it.

"Parvin," Mom said, using the super-Iranian pronunciation of my name as ammunition, "it's your heritage. It's important to your family."

"Maybe if you spoke Farsi to me, I wouldn't need to go to Farsi school!" I pointed accusingly at Dad.

"You know that's not fair," Dad started. "Your mother doesn't speak Farsi. It's rude."

"That makes zero sense, Dad. When am I supposed to speak it then?"

"Parvin—" Mom began again, but I was too angry to listen.

"Nemikhaam!" I said back to her in a flawless accent.

"What'd she say?" Mom turned to Dad.

"She says she doesn't want to," Dad said, giving me the angry eye.

"I just had my heart broken, and now you're telling me I have to go to school on a *Sunday*?" I replied, using my most Reasonable Adult Voice. Only it came out as a wail.

"Yes," Dad said flatly.

"I'M NOT GOING," I shouted, stomping up the staircase.

"PARVIN," Dad shouted back. "NO STOMPING." *Stomp-stomp*. Too late. *Stomp-stomp*. I stomped past the kitchen and up to the second floor, where I slammed my door.

There was zero chance I was going to stupid Farsi School.

. . .

FARSI SCHOOL
11:00 A.M.

I had lost the Farsi war. I was so mad I had to go that I
turned into deadweight. Mom had to practically force me
into a pair of jeans and wash my face for me, and I refused
to even buckle my own seat belt in the car.

It's not that I didn't love my Iranian heritage or anything. It's more that I wanted to spend my weekends like
a normal high schooler, and that did not involve going to
some moldy basement in Northwest DC where everyone
could see my red eyes and stretched-out curls after crying all
weekend. I didn't even have lip gloss on, which was a first.

"All right, everyone," Aghayeh Hazemi began from the
front of the classroom. He was the school administrator, and
we rarely saw him unless we had to hand him monthly checks
from our parents. Where was our old teacher, Khanoumeh
Rezai? Not that I was anxious to see her again. She always
motioned to slap me upside the head because I sucked at
conjugating verbs. "There are no irregular verbs in Farsi."
she'd yell. "So why do you always get them wrong, Parvin?"

"As many of you know, Khanoumeh Rezai has retired—"
Aghayeh Hazemi began. I locked eyes with Hanna, an older
girl in my class, and she gave me a big grin. Hanna was by
far the coolest person in Farsi school, and rumor had it she
spent weekends going to hookah bars with Saudi princes
who couldn't get enough of her dark skin, full lips, and
sunflower eyes. I couldn't believe she just smiled at me. I
guessed Hanna wasn't a big fan of Khanoumeh Rezai, either.

"So," he said. "I know you're only in intermediate Farsi,

but given the circumstances, we're going to be joining your class with the advanced students." There were only five kids in my intermediate class, and we all groaned, except little Laleh, who was nine years old and easily the best in our group. Most of us could barely get through the alphabet, much less the poetry we had to read. Advanced Farsi would be a bloodbath.

"Don't worry," Aghayeh Hazemi replied. "The advanced students have volunteered to help you transition into their classroom and be your 'study buddies,'" Aghayeh said with air quotes, his Iranian accent making it sound like "eh-study buddies."

"Great," I said flatly. I didn't have to pretend to be a quiet human being at Farsi school. There was nobody here I was trying to impress. I put my head back down on my desk, wondering if Wesley even knew where Iran was on a map.

"Awesome," Hanna echoed, in my same flat voice.

"Sigh," said Hamid, a high school junior who hated coming here as much as I did.

We looked back to see if Morteza was going to chime in, but he had already fallen asleep. Laleh shrugged.

"Cool," she said gamely. Suck-up.

"All right, follow me. Befarmain!" Aghayeh Hazemi said, opening the door.

As we walked through the hallways, I jealously eyed the younger grades that basically got to go to the playground or do arts and crafts as long as they spoke in Farsi. That's where I'd started, and most of the students I'd begun with had dropped out by the time we had to learn to read and write.

The alphabet was probably the hardest part of learning Farsi from English, since it reads from right to left and has different letters. Not only that, but written Farsi is a completely separate language from spoken Farsi. It's like reading medieval English versus speaking the way we do now. The kids who'd grown up speaking Farsi were just as screwed as non-speakers like me when it came to reading and writing. Learning ketabi, or "bookish," Farsi had really thinned our ranks.

Dad had driven me to class as usual, and I knew he was still hanging out in the parking lot with the other Iranian parents as they cracked pumpkin seeds between their teeth and chugged black tea, gossiping about who was marrying whom and who was trying to risk a visit back to Iran. I bet the real reason he made me go to school was so he could hang with other Iranians for two hours. After all, Sundays were pretty much the only time I ever heard Dad speak Farsi other than when he's ordering kabob from somewhere.

Aghayeh Hazemi opened the door to a classroom at the other end of the building and motioned for us to go in. Instantly, ten heads swiveled to look at us. Most of the kids in this class were older, though there were a couple who could have been younger. Those were probably the kids who had been born in Iran. The majority of my classmates had been born here, like me, and had never gotten a chance to speak Farsi unless it was with their parents. Or when we were thanking our relatives for the money they gave us at Iranian New Year.

But unlike me, almost all the kids at school were full Iranian, not half. I recognized a couple classmates from seeing them at Iranian New Year parties, but nobody I knew well enough to say hi to.

Sprinkled throughout the classroom were five empty

seats, none of them together. Hanna gave me a sad shrug and headed to sit next to the only girl with an open seat. I put my head down and grabbed the closest open chair.

"Hey," the guy next to me said. He had deep brown eyes and eyelashes that were even longer than mine. "I'm Amir." He held out his hand.

Amir was as Iranian as it got. He wore a gold chain (classic Iranian-boy jewelry) and a long-sleeved Adidas shirt. Why were Iranians obsessed with Adidas?

"Parvin," I replied. His hand grasped mine, and I felt a little better.

"Welcome, welcome," Aghayeh Khosrowshahi, our new teacher, said from the front of the class, making his *w*'s sound like *v*'s. "To all the new students, don't worry, we will be going slowly to get you up to speed. Each of you is already sitting next to your study buddy, who will help you get caught up. Oh-key?" His wild bushy white eyebrows made him look more like a mad scientist than a language instructor.

"Oh-key," he continued. "Please turn to page sixty of your poetry books. Today we will be learning about *Layla and Majnun*, the precursor to *Romeo and Juliet*. It is written by Nizami."

Amir opened his book up in the middle of our desks, sharing with me until I got my own. Aghayeh Khosrowshahi gestured to a boy up front to start reading out loud in Farsi. "Befarmain, Bobak."

"Once there lived among the . . . ??? . . . in Arabia a great lord, a . . . ??? . . . , who ruled over the Banu Amir," Bobak read easily in Farsi. *"No other country flourished like his and . . . ??? . . . carried the sweet scent of his glory to the farthest horizons."*

I struggled to catch up. There were a lot of new words that I hadn't seen before. Which line were we on? I think Amir could sense my eyes roving all over the page and pointed at the corresponding Farsi script with his thumb. Aghayeh Khosrowshahi called on the next student, and they picked up where Bobak left off, reciting in flawless Farsi.

Amir used his finger to track each word as it was spoken so I could follow along, which was nice of him. I moved closer to get a better look, and I smelled rosewater, and something deeper, like cologne. I followed his fingers, reading the poetry as quickly as I could but always a word or two behind. By the time it was my turn to read out loud, though, no amount of silent coaching from Amir could help.

"If prayers remain . . . unanswered, do we ever reflect that it may be for our good?"

My tongue felt fat in my mouth, the Farsi I'd learned from last spring gone thanks to summer break. I had no idea what I was even saying.

"We feel sure that we know our needs . . . yet the future is veiled from our eyes," I stumbled out loud in Farsi.

The hardest thing about reading in Farsi is that the vowels aren't written the way they are in English. There is an *a* and a *u* vowel, although sometimes the *u* becomes an *o*, *v*, or *w* sound, so it's basically an ambush in every word. There isn't really an *i* sound like the *i* in *Ireland*. Instead of an *i*, Farsi uses a *y*, which is actually an *ee* sound in English. That's why my name is spelled *Parvin*, even though it should have been spelled *Parveen*—because someone from Iran (pronounced EE-ran) decided that's the English translation.

To read a word out loud, you have to guess what the sounds connecting each consonant are or know the word already. Like spelling Washington "Wshngtn." Sometimes there are little accents and squiggles to help you figure out pronunciation, but there weren't any in this advanced book. By the time I got to reading the last word out loud, I was so frustrated I wanted to throw Amir's stupid Farsi book across the room.

"It's okay, khanoum," Aghayeh Khosrowshahi said kindly when I finished. I could feel moisture prickle at the corner of my eyes. How many times was I going to be humiliated in front of an audience this week? Amir went after me, his pronunciation perfect. I looked at his skin, at how much tanner it was than mine. It wasn't fair—he was definitely full Iranian. His parents probably even spoke it at home.

By the time class was done, I felt like my brain had been thrown into a salad spinner. Hanna, Hamid (pronounced Ha-MEED), Morteza, and even little Laleh looked dazed, too.

"For homework, please translate the first five verses of the poem in chapter two to English. And no parents!" Aghayeh warned. Drats! I had been banking on Dad's help.

Hanna approached my desk. "I didn't understand half of what Aghayeh Khosrowshahi said. Did you?"

I shook my head. "Amir had to help me." I gestured to him. "Amir, this is Hanna, from my intermediate class." I didn't know if I'd actually talked to Hanna before. She was definitely too cool to hang with me. At least this class was putting me in the orbit of a high school senior.

"Hey, Hanna," he replied.

Hanna smiled. "I think your dad's my dentist. Well, I

guess I'm gonna go bang my head against a wall and hope I can finish this homework."

"Godspeed," I said solemnly. Because I was going to have to do the same thing.

"Khodafez!" *Bye!* Hanna walked away.

"So, when do you want to meet?" Amir asked.

"What do you mean?" Maybe if I told Dad how hard class was today, he'd stop for ice cream on the way home out of guilt.

"For your homework? I'm supposed to help you complete assignments," he said, looking at me like I was stupid.

"Oh." I hadn't counted on Amir *actually* being my study buddy. I thought that was just something the teachers had said to make us feel better about the switch. I didn't know what I was supposed to say. *No, thank you, I'd rather fail since there are literally no grades in this class*?

Amir sighed. "Listen, I agreed to tutor the intermediate students because that means I won't have to help my dad out at his dental office. We can just meet for half an hour, okay?"

It was as if Amir had read my mind. Meeting for half an hour was just enough to help me in this class, but not enough to become a drag.

"Yes, please," I replied quickly.

He slung his bag over his shoulder and walked out with me. "Which school do you go to?"

"Polk," I replied.

His eyebrows raised in surprise. "Same. Are you a freshman? Is that why I haven't seen you?"

I nodded.

"Okay, well, wanna meet after school this week? I could

meet you on the bleachers." He looked at his phone, checking his calendar. "How about Wednesday?"

Who were we? Stockbrokers? Who used a calendar in high school?

"I'll pencil you in," I responded, equally serious. Amir laughed.

We were walking through the hallway now, following the rest of our class toward the main exit. "What's your last name?" Amir asked.

"Mohammadi," I said. "What's yours?"

"Shirazi." We were quiet then, walking up the stairs. It wasn't awkward, though.

"You're half," he said. It wasn't a question.

"Yep." A lot of Iranians could tell straight off the bat that I was half. Aside from my skin color, I looked pretty much the same as them. There were plenty of Iranians who were fairer than me, though. I didn't know how they could always tell I was half. They just *knew*.

We were in the parking lot now. I spied Dad drinking tea from a thermos with another parent. I bet he hadn't moved since we started class.

"You should leave now," I warned Amir. "If you meet my dad, he'll want to know who your parents are and whether we're related, and then we'll be stuck in this parking lot forever."

"Wait, are we related?" asked Amir.

I shrugged. "Probably." He laughed again.

"You're funny, you know that?" Amir said.

I crossed my arms defensively. Was he going to call me loud and too much, too? But instead he waved and walked away, the scent of rosewater following in his wake.

Tuesday

HOMEROOM
7:30 A.M.

The first day of school was always so depressing. It was too hot, nobody wanted to be there, and the teachers all had this sad optimism as if they were telling themselves *This year is gonna be different*. I could already feel my summer freedom slipping away as I sat next to Ruth in homeroom. Unfortunately, Fabián was in another class. At least Wesley was nowhere to be seen.

I'd worn my least "loud" first-day-of-school outfit and had on jeans and a plain T-shirt. Gone was the sparkly silver eyeshadow Ameh Sara had taught me how to apply; I exchanged it for a "natural" look (that somehow still took as much time as my sparkly makeup routine). Not only that, but I'd shaved my arms, plucked my eyebrows, and straightened my huge curls that were "loud" in their own way. My hair had so little volume I actually looked related to Mom, who complained about her lank blond hair all the time.

"Partin . . . Mohammad . . . ?" Ms. Payne struggled to pronounce my name for roll call. Here it was: my first challenge as the Non-Loud Parvin from the movies. How would *she* handle this situation?

"Er, it's pronounced PAR-veen. And my last name is Mo-HAM-mad-i. With an *i* at the end," I said politely. See? I didn't have to give a lecture on how all names from the Middle East were spelled to be as phonetic as possible. Why she had thrown a hidden *t* in there, I would never know. But I stood firm, stated my case, and got to slip into the background again. Perfect first test as a quiet woman.

Ms. Payne made a note and smiled. "Where is your name from?"

Good grief, what was this? An interrogation? If I told her my name was Iranian, she'd probably make some bizarre comment about how she loved hummus or something, which wasn't even from there. Oh no, I was snowballing, but Ms. Payne kept staring at me expectantly.

"Well," I began, my mouth suddenly dry, trying to figure out how to not make this weird. "I was born in America. So, I guess it's an American name."

Ms. Payne's lips went very thin, but she didn't say anything before moving on to Teddy Nelson. Phew. Dodged a bullet.

"Parvin." Ruth tugged on my arm. "Is your shirt inside out?"

I looked down. Oh no. Being two different Parvins had me so turned around I couldn't even put on a shirt properly. There was no way I could just raise my hand and say, *Excuse me, I need to go to the bathroom because I put my clothes on wrong.*

Panicking, I did the old tilt-your-head-back-and-pinch-your-nose-like-it's-bleeding pantomime that lets you slip out of class with the teacher giving you an understanding nod. Ms. Payne waved me on, probably relieved she wouldn't have to deal with me for ten minutes.

• • •

BATHROOM
7:45 A.M.

Egad. A girl in one of the stalls just unwrapped what sounded like a massive tampon, and the sisterhood code required that

I pretend not to notice. In middle school, periods were so embarrassing you straight-up acted like you couldn't hear someone crumple a pad into the tiny trash can in the stall. I bet the same rules applied in high school.

Hmm. There was smoke coming out of her stall now. It smelled like cotton candy.

Oh, wait. She was unwrapping a vape pen, not a tampon.

Her stall banged open. It was Becca, the scary girl from orientation. Too late, we'd made eye contact. Quick, say something!

"I thought you were unwrapping a tampon," I said nervously, pretending to wash my hands. *WHY DID I SAY THAT?*

She remained silent. She had on enough black eyeliner to outfit an entire Intro to Theater class.

"They should sell vape pens like tampons," I went on, the word diarrhea just tumbling out of my mouth. "You know, like light, regular, super—"

"What?" she snarled, drying her hands by shaking water onto the floor. Upon closer inspection, she looked old enough to be a senior. I gulped.

"Um, your tampon," I said weakly, my heart forgetting to pump blood to my brain. "I thought you were smoking it?"

She flicked water into my eyes before stomping away.

Why had I opened my mouth? Why did I let those words spill from my brain without invitation? I'd barely been in school for an hour and had already failed my Quiet Parvin mission.

I flipped my shirt right side out in silence.

• • •

ENGLISH CLASS
9:00 A.M.

Our required reading list this year was so thick I could barely fit the books in my locker, much less carry them in my backpack. Maybe it would be easier to get a Homecoming date if I toned up a bit, though. Maybe this was an opportunity to get Michelle Obama–like arms.

Ruth caught me doing reps with *The Count of Monte Cristo* under my desk as Mr. Nuñez went over the syllabus.

"What are you doing?" she hissed.

"Getting swole," I whispered back, flexing my biceps.

Ruth tilted her face up and looked to the heavens as she slowly exhaled. News flash, Ruth: God probably had better things to do than worry about my new dedication to fitness.

"If you embarrass me today, I will never speak to you again," she muttered, her face deadly.

This coming from someone who let her mother dress her in Hello Kitty for her first day of school.

And not in a cool way.

. . .

LUNCH
FINALLY

It was still nice enough to sit in the courtyard, which meant we didn't have to deal with the cafeteria. I had a feeling that the second fall ended, me and the freshmen sitting outside would have to fend for ourselves at the lunch tables indoors, probably upsetting some kind of weird social hierarchy that was established by the seniors. I was not looking forward to it.

How did people even know where to sit? It was like this big unspoken map where it was just understood that certain groups sat in certain places. Middle school had, like, five tables. Here, I counted at least thirty. Ruth and I were living on borrowed time by eating in the DMZ that was the courtyard.

I spied Wesley sitting at one of those indoor tables through the window as he chuckled with his fellow khaki friends. I wondered what it would be like to sit next to him every day. In my fantasy he'd offer me some of his lunch and we'd split a soda, his arm protectively around my shoulder as he told a joke that the entire lunch table laughed at.

Nobody would mispronounce my name or ask if my eyelashes were real. Nobody would make me feel like I didn't belong. Instead, his group would invite me to their cool golf parties and beg me to sit with them at a town hall meeting, or whatever it was they did. Then Wesley would pass me a bag of Hot Cheetos, and I'd know it was True Love.

"Why?" Ruth groaned as she opened up her lunch box. "It's not like it's a different message, either."

I snapped back to reality, my radar for things that could potentially embarrass me going off. "Oh no," I replied, staring at the note in Ruth's lunch. Please tell me Mrs. Song did not write what I think she did.

Ruth held up the paper, her fingers holding the tiniest corner of the offending note. It was the same note that Ruth's mom had put in her middle school lunch every day, too.

You are filled with Jesus's light. He loves every fiber of your being, it said in Mrs. Song's perfect script. It was then followed with the words, *And remember: no boys* :) The note was the size of a five-by-eight-inch index card and could probably be seen from outer space, like the Great Wall or Australia.

How could Ruth's mom still do this? We were in high school now. We had real bras. It was a war crime at this point.

"I mean, at least Jesus loves you," I offered, trying to cheer Ruth up. "I feel like you should laminate it, though? Save her some time?"

Ruth thunked her forehead onto the table. "Do you think my mom would be okay with me not being straight? Or would she be even more harsh?" Ruth asked.

"Ummm," I replied helpfully.

The truth was, I had no idea. Ruth's mom was so strict it was scary. She could either take Ruth being pansexual as the worst thing ever or a miracle from God that her daughter could fall in love with someone who couldn't get her pregnant before her first PhD. Mrs. Song was a big deal in the Washington DC academic crowd and expected Ruth to be just as famous in her own field one day.

I put my hand on hers. "Don't worry, Ruthie. At least she packs you lunch."

All my parents had ever packed me was a stray cookie and maybe a stick of chewing gum.

Ruth glared at me over her crossed arms. "I know what you're trying to do."

"What?" I asked innocently.

Ruth sighed, opening the metal containers inside her lunch box. She began stacking tiny side dishes of Korean food on our table. Little dishes of kimchi, pickled cucumbers, scallion pancakes, acorn jelly, and potato salad peeked out of each one. My mouth watered. Ruth's mom made her the most amazing meals, and she always packed extra for me. That didn't stop Ruth from whining about carrying enough food for two to school every day, though.

Fabián sat down with us just then, slamming his over-flowing tray of fries onto the table. I envied him—his parents gave him a big allowance to buy lunches and order delivery since they traveled so much for work and were never home to cook.

"Hola, chicas," Fabián said with a grin, popping a fry into his mouth.

I'd known Fabián and Ruth since elementary school, when the three of us had teamed up against Spencer Tunstall for making fun of Fabián for going to dance class. The cherry on top had been when Fabián beat him in the hundred-yard dash in fourth grade and proudly announced to Spencer that he'd just lost to a gay kid. No joke, that was actually how Fabián had come out to our school: in the form of a savage takedown. Ruth wasn't ready to come out, though. For reasons I still didn't understand, I didn't have to come out for liking guys.

It was a mystery.

Fabián's first-day-of-school outfit was excellent: a white T-shirt with the sleeves rolled up that made his copper skin glow. His blue jeans were artfully ripped, and his black hair was slicked back to look like a 1950s heartthrob. All he needed was a vintage motorcycle to complete the look.

"Nice fit," I said, giving him a slow clap. Ruth grinned—she'd helped rip the jeans he was wearing. Today was finally the day for him to show it off. Too bad I had been too use-less to help Fabián with his outfit over the weekend.

Fabián bowed low. "Thank you. It's not easy looking like such a snack all the time."

I cackled, the sound echoing across the courtyard. A girl at the other end shot me a dirty look, and the laugh died in my throat as I remembered that cackling was a decidedly not-quiet way to laugh. Fabián ran a comb through his hair.

"Now that I've bestowed you with praise, can you please tell Ruth to share?" I whined. She kept batting my hand away with a chopstick every time I tried to steal a piece of food.

Fabián took one look at the kimchi Ruth had brought and put his hand on mine, gazing sadly into my eyes.

"As your friend, I feel like this is for the best." He wrinkled his nose.

"Hey!" Ruth shouted, offended.

"See? I'm the only one who appreciates Korean food here. Better to let me have some," I pointed out.

"You could always pack your own lunch this year, you know," Ruth said.

I pouted.

Ruth grudgingly pushed the metal container of kimchi toward me, and I ate a couple more pieces, amazed I was a High Schooler now, Eating Lunch, in my High School. Fabián dipped his French fries into enough ketchup to fake an accident.

I could see his eyes wander, scoping out everyone in the courtyard, taking it all in. I caught him staring at a senior boy by the water fountain, and he grinned.

"Homecoming is the first weekend of October," I said, pointing at Ruth with a metal chopstick, focusing us back to my mission. "Maybe you could find a cute girl and you, Fabián, could seduce some hot jock. Meanwhile we still need to find a date for moi."

"How are you going to get a date in a month?" she asked.

"I have a plan." I clutched the crumpled list I'd made at our sleepover, the one I'd been carrying in my jeans pocket all day. "Oh, I have a plan!" And then I started my evil laugh, the one that Ruth and Fabián said was legitimately scary. Ruth looked terrified.

Just then, a passing junior looked at me like I was crazy. I choked to a halt. I'd seriously underestimated this whole being-quiet thing. How did quiet people explain their plans without laughing like an evil genius? Maybe they just passed polite notes back and forth.

"Hey, how's your first day coming along?" a voice interrupted. I looked up—it was Matty, our tour guide from orientation. Fabián swooned again.

"It's going," Fabián replied, his voice cracking. Was Fabián nervous? I couldn't wait to make fun of him for this later.

"And how about you—Parvin, right? You feeling better?" Matty turned his gaze to me, and I found myself gaping like a fish, just like Fabián. I was close enough to see his thick eyelashes, and how his brown hair curled a bit at the ends. His eyes were an intense green, and his forearms were all corded muscle. He was nothing like the guys in our year who had chicken legs for limbs, Wesley included.

"Parvin?" Ruth poked me.

"Oh yeah, much better." I laughed. Why was I laughing? What was so funny?

"Glad to hear it," Matty said, rapping his knuckles on the table. He flashed Ruth a smile and asked how she was doing, too, but I didn't hear her answer. Matty was so cool. He smelled good, and I was pretty sure he had his learner's permit. Plus, he wore the shirt of a hip band no one had ever heard of—a true sign of status.

What if I got Matty to take me to Homecoming? That would show Wesley, for sure.

"Jeez Louise," Ruth said out loud, as soon as Matty walked away. "Parvin . . . I can tell you're planning something. And please don't say it's another prank."

Fabián gave me a cold look. He hadn't brought up the warm water from the sleepover, but I knew it had worked when he'd gotten up suddenly that night to use the bathroom, muttering, "Damn it, Parvin."

"No, no, it's not that," I said, taking one of Fabián's fries, deep in thought. I could feel the maniacal gleam in my eye flicker on, the one that Wesley had seemed to love so much until he'd learned what slacks were. But this time, I'd plot *against* him, and not by his side.

"What if I went to Homecoming with Matty?" I said, laying out my plan.

Fabián guffawed. "He's a sophomore. And I'm pretty sure he's gay."

Ruth coughed. "Actually, he's bi."

Fabián and I snapped our heads back to Ruth so quickly they almost fell off our necks.

"Didn't you see his pin?" Ruth continued. "On his bag? It's the bisexual flag. He said he was a GSA member, right? So . . . there you go."

"But you have a lot of pins on your bag, Ruth," I said. "I don't see the pansexual one."

Ruth shuddered. "I can't just put my pin on there. What if my mom googled my flag's colors?"

"Okay, okay, back to Parvin's wild idea—" Fabián started.

"How are you gonna get Matty to ask you to Homecoming? Or get him to say yes if you asked him?"

"*I* can't get him to go with me . . . but New Parvin can," I replied. "I'll be quiet and restrained, and the things holding me back from a boyfriend will disappear. I'll be like those women in the movies we watched and fix it all. And then I bet someone as cool as Matty will want to date me."

Luckily, I hadn't embarrassed myself in front of Matty too much, other than hiding under a water fountain after Wesley dumped me. In fact, Matty had barely heard me speak at all, which was probably a good thing.

"Or," Ruth began, "maybe you could just go to Homecoming with your friends? And take some time to get over Wesley, since it sounds like he really hurt you?"

I thought about it for a second. "Nah."

"I saw him first at orientation. Technically, *I* should be scheming how to get him for Homecoming. Plus, he's Latino, which means we'll have adorable bilingual children," Fabián pointed out.

"Please, Fabián?" I wheedled.

Fabián sighed. "He's my competition for the fall play, you know."

"You *did* already get asked to Homecoming today," Ruth revealed. "By that sophomore with the green hair."

Fabián drummed his fingers on the table. "Yeah, I'm still not sure if I want to go with Austin," he replied. I knew it. Fabián was too impressive to be dateless for long. Why he hung out with us was truly an enigma.

"Please, Fabián? I need your blessing. Or whatever people bless." Dad was Shiite Muslim and Mom was Episcopalian. Who knew how blessings worked?

"Fine." Fabián rolled his eyes. "I bless this stupid Matty scheme. But you have to promise to be real with us and not whatever version of yourself you're using to bait boys."

"Hey!" Ruth shouted. "I didn't give my blessing. And I don't think I will." She crossed her arms, looking between Fabián and me.

"Ruth"—I patted her gently—"you've been outvoted."

. . .

BAND
1:30 P.M.

This high school was so massive I got lost on my way to band, even though I'd had the tour only a few days ago. The band room wasn't even connected to the school—it was in a completely different structure on the other side of the main building that you had to access by exiting the front door, walking under a couple weird overhangs, then huffing and puffing up a hill to make it on time. After lunch, Ruth had stormed ahead without me, saying that this plan was the worst thing she'd ever heard. I got to the clarinet section just as the bell rang, and our band director, Ms. Kaiser, called the class to order.

"All right," she said, tapping her baton on her music stand. "Today, we're just going to sort everyone into chairs. We'll start with the chromatic and then a random scale that will be different for each student." I turned around, wondering whether I was just seeing him out of the corner of my eye or if he was really there. Yes! There, in the trumpet section, was Matty. My plan was already off to a great start.

And then, to my horror, Ms. Kaiser started auditioning the flutes . . . in front of the *entire class*. Usually for an audition you went into a separate room where your band instructor tested you on scales and a prepared piece (usually behind a curtain so they weren't biased), but doing it in front of other students was unheard of . . . at least in middle school.

I had been playing the clarinet since sixth grade, when our elementary school's band teacher said that anyone who played an instrument would get to be excused from regular lessons for two hours a week if we joined. Of course, I signed up. Anything to skip class for two hours. Ruth had always wanted to play the clarinet, so I picked the same instrument as her.

Mom and Dad had agreed that playing an instrument would be good for college applications, so it stuck. All throughout middle school, no one had taken band that seriously (except Ruth, of course). But now, I could tell that high school band was going to be a major commitment. What had I gotten myself into? And was it too late to quit?

Matty sat in the brass section, laughing about something his friend had whispered to him. I could almost feel his presence behind me and felt hyperaware that we were in the same room even though we didn't know each other well (yet). I wondered if he could please turn around and cover his ears during my audition. How was I going to get him to ask me to Homecoming if he heard what a terrible clarinetist I was?

"Ruth," I whispered. She was already fingering the chromatic scale on her clarinet. "I think I am going to have a nosebleed."

Ruth rolled her eyes. "Didn't you practice at all over the summer?"

I shook my head. I'd been too busy dropping fries near people snoozing on the beach so they could be woken unpleasantly by loud, squawking seagulls digging for food.

The person I dropped fries with would now remain nameless. Needless to say, clarinet practice had not been high on our list of activities over the summer.

Ruth didn't even bother responding. She just sat there, cool as a cucumber, her scales already memorized while she ignored me. Ms. Kaiser finished with the flutes, where sophomore Yessenia López got first chair. She smirked at the rest of us and skipped proudly to the front row.

I fiddled with my clarinet, adjusting the reed and mouthpiece and doing my best to run my fingers over all the little keys and finger holes. I actually wasn't too bad at the chromatic scale, aka the scale where you played every possible note the instrument could belt out, in order. But deep down I knew that whatever random scale I was tasked with would be a disaster, since I always confused them in my head.

Too soon, Ms. Kaiser turned her attention to the clarinets. I could actually feel my heart pounding in my chest, which wasn't fair, as it wasn't at the right tempo.

Ruth auditioned first with her perfect embouchure, the corners of her mouth tucked neatly around her clarinet reed. Her scales were flawless, her fingers flying over the keys like a spider scuttling up a branch. Then Ms. Kaiser pointed her hatchet at me. I took a deep breath, my hands already trembling over the keys. *Dear God, or Allah, or whoever is listening—please let me nail this audition.*

My brain felt like it was going to explode from nerves, but luckily my fingers remembered the whole chromatic scale, and my muscle memory kicked in as I played. I could feel everyone (including Matty) stare at my back.

My mouth still felt weird without braces, though, and it got really sore toward the end of my scale. I exhaled after I played the last note, my fingers shaking. Ms. Kaiser frowned and wrote something on the pad she kept on her music stand. My body stayed tense, waiting for her to announce the random scale she wanted me to play.

"Play the C scale, please," she said, peering at me with her big circular glasses.

I gulped so loudly I was sure Matty could hear it all the way in the back row. The C scale was, technically, the easiest scale when played in the privacy of your own home. It started off all right, but then when I forgot to play a B natural (which was a very rude fingering where you essentially gave your clarinet the middle finger), it all went downhill.

I soldiered on, but my mouth was already so tired I could hear the pitch of the clarinet go wonky, and then I missed another note. Matty must have thought a loud Canada goose was honking, and not a freshman clarinetist. That was truly the only way to explain the noises emitting from my instrument.

To top it off, I accidentally started going back down the scale when I was supposed to go up a second octave, that's how much I was panicking. When I reached the last note, the muscles around my mouth just about gave out. I needed to go to church/mosque more often. My prayers had no juice.

I opened my eyes, unaware I'd even closed them. My thoughts seemed to catch up to my body just in time for me to notice that I was covered in an inch of sweat. I watched Yessenia whisper something to the flutist next to her, who giggled and looked right at me. Please tell me Matty went to the bathroom for my audition. I couldn't bear to look around and check.

The room was silent. I wanted to die. But it wasn't until Ruth squeezed my hand that I knew I'd really messed up.

Ms. Kaiser grimaced as she took notes on my audition. I didn't know what felt worse: wallowing in heartbreak in the privacy of my own Netflix queue, or knowing with absolute certainty that I'd blown it in front of a whole classroom of people. Who was I kidding? This was way worse.

Ruth got third chair, which was pretty good for a freshman. I quietly hyperventilated and waited for Ms. Kaiser to give me my seat assignment, but it never came.

"Miss Mohammadi," she said finally, "please see me after class."

A low "ooooh" noise rippled through the band room, the noise specifically reserved for bad kids, and I wanted to evaporate into my chair. Ruth looked at me apologetically as she moved to the front row while the clarinet section reshuffled. I just stayed in my spot, trying to make myself invisible as Ms. Kaiser moved on to the French horns. I had never felt so devastated in front of so many people.

It was only my first day of high school, but I was pretty sure I failed it.

. . .

MS. KAISER'S OFFICE
2:45 P.M.

The bell rang, and I could hear all the band students head to the main building where our lockers were. I should have been one of them. Instead, I sat in Ms. Kaiser's office, awaiting my doom.

Her office was full of so many different knickknacks it was hard to know where to look. Sheet music, photos of students, vintage instruments—she had her whole life crammed into shelves and even hanging from the ceiling. There was so much stuff in there that when Ms. Kaiser sat behind her desk, the pattern on her shirt practically blended in with the instruments behind her. I jumped when she turned to look at me.

"Miss Mohammadi," she started, staring evenly at me from across her huge wooden desk. "Do you know what a bassoon is?"

I blinked back at her. "A bassoon? Like . . . a . . . bassoon?" I repeated stupidly. Where was this going? Ruth, Fabián, and I were supposed to walk home from school together today. I hoped they were waiting for me.

Ms. Kaiser nodded, her mouth twitching. She had the type of face that looked like it was made from marble, she was so tough to read. "It's a type of musical instrument. Similar to an oboe, but bigger."

I nodded. "Cool?"

She shook her black hair out of her ponytail and ran her hands through it. Suddenly, she seemed very tired.

"Look, we have too many clarinets. You had braces, right? And I'm guessing you wear a retainer at night?"

My eyes widened. How did she know?

"Your embouchure. I can tell by the way you got tired halfway through playing."

Oh.

"Yeah," I replied. Had I done something wrong? Besides be terrible?

"We need a bassoon player," Ms. Kaiser said flatly. "Would you be interested in learning? If not, you can still play clarinet, but you'd have to be last chair."

I didn't know what to say. It was only my first day, but I

was already being asked to give up an instrument I'd been playing for three years.

"The bassoon is a double reed. Your mouth won't get as tired. And it's a lot less competitive," she explained, as if that would make me feel better. "It could be a good fit."

"Can I think about it?" I asked.

Ms. Kaiser nodded.

I headed for the door. "How do you spell it?"

"Excuse me?" Ms. Kaiser replied.

"Bassoon. How do you spell it?"

She told me, and I left.

. . .

THE WALK HOME
3:00 P.M.

Emergency Hot Cheeto meeting. Obviously, I couldn't partake because none of the women in the movies I watched ate junk food. Fabián shoved a bunch into his mouth at once to "get enough heat," as he liked to say. Ruth sucked the neon-orangey-purple Cheeto crumbs off her thumb as we took the creek path home.

"I don't understand," Ruth said, looking at a photo of a bassoon. We'd image searched it, and the results were . . . not great.

"It's like a bedpost, but with a reed stuck into its side," I explained, looking at the photo. Or maybe I was looking at it upside down. I flipped the phone over. Maybe that was how it worked.

Fabián took the phone, his nose near the screen to get a good look.

"Pass." He handed it back to Ruth.

Ruth frowned. "It's so big. How do you even hold it?"

I took my phone back and searched some more.

"Oh my god," I said, chewing a Cheeto (I was only human, after all). "You don't hold it. You sit on it."

"WHAT?" Fabián said, snatching the phone back. It was true. There was a little leather belt attached to the bottom end of the bassoon, and you laid that belt across your chair, offsetting the weight so you held it sideways like a saxophone. The rest of the bassoon pointed upward, while the lower half's weight rested on the belt. That you sat on. Ruth's eyes went wide.

"I've never heard of an instrument you had to sit on to play," she said.

"This is incredible," Fabián said with a snicker. "I can't believe it makes music. It looks like a rocket launcher."

"What was Ms. Kaiser thinking?" I groaned out loud. "This is the least sexy instrument known to humankind." Ruth didn't say anything. Because I was right.

Fabián scrolled through the page, looking at more photos. Then he gasped.

"Oh my god!" he said, his voice sounding almost angry.

"What? What?" we asked.

"Do you know what you call a bassoon in German?" Fabián said, his voice uncharacteristically serious.

"Der bassoon?" I asked. I didn't know. I didn't speak German.

"'Fagott,'" Fabián said, reading from the phone. We were quiet. I didn't feel comfortable repeating that word.

Ruth handed me the entire bag of Cheetos. She must have felt really sorry for me. "Maybe you can quit band? It's not too late to change electives, you know."

"And to not subscribe to homophobia," Fabián added.

I kicked a rock, sending it scuttling into the creek. Ruth's advice made sense. It's not like I was any good at band, anyway. Mom and Dad would be bummed I was quitting, but they'd understand. The mortification of being last-chair clarinet was way too much to bear.

But then again, band was the only class I had with Matty. How else was I supposed to get him to notice me?

I did not anticipate having to think this much on the first day of high school.

Maybe this was why they didn't assign us homework.

. . .

MY ROOM
8:00 P.M.

After spending the entire afternoon stalking Matty's social media accounts from Homecoming HQ (aka my room), I was confident I had picked the perfect target.

My research showed that, besides being super cute, he was:

- On the honor roll
- The owner of the most perfect pair
  of dimples ever witnessed by humankind
- An example of green eyes that sparkled
  with every glance
- A trumpet player
- A Nice Person Who Wouldn't Dump
  Someone at Orientation

His hobbies included:

- Doodling on his Converse sneakers
- Speaking fluent Spanish (he's in Spanish 4, as a sophomore!)
- Wearing tees with cool band names
- Theater, GSA, Band, *and* Jazz Band
- Making my heart gallop with a single glance

And I *will* make him ask me to Homecoming. Or I'll ask him. I haven't decided yet.

Wednesday
WALK TO SCHOOL
7:15 A.M.

This morning on the creek path, Ruth and I did our special dance that we call the Wiggle. It's used only in the direst of emergencies, like when you're anxious or scared or you have to decide whether you're going to play a homophobic musical instrument. To pull it off you have to act like you've gotten a shiver and your hands have lost control at the same time. The result = the Wiggle.

Wiggle-wiggle.

Wiggle.

WiiiiiGgglllleeeEeee.

Ruth even made an accompanying noise. It sounded like a mouse going through the Hadron Collider. I know because when I asked her what it was, that was her explanation.

Fabián was already at school to sign up for his after-school clubs, but I wished he were here this morning to give me advice on what to do about the German bassoon fiasco. The two of us wiggled our way through the trees, past the kudzu vines and the little bridge that took us over the streambed. That's when I heard a twig snap. I froze.

There, on the other side of the bank, was Teighan, and she looked horrified by our dance moves.

"What is it?" Ruth whispered. She still hadn't seen Teighan. Aghast, I just motioned for us to keep walking until we burst into the back baseball field. Oh god, had Teighan witnessed our whole performance? I was pretty sure Quiet Women did not Wiggle. I had no doubt she'd tell Wesley about it over a glass of milk and a crustless sandwich, or whatever their stay-at-home moms made for them. My body buzzed, the mortification I hadn't felt since orientation surging through me again.

I exhaled slowly, trying to shake it off. It was actually not sweltering today. Usually it was so swampy and humid here that summer lasted until October. But today was mild enough that I didn't have to shave my arms and could wear a cardigan with my jeans and a blue tee. Instead of cool makeup, I had just thrown on mascara, eyeliner, tinted Chapstick, neutral foundation, neutral concealer, a skin-matching blush, and brown eyeshadow to keep it simple. Plus, my hair was in a slicked-back ponytail thanks to my straight hair from yesterday. I hadn't realized how boring dressing "not loud" would be. I almost looked like one of Wesley's church friends. I wished I could have worn bright blue eyeshadow with the tie-dyed skirt Ruth had made for me.

My phone chimed.

7:18 AM SARA MOHAMMADI: How are you feeling, ameh? Better, I hope?

7:18 AM PARVIN MOHAMMADI: Don't worry, Ameh, I've got a plan to make sure no boy ever breaks my heart again!

7:20 AM SARA MOHAMMADI: Afarin, Parvin joonam! That's what I like to hear. Who needs boys anyway? 🌿

I grinned, putting my phone away.

"So, what are you going to do?" Ruth asked, lugging her giant lunch. "Are you going to stay with the clarinet? Or switch to bassoon? Or quit band?"

"Ugh, Ruth, you know I have no idea," I whined.

"If you switched to bassoon, you'd be first chair," Ruth said, smirking. "Get it? Because you'd be the only chair."

I hate band.

. . .

ASSEMBLY
7:30 A.M.

How many assemblies did this school have? In middle school they just made a lot of announcements over the loudspeaker instead of forcing everyone to shuffle into the auditorium. Luckily, Fabián had saved us a seat far away from Wesley and Teighan_23.

"James K. Polk," Principal Saulk boomed, walking onto the stage. He had one of those microphones that clipped over his ear, the kind that made you feel like you were watching a TED Talk.

"Does anyone know why this school is named after our eleventh president?" he asked, scanning the audience as if he thought someone was going to raise their hand. News flash: Nobody raised their hand.

"James K. Polk was one of the few presidents who accomplished everything he set out to do in office. And he did that by creating *very* actionable goals."

Fabián got out a sheet of paper and started scribbling something. It was a Would You Rather? chart. I grinned; this was one of our favorite games. He handed it to me, and I began writing the first question while Ruth shot us a dirty look. Sometimes it felt like Ruth was the angel on my shoulder, reminding me to be good. But Fabián was definitely the devil.

"Actionable means realistic. And when President Polk was elected, he set out to accomplish just four things. Four things that he completed while in office . . . and he never ran for a second term."

Would you rather . . . go to Homecoming with Principal Saulk or James K. Polk?

Fabián chewed his pencil, thinking. "Was James K. Polk hot?" he whispered.

I shook my head. James K. Polk was dead. And very moldy by now. Fabián circled him anyway.

Principal Saulk continued pacing the stage, like he was recording a comedy special and not our freshman welcome assembly.

"James K. Polk's four goals were to cut taxes, make the US Treasury independent, annex the territory of Oregon, and win California and New Mexico from Mexico."

Fabián suddenly booed. A couple other Mexican kids joined him. Principal Saulk looked uncomfortable.

"¡VIVA LA RAZA!" someone shouted. I started booing, too, out of solidarity. People were getting out of their chairs now, and Fabián and I stood up with them as we jeered loudly.

"Okay, okay, fair enough. Maybe not the best example of actionable goals." Principal Saulk chuckled nervously.

The crowd kept booing. I knew loudly heckling a school administrator was something Quiet Parvin shouldn't be doing, but the bells of justice must ring. This might have been the best thing that had happened at high school so far. Ruth looked supremely uncomfortable.

"Enough!" Principal Saulk shouted. "If you need to talk to anyone about the trauma of the Gadsden Purchase of 1853, I encourage you to reach out to our head counselor, Mrs. Everly. Now, what are four goals *you* want to accomplish this year? Please write them down," he directed us.

I sat down and got out my notebook, then I stared at the blank page. What the heck *did* I want to accomplish this year?

I looked over at Fabián's paper. *Not . . . commit . . . genocide,* he wrote. That was a good one.

Ruth, of course, was already done. *1—Make first chair clarinet, 2—stay on Honor Roll, 3—get a 4.0 GPA*. I looked closer. In tiny script she'd added, *Come out to my mom,* as number 4, with an asterisk. At the bottom of the page, she'd written, **Reach goal*.

I smiled. I was proud of Ruth. She had a good list.

Maybe she wasn't going to wait until graduation to come out to her mom after all.

I tapped my pencil on the page.

1—Go with Matty to Homecoming.

Fabián read over my shoulder and whispered, "Good luck with that." I swatted him away.

2—Pick an instrument/decide if I want to stay in band.

3—Get better at Farsi.

4—Finally understand how leap years work.

"Parvin, number four isn't a real goal," Ruth whispered, clearly spying. I sighed.

"Ruth, how can there be one-fourth of a day left over at the end of every year? How?"

"It has to do with the rotation of the Earth. What do you not understand? Besides, you can google that in two seconds. It's not a real goal."

I scribbled out the leap year goal and angrily wrote in a new one.

4—Make a new friend.

I glared accusingly at Ruth. She glared back.

"Yeah, a *cute* one," Fabián whispered.

The auditorium was silent with the sounds of papers shuffling around. Suddenly, someone raised their hand. Principal Saulk blinked a couple times, like the hand was a mirage in the desert.

"Yes? Mr. . . . ?"

"Cheng," a voice finished for him. It was Emerson Cheng, the arsonist from our middle school. He wore baggy pants and a gold chain around his neck.

"Cherry Bomb Cheng goes to Polk? How did I not know this?" Fabián hissed, already texting someone about this new development. They had a long-standing beef, in that Emerson always set off the fire alarm with fireworks at school dances just when Fabián was getting the crowd heated up.

"Emerson's eyebrows grew back in," Ruth observed.

"Oh yeah," I replied. "He actually looks pretty cute now."

"Parvin. He's a pyromaniac," Ruth chided me.

"Don't worry, Ruth, I'm a Leo." I patted her arm gently.

Emerson stood up in the middle of the auditorium, facing Principal Saulk.

"Principal Saulk, what does the *K* stand for?" Emerson asked.

"Excuse me?" He blinked back rapidly, fiddling with his mic pack.

"The *K*? In James K. Polk? Our eleventh president?"

The whole auditorium was staring at him now, but Emerson didn't seem fazed.

"I . . . er . . . ," Principal Saulk said, his face turning bright red. "Well . . . I . . . I don't actually know," he finished, his voice trailing off.

The entire freshman class was drop-dead silent. Fabián tried hard not to laugh.

"Okay," Emerson said.

"Yep." Principal Saulk nodded back to him, as if the matter were settled.

This high school was already robbing me of a real education.

• • •

INTRODUCTION TO VIDEO
10:00 A.M.

I signed up for Intro to Video because I thought I'd learn how to make cool eyeshadow tutorials and help Fabián with his own videos. Instead, I was learning I was the only girl in this class.

At least Wesley didn't take this elective. That meant I'd never have to see him in class, which was a relief. He probably signed up for Technical Drawing, or whatever stupid people did. *Why didn't I sign up for Technical Drawing?* I suddenly thought, panicking. *Snap out of it, Parvin! You've got a new plan now.* Besides, I could barely draw, much less technically.

Our teacher, Mr. Clarke, had already assigned us a project: Make a one-minute video introducing yourself. We had to check out cameras from school and then edit the videos together in class next week.

Part of me wanted to just get the one-minute video over with, but a smaller, tinier part of me was actually excited about the assignment. Like, maybe I could even learn enough to help Fabián light his videos so they'd look super professional, since he only used the overhead lights in his basement. Or maybe I could even learn enough to teach Ameh Sara when she came to visit, so she could add another skill to her résumé. But it was probably safer to just be Non-Loud Parvin and record something boring.

Unfortunately, my desk mate was a guy who insisted we call him "Sir," like a knight. I could barely get people to pronounce my real name correctly, but here I had to deal with this dude who thought he was actually royalty or something. Not that you'd mistake him for someone with noble blood. Sir had stringy brown hair and greasy pale skin. He also had a deep obsession with his floor-length trench coat, as he refused to take it off even though he was clearly sweating.

"Hey," he said, looking at the Vampire Weekend sticker on my laptop. "That's cool."

What was I supposed to say? *Thanks for validating my music choices?* Or *Do you even know who Vampire Weekend is?*

Instead I gave a chilly thanks.

He nodded back at me, as if waiting for me to provide more conversation. I could feel Mr. Clarke walking our way to make sure we'd finished our list of favorite movies for our in-class assignment. I didn't need both Ms. Kaiser *and* Mr. Clarke thinking I was a complete failure. I turned back to my work.

"Hey," Sir said again, poking me with a pencil. Oh my god. Why couldn't he leave me alone? I bet Ruth didn't have to deal with this kind of harassment in Creative Writing. To top it off, Fabián was in theater with Matty right now. I tried not to think of the great time they were probably having.

I turned toward Sir, attempting to look polite, but I had to work extra hard since my eyebrows were so thick they made me look angry all the time.

"Where are you from?" Sir asked.

"What?" I was clearly from the DC-Maryland-Virginia region, aka the DMV, like everyone else in this godforsaken place.

"Like . . . where were you born?" Oh no. I knew what was happening. It was the dreaded why-aren't-you-as-white-as-me? question.

"I was born at Washington Hospital Center." I smiled. It wasn't like I was embarrassed of being Iranian, but it wasn't great having to explain why your eyelashes were twelve feet long or why your last name was hard to spell. Besides, Wesley wasn't in this class, so I decided to have a little fun and go back to my mischievous ways.

"No, like, where are your parents from?" Sir pressed.

"Ohhh," I replied, pretending to understand. "My mom's from Colorado. And my dad grew up here—he went to Polk, actually."

I struggled not to laugh. I knew Sir wanted me to explain how my dad was originally from Iran, but why did I have to be a mind reader? I was 100 percent American. I was allowed to act like it.

Sir grimaced, frustrated. "That's not what I—"

"Sir, Parvin, please focus on the assignment," Mr. Clarke called out. Time to really mess with Sir.

"Mr. Clarke, what's the name of that movie that won the Oscar? With that guy doing the play about a salesman? It's one of my favorites, but I can't remember the name." That was a lie. My favorite movies were rom-coms or animated films. The movie I was thinking of had neither romance nor cartoons, but it hadn't stopped me from sneaking downstairs to watch it through our staircase during one of Mom and Dad's date nights (blergh).

"Oh! *The Salesman*," Mr. Clarke replied. "That movie's from Iran—yes, I believe it won the Foreign Film Oscar. Great choice, Parvin. Albeit . . . a little mature for you," he said, frowning. "Are you Iranian?"

"Yes." I beamed. "I am."

Mr. Clarke just smiled, then turned to help Emerson

Cheng with his own favorite films (anything with The Rock in it, as it turned out). Sir gaped at me.

"Why didn't you just say you were Iranian?" he whispered, clearly annoyed. You'd think someone who'd written the *Lord of the Rings* trilogy as one of their favorite movies would be a little more patient with getting to know someone.

I shrugged. "You never asked." And then I hid my face in my arm so that I wouldn't cackle.

. . .

LUNCH
12:00 P.M.

"I always just tell people I'm Korean." Ruth shrugged after I told her about the Sir incident in Intro to Video.

"Yeah, but you shouldn't *have* to, right?" I asked. "It's not really any of their business."

Ruth nodded, sitting across from me. "True. But I *look* Korean. You look . . . er . . . well, you could be from anywhere," she added. Sigh.

Ruth stared off to the other side of the courtyard as I ate bits of kimbap from her lunch box. Ruth was also not thrilled with her new elective. "Mr. Simmons wants us to expand on our four goals for Creative Writing," she said anxiously.

"That should be easy, right? Just write about getting good grades and the clarinet and stuff."

"I have." Ruth dropped to a whisper: "But he wants all four. Including the one I wrote about coming out to my mom."

Just then, I spied Matty walking across the football field with a couple juniors and seniors. It looked like they were leaving campus for lunch, and I watched all of them pile into a beat-up minivan. Maybe if Matty and I date, I'll be able to leave campus for lunch, too.

"Parvin!" Ruth clapped. "Hello?!"

I sucked my eyes away from the parking lot and back to Ruth. Her face looked flushed, and I could tell she was truly freaking out. I snapped out of my daydream.

"Huh?"

"My teacher wants me to write about coming out to my mom, remember?" Ruth huffed.

"Just make up another goal. You don't have to come out to your Creative Writing teacher. That would be a violation of the Geneva Convention, or whatever it's called."

Poor Ruth. Most assignments came really easily to her. I was pretty sure she'd never had an essay topic she hadn't outlined within hours of it being assigned.

"Maybe your fourth goal could be something like 'I'll give my friends extra peanut butter cups,'" I offered.

"Parvin! Be serious," Ruth cried.

"Okay, okay," I said, thinking. "Well, you're worried about sharing something important with your mom, right? Maybe you don't have to mention that you are into boys and girls and nonbinary people. Maybe you could just talk about sharing more parts of yourself with her."

Ruth chewed, thinking. She always squinted hard when she was considering taking any of my advice.

"Yeah," she said slowly. "That just might work. I'll do a rough draft tonight and see how it feels."

"There we go." I grinned. "Now can I have your Hot Cheetos?" I said, pointing to the bag she was trying to hide in her backpack.

Ruth laughed. "No."

Just then, the loudspeakers crackled on. "Whoever stole my parking sign, please return it to the front office," Principal Saulk demanded.

Ruth shot me an accusatory look.

"What?" I said. "I did that after I ran into Wesley and Teighan—I needed a confidence boost."

"That poor man," Ruth chided me.

"Fine, fine, I'll return it tomorrow before school and say I found it in a bush somewhere." No one would believe a quiet, mousey freshman like me had done it, anyway.

"This is Principal Saulk of James *Knox* Polk High School, by the way," he added on the loudspeaker. "That's James *Knox* Polk. Thank you."

...

BLEACHERS
3:00 P.M.

I'd almost forgotten about my Wednesday study-buddy session, but Amir had thoughtfully sent me a calendar invite. Needless to say, it was the only event on there. After school, he came trudging up the bleachers with his Farsi books, and I settled in for what was going to be the longest half hour of my life. I doubted I'd learn anything useful, but hoped to at least get our Farsi homework done.

"Hey," he said, and smiled. I smiled back. Thank goodness Amir was nice, which would make these tutoring sessions easier. He wore jeans and a long-sleeved Team Melli jersey, which was the Iranian national soccer team. He looked, if possible, even more Iranian than the last time I'd seen him. "How's your first week at school going?"

I shrugged. It was only our second day but already it felt like a lifetime. "Fine," I replied, trying not to think about how I'd started school by being unceremoniously dumped at orientation. "What about you?"

Amir groaned. "I already have so much homework. And my teachers say this will be nothing compared with junior year."

I winced sympathetically. Thank god our teachers hadn't assigned us any reading yet. All I really had to do was start thinking of my intro video and decide if I wanted to play the bassoon. Which, once I thought about it, was actually a lot.

"I noticed you were tripping yourself up on some of the letter combinations in Farsi, so I thought I'd break them down for you."

"Letter combinations?" I asked. Wasn't every word a letter combination?

"For example," Amir began, getting out a sheet of paper. "Here's an alif," he said, drawing an ا.

"And here's a laam," he continued, drawing a ل.

I yawned. "Yeah, I know that." Dad had given me Farsi alphabet blocks when I was barely a year old. This was, literally, child's play.

"Okay, but what you don't know is that when you have a laam and an alif together, it makes this symbol," and then Amir drew a لا.

"Aha!" I shouted. "That was the stupid symbol that kept messing me up during my reading."

Whoops. I'd just shouted, pointing my finger accusingly at a piece of paper in a decidedly not Quiet Parvin way. But I guess I didn't have to pretend to be less loud or passionate around Amir. Everyone knew Iranian kids only dated other full Iranians, which meant Amir would never be an option for Homecoming anyway. Plus, we probably *were* related.

Amir laughed. "I know. But it's just an *L* and an *A* connecting. So, you pronounce it 'La,'" he said, giving it a soft *A* sound.

I nodded, copying the combination into my own notebook. For a language with zero irregulars, Farsi was a slippery beast. Maybe this tutoring stuff wasn't such a waste of time after all.

"Wanna learn some more?" Amir asked.

I nodded. These were the things I'd missed out on by jumping straight into Advanced Farsi. It was useless trying to ask Dad for grammar help because he'd always answer my questions with things like "I don't know why it's like that, it just is!" or "I don't know how to conjugate a verb, I just do!"

"Parvin, you there?" Amir asked. He had shaggy curly hair, and he kept running his hands through it. He had another letter combination written down.

"Yeah, sorry." I focused back on the paper in front of me. Amir scooched closer, and I smelled that rosewater scent again.

• • •

DINNER
8:00 P.M.

Mom and Dad felt bad about how much time they'd been spending at work, so they actually cooked dinner tonight. Mom had clearly been the lead chef, as it was some kind of food hybrid with green chilis that she called "Colorado Cuisine." I took a cautious sniff at our kitchen island. If this was her culture, maybe it was for the best that we didn't cook it too often.

"What?" she asked, her apron covering the black-and-white sweater she wore. Mom loved wearing graphic prints, which looked even funnier against her frumpy apron. Her straight blond hair was more normal today, in that there were no pens or pencils stuck into it. I took another whiff, trying to decide if I wanted this food in my body.

"It's green chicken chili," she added defensively. I spooned a bit out of the soup pot, turned the spoon over, and watched it glop back into its chunky green depths. "It's a family recipe," Mom wailed, as if that explained it.

Mom's family was a mix of Scottish, Irish, and English, so her heritage usually came out in random dishes she suddenly decided to feed us. Even though her ancestors weren't born here, I noticed how nobody ever asked her where she was from or commented on her features. Mom looked like the Americans on TV and in magazines, with their long legs, blue eyes, and shiny blond hair. Next to her, I looked like a big question mark.

Just then, Dad walked in and sniffed the chili pot.

"What is it?" he asked her.

"Can't you tell?" she cried. Dad and I looked at each other, as if silently agreeing that we should just eat and not ask questions.

"Yum," Dad said unconvincingly.

"Mm-mm. Chili is the best," I agreed. Mom's eyes narrowed as she watched us, almost daring us to say her cooking sucked before we'd even tried it. Dad, American Hero that he was, took an experimental bite.

"Sooo good," he assured her. Mom relaxed, her eyes crinkling into a smile as she turned away. Dad shook his head at me and mouthed, *Don't eat it.*

"I saw that," Mom said icily.

We were doomed.

...

BATHROOM
10:00 P.M.

It was almost bedtime.

"Mom?" I called out from my bathroom. Thank god I had my own, for situations exactly like this. I'd already tried video chatting Ameh Sara, but she didn't pick up. I was down to my last resort—and by last resort, I mean asking my own mother for help.

Mom peeked her head in. "What's up?"

I pointed to my leg. There, on my thigh, was a hair that looked like it was trapped in my skin. It was starting to hurt, like a pimple that you couldn't see yet but knew was lurking below the surface.

"Huh," Mom said, looking closer at the bump. "Is that an ingrown hair?"

I shrugged. How was I supposed to know? "You're the expert," I whined. Mom usually helped me wax in places I couldn't reach, like the backs of my arms and legs.

Mom frowned and got out her phone. "I've heard about these, but I've never had one myself."

I rolled my eyes. Mom didn't even have to shave her thighs, that's how light her hair was. Meanwhile, she still wouldn't let me get laser hair removal, saying, "We don't fully understand the technology yet." *Please*. Every full Iranian girl got laser hair removal. That, or a nose job.

"Okay, it says here that you shouldn't pick at it, and apply a topical solution like . . ." Mom trailed off. "Oh, it's just an ad for a skincare cream."

I sighed.

"Don't worry, sweetie, I'm sure it will grow out," she said cheerfully. Easy for her to say—she didn't have a red pustule sprouting from her thigh like one of Zeus's lesser children.

"Yeah," I replied. "Thanks."

Mom closed the door, as if she were saying to herself, *Problem solved*.

News flash: The problem was not solved. It was like when I wanted to get my eyebrows waxed and Mom insisted on doing them at home with an in-home wax strip kit. It took three months for my right eyebrow to grow back. This, too, seemed beyond her. How we shared the same genes I would never know.

I looked in the mirror, trying to find any bits of Mom in my face. I had Dad's tan skin, although it looked like mine had been watered down. My brown hair looked messy next to Mom's straight blond hair, and I could never get it to turn into the loose curls that girls like Teighan styled on Instagram. On top of everything else, my nose had this sharp hook that could only be described as a black-diamond ski bump. Mom's nose, however, was a cute bunny slope. I looked nothing like her.

I pulled up a photo of Dad on my cell phone and stared hard in the mirror. If anything, I looked like a female clone of Dad. That would have been okay if there were more girls who looked like me on TV or in magazines, but all I had to compare myself to were people in my Farsi class and Ameh Sara, who were full Iranian, not half like me.

All of those girls were stunning, with moms who knew how to make the best of their daughter's features because they looked like each other.

In the end, I stayed up all night watching YouTube videos of people pushing ingrown hairs out of their skin. It was fascinating, like popping a pimple. I was addicted.

Then I tried popping mine out like in the videos, but it wouldn't budge. After that I tried shaving over it, using a tweezer, and straight-up using my fingernails to pry it out. Nothing.

The ingrown hair was really throbbing now. Was it supposed to hurt this badly?

Desperate, I got out my wax kit. Mom had finally let me buy my own wax melter that I kept under my bathroom sink. I plugged it into the wall, then put a couple chunks of solid blue wax into the melting bowl. Soon, the wax had heated enough to turn liquid, and I stirred it with a Popsicle stick until it was the right consistency.

I smeared some of it onto my thigh, waited for it to harden, then ripped it off.

Sigh. The ingrown hair was still there. Maybe I wasn't doing it right?

I tried it again, but I must have heated the wax too much this time because it started dribbling down the back of my thigh. Oh god. I couldn't see back there and figure out how to pull it off. It had coated my entire leg now. How was I supposed to remove it?

Water, I thought to myself. I turned on the bathtub

faucet and waded in, letting my legs lie against the porcelain tub. I reached my hand below my leg, ready to wipe the wax off, and—

Oh my god. The wax had fused with my bathtub. It had stuck to the enamel.

"MOM!" I called out again. She barged into the bathroom and saw the blue wax clearly glued to the tub. "I couldn't wash the wax off and now I'm stuck," I explained helplessly.

Mom shook her head, eyes wide. "Oh, Parvin. What are we gonna do with you?"

The worst part was that the ingrown hair was still there.

And that my mom had to practically cut me out of my own bathtub.

Thursday

BAND
12:45 P.M.

I told Ms. Kaiser I'd go ahead with the bassoon. Instead of sulking in the last clarinet chair, I might as well give the new instrument a shot. I figured Matty would probably find me playing a new instrument more interesting than being the worst at the clarinet. After all, I only had a month to get a Homecoming date, and I would take any potential advantage I could get.

Ms. Kaiser seemed relieved when I said I'd switch in band today. "Here, let's go get it for you," she said.

We walked into a dusty closet to the side of the band

room that was packed with instruments. I sneezed. She began opening and closing a bunch of random cases, a lot of them filled with instruments I'd never seen before.

"Mellophone . . . marching euphonium . . . sousaphone . . . bass clarinet," she mumbled to herself. "Aha, here we go." She took down a long, flat, rectangular case. Then Ms. Kaiser opened it up slowly, almost reverently, and showed me all the pieces.

"See that, Parvin? The keypads are made out of kidskin, or baby goat. That's why it's so soft."

I looked down, horrified. I was the only one in band with an instrument that was Not Vegan. Not that I was vegan. But still.

"Here's the bocal," she said, taking a long squiggly metal piece and sticking it into the main bedpost part. She attached a little chimney to the top of it. It looked like a ginormous pretzel that had folded in on itself, with a hole at the top for Santa to come down and deliver presents. She handed it to me, as if I knew what to do with it.

I was starting to seriously doubt my commitment to bassoondom.

I waddled out of the closet with the bassoon, and she showed me how to sit on the leather belt attached to the bottom, which helped offset the weight of the four-foot-tall instrument. I laid the belt across the chair, then . . . I sat on it.

Dear God, when I die, please don't let it be while sitting on a bassoon.

"Here, Parvin—it's the login for a tutorial website. There are a bunch of beginner bassoon videos I want you to go over for the rest of class. You can use a practice room while we rehearse."

"Okay," I said, taking the piece of paper with the URL on it from her. She headed toward the podium.

"Cool instrument," I heard someone say behind me. I turned. Matty Fumero was admiring the wooden serpent that I'd somehow agreed to play.

"It's a bassoon, right?" he asked, walking up to me. But I couldn't answer. My face had frozen into a pathetic grin, as if I was happy all the time and this was just how I normally looked. It worked! Switching to bassoon had worked, because Matty was talking to me now.

"Yeaahhhp," the air between my teeth expelled from my mouth.

"Nice," he said. I nodded back, the top of my bassoon nodding with me. He headed back to his chair and emptied the spit valves from his (vegan) trumpet. Success!

I turned to my music stand, thinking. All throughout orientation, and that time at lunch, I had been pretty quiet around Matty, even though Ruth or Fabián would *never* describe me as soft-spoken. But it seemed like the quieter I was around him, the more he responded to me. So far the only words I'd said to him were my name, *better*, and *yeah*, yet he still seemed under the impression that I was a normal, not too-much person. It could only mean one thing: My Quiet Parvin plan was working.

"You gorgeous bedpost," I whispered to my instrument. "It's me and you, kid."

Or was it *kids*, because of all the baby goat skin?

To be googled.

· · ·

WALK HOME
3:00 P.M.

Ruth and Fabián had Gay-Straight Alliance today. That meant I was walking home alone, completely abandoned by my friends, lugging a hundred-pound bassoon case.

Now that I had chosen Matty as the target for my Homecoming plan, I needed "actionable" steps on how to win him over. I couldn't just be quiet around him (though that was important, and it seemed to be working). I needed clear direction on what to do next.

I got out the Notes app on my phone and began brainstorming, thinking of all the steps that happened before the guy and girl fell in love in the movies, and how I could recreate them with Matty.

ACTIONABLE
MATTY FUMERO STEPS:

- Have him initiate a conversation with me (CHECK!)
- Talk for longer than two minutes
- Laugh at one of his jokes
- Compliment him on something
- Make physical contact (hug? elbow touch? accidentally run into him?)
- Have sustained eye contact (every movie had this)
- ??
- ???
- Go to Homecoming together, make Wesley jealous, etc., etc.

My phone buzzed, letting me know that Fabián was starting a livestream. I clicked it open to reveal him in the school gymnasium.

"¡Hola, familia!" he sang out. "GSA doesn't meet for another fifteen minutes, so I wanted to show you all some stuff I've been working on."

Who was holding the phone? Was it Ruth? I thought jealously. The phone kept moving, which meant someone was helping Fabián film. He pressed play on the music and began dancing to a slow R & B song. It was amazing how his body moved like liquid, and he unrolled his arms and legs so gracefully it was easy to forget you were watching a fourteen-year-old and not a dance master.

The slow song matched Fabián's syrupy moves, and I could see the number of viewers jump from hundreds to a thousand. Luckily, Fabián never shared his location or anything like that, but still. He was famous enough now to have rabid fans, and I could see them comment things like "MARRY ME, Fabián!" or "Ughhh, I luv u so much xx" in the live feed. But Fabián couldn't see them as he slowly spun around, finishing with his hands on his hips.

"Thanks for watching, familia! Chau!" He blew a kiss to the camera, and the stream ended.

"Parvin?" a voice called out. Dear god, what now?

I turned. Or rather, I waddled around. This bassoon case was no joke—it was a big, flat rectangle that was not very aerodynamic. Should a gust of wind blow, it was definitely taking me down with it.

It was Wesley. I wished my heart didn't race every time I saw him. It made getting over him much, much harder. Didn't he live a good twenty minutes away by car? Oh, wait . . . he was probably visiting Teighan, his new, perfect girlfriend.

"Hi, Wesley." My voice cracked.

My hair was straight, my outfit was an inoffensive jeans and black blouse combo, and I'd waxed my mustache last night, making the skin there so red I had to wear concealer on my top lip. But still, I felt vulnerable. I walked a little faster toward the creek path, hoping that was all he had to say to me. Besides, I had to go home and learn how to assemble my bassoon and potentially figure out how to sit on it again.

But Wesley hurried to catch up to me, which made me happy, even though I knew it shouldn't. Curse you, feelings!

"So . . . ," he began. He wore another polo shirt and khakis, the spitting image of a youth group leader. After seeing him run rampant at the beach, he looked completely unlike himself. Where were his cutoff shorts and cartoon tees? This new Wesley was bewildering. "How are your classes?" he asked.

"Fine," I replied.

I wasn't about to give him the satisfaction of a real conversation. I knew that the less I said, the less I would seem like that girl on the beach who he talked to for hours on end, the one he'd decided wasn't good enough. Besides, this bassoon was very heavy, and I didn't have a lot of words to spare.

"Cool," Wesley said, undeterred. "I replaced the saltshakers at our lunch table with sugar."

I didn't say anything. I just raised my eyebrows.

"Yeah . . . That was an easy one. But Teighan wasn't exactly thrilled when she poured sugar all over her fries."

What was this, a confessional? That prank was pretty tame, all things considered. Still, I would have loved to see Teighan try to eat French fries with sugar on top. I remained strong, keeping my chuckles to myself. I could still smell his intoxicating brand of soap wafting over, though. *Stay firm, Parvin.*

We were at Teighan's street now.

"Well, it was good to talk to you, Parvin," Wesley said quietly, looking into my eyes for once. *I am an ice queen,* I repeated to myself. *I don't melt for any man.*

"Tell Teighan I say hi." I smiled back. I'd said two sentences this entire conversation, and I could tell it made Wesley feel uncomfortable.

He winced, then stalked off.

I headed toward my house, bassoon in tow. What the heck had just happened? Why was Wesley trying to talk to me after he blasted my heart to smithereens? The worst part was that Ruth and Fabián weren't here to tell me what they thought about the whole thing. I was the only one who could dissect our conversation, which would probably make me feel even more miserable.

But what did I care? I had moved on, hadn't I?

My plan to get Matty to ask me to Homecoming was just getting started.

. . .

MY ROOM
9:30 P.M.

It was late enough for me to Skype Ameh Sara over in Tehran. She'd been sending me WhatsApp messages asking how school was going, but it wasn't the same as talking face-to-face. Her screen popped up, and this time she was fully dressed in a bright yellow chador and a long-sleeved black shirt. Even though it was still Thursday night in my bedroom, it was already Friday morning in Iran.

"Sob bekheir, Ameh," I said, wishing her a good morning.

"Sob bekheir, Parvin joon. How are you? You look better."

I felt better, too. Having a plan was a good feeling. "Thanks, Ameh. How's school?"

Sara shrugged. "It's okay. The sanctions make it hard to buy art supplies."

I had heard about the US putting up sanctions against Iran, saying that Iran was a threat to democracy or whatever.

"My maman is having a hard time getting her insulin shots, for her diabetes . . ." Sara trailed off.

"Oh no." I grimaced. "She needs those, right? Other-wise . . ." I didn't know what else to say. Not having insulin shots meant you could lose a limb or go blind. It was really, really serious.

"It's okay, azizam." Sara waved it away. "When I come visit you, I can stock up on medication for my mom and my friends. I've already got an extra suitcase that I'll bring and fill up there."

"What other stuff do you need, Ameh? Maybe I can get it for you?"

"Oh, Parvin joonam. You don't need to do that. But maybe when I'm there you can help me shop, okay? I won't know where to go."

I nodded. "Of course." This would be her first time in the US. It would probably be really disorienting. I could be her tour guide, for sure.

"How is school for you?" she asked. I had almost for-gotten why I'd Skyped her in the first place, but now it felt small in comparison to her hunting down insulin in Tehran.

"Well," I began. "Like I texted earlier, I've come up with a plan."

"Yes, the plan." She clapped her hands. "Go on."

"So, unfortunately I told Wesley I had a date to Homecoming, even though I don't." Sara was already frowning. "But it's okay," I backtracked. "Because I've figured out how to get a date."

"How?" she asked, brows narrowing. Our eyebrows were probably the most expressive parts of our face, they were so thick. It was nice seeing mine mirrored in her delicate features and not Dad's furious ones.

"I'm setting my sights on someone better than Wesley. His name is Matty Fumero, and he's really nice and cool. Plus, he's a sophomore."

Sara said nothing, her face in full-on frown mode. "Why you are rushing to get another date?" she demanded. "Why do you need one at all?"

"Well . . . because . . ." There was no way to explain this without sounding stupid. "Wesley was my first boyfriend. Nobody ever liked me before that. And I want to prove to him that I can be liked again, you know?"

"People already like you, though," Sara pressed. "I don't know if I like this plan."

"It'll be great, Ameh! You'll see."

"You are perfect the way you are, azizam! Without anyone else." Sara gestured emphatically through the computer screen, but I wasn't about to fall for her same pep talk again. Last time she told me how great I was, I felt good for maybe a couple hours before realizing that friends and family complimenting you meant nothing if you didn't have a boyfriend to back up their claims.

Just smile and nod. "Thanks, Ameh."

"I love you, azizam."

"Man dustet daram, Ameh."

Sunday

FARSI SCHOOL
10:55 A.M.

"Dad, what do you *do* while I'm in Farsi class?" I asked as we pulled up to the church that Sunday. I'd spent most of Friday and Saturday night trying to record my intro video and failing. Making videos was harder than I'd thought. It made me appreciate Fabián's social media skills even more.

Dad put the car in park and shrugged. "I just talk to the other parents, that's all. It's nice."

"Do you miss speaking in Farsi all the time?"

He laughed. "Where is this coming from?"

It was my turn to shrug. "I'm just curious. It must be weird speaking one language and then switching to another for the rest of your life."

He looked out the windshield, searching for an answer. "Speaking Farsi reminds me that I was born somewhere else, that I come from Iran. Sometimes I can go for days or weeks forgetting that I've got this whole other piece of me. And then I come here, and I get to remember again. It's hard without my dad here anymore. He kept that part alive."

He turned to face me, his eyes sad. I could tell he missed his dad a lot.

"When Ameh Sara comes, you'll get to speak to her in Farsi, right?"

His face brightened. "Yeah, I'm looking forward to that. She should be here in a couple weeks. Now hurry or you'll be late, and you won't be able to speak to your ameh in Farsi."

"Khodafez," I mumbled.

He kissed my forehead, and I shuffled out of the car.

"Everyone," Aghayeh Khosrowshahi began from the head of the classroom, "today we have a new student."

I looked up from the poetry Amir and I had been reading to see a girl standing near the classroom door, one who looked even less Iranian than I did. *Yes!* I silently screamed. I wasn't the least Iranian person here anymore. Now, there was somebody even more watered-down than I was. *Ha-ha-ha-haaa!*

"Please welcome Azar Rossi. Khosh amadi!" *Welcome!* "Why don't you tell us a little about yourself?" he prodded Azar. She had curly hair like me, but light sunflower eyes and skin with pink undertones, unlike my olive ones. Everyone in class had olive skin except Hanna, who was Black Iranian.

Azar took a breath and then began spouting off a bunch of stuff in rapid-fire Farsi. She had a husky voice, like she was getting over a cold, but her pronunciation was perfect. You could tell she wasn't translating words in her head, either. She spoke fluidly. Amir leaned in, trying to catch up.

When Azar finished, Hanna gave a stunned, slow clap. I still had no idea what the girl had said. I looked to Amir for help, but he was equally dazzled.

"Barikalla!" Aghayeh Khosrowshahi cried. *Well done!* "I meant you could say a bit about yourself in English, but this is better."

What gives?! I wanted to scream. I finally got a classmate who looked less Iranian than I did, but she was a professional linguist or something. Even Laleh looked impressed. Laleh, who was nine years old and in Advanced Farsi.

"She said she loves music and writing song lyrics, and that she goes to James K. Polk. She also said she's taking this class because she never learned to read or write in Farsi," Amir finally whispered back.

"Thanks," I replied as Azar took a seat toward the back. *Hah! She's illiterate in Farsi*. At least I could read and write. The thought cheered me up as I opened the new workbook I got so I wouldn't have to share with Amir anymore.

"Out of curiosity"—Aghayeh Khosrowshahi turned toward Azar—"do you speak any other languages?"

Azar cleared her throat. "Um. Spanish. And Italian."

God help us all.

Monday

BAND
2:00 P.M.

By Monday afternoon I was getting the hang of this bassoon thing. I could sit on the strap—no problem now—and all the little keys were slightly less intimidating.

Luckily, the bassoon parts were way easier than the clarinet parts. I just made long, low honks of the same note, over and over. I forgot that since this instrument was deeper-sounding, I wouldn't have as many fun melodies or main themes. Today in band I just blared like a sad, lonely tugboat.

I looked over at Ruth, who was running through the main

tune of today's music like a demon, her fingers whipping over the keys too fast to see. And then I looked at my own fingers. My hands barely reached some of the keys at the bottom register.

Maybe I'd made a mistake. Maybe I should have just quit band.

But then I thought of Matty being a mere three rows behind me, *in the same room*. No, this was my mission and I had chosen to accept it. For better or worse.

Still, I was feeling low by the time band ended. Ruth threw an arm over my shoulder.

"Cheer up, Parvin," she said. "It almost looked like sound was coming out of your instrument—"

"Hiiiii, ladiessss," a super high-pitched voice interrupted.

We turned around. Yessenia López, first chair flute, was smiling at us. Why was she smiling? I was immediately suspicious. We were lowly freshmen—why was a cool sophomore girl talking to us? I wondered if the rules of popularity didn't apply the same way they did in band, though. After all, who were we kidding? Everyone in band was a nerd.

"I'm having my quinceañera this Saturday," she said, handing us invitations. I'd never received a physical invitation in my life. It was covered in sparkly glitter and had a white dress on the front.

"Oooh," Ruth squealed. "This looks so cool." She seriously had zero chill.

"Who else is invited?" I asked.

"Cool woodwinds only, for sure," Yessenia replied, her face turning serious. "And I'm inviting cute boys, too." She gave a pointed look to Matty, who was packing up his trumpet.

Wait, did Yessenia have a crush on Matty, too? But this meant that Matty was going to the party!

"Speaking of—you're friends with Fabián Castor, right?" Yessenia asked, fanning herself with an invite. "Maybe you could pass this on to him?"

I plucked Fabián's invite out of her hands. "We'll be there." I smiled back, my voice going up an octave to match Yessenia's. *Oh, we'll be there all right.* I still needed to laugh at one of Matty's jokes and possibly crash into him to initiate physical contact.

Yessenia sauntered away, stopping to talk to Matty.

"Ruth," I whispered. "This is it! My big chance to get Matty to notice me."

Ruth ignored me, marveling at the glittery envelope. "Do you think she got these custom? Or made them herself?"

She lovingly stroked the card stock. I knew she would definitely add it to her memory book. We'd never been invited to a quince before, and the prospect of a party with good stationery had caused her eyes to gloss over as she fantasized about the thank-you note she'd send afterward.

"Ruth," I said, shaking her by the shoulders. "Focus! Matty is going to be at the party. This is huge! I'll need to wear my cutest dress if I want to stand out from Yessenia. And ask my aunt Sara how to do my makeup. And start rehearsing our small talk, and—"

"Or maybe . . . maybe it's from an online card store?" Ruth continued, still in her own world.

"It's custom, Ruth. See? It says so on the back." I showed her the name of the designer.

"I knew it," Ruth shrieked. "Jeez, Yessenia sure is classy." Ruth had just complimented my competition for a

Homecoming date, but it was too late, the Ruth Crafting Train had already left the station, and there was nothing to do but watch it chug away.

"Here, Ruth." I sighed, handing her my invite. "You can have mine, too."

She squealed. "Thank you, P."

I was the best friend in the world. All bow before me as I bestow ye with friendship.

"Do you think Fabián will let me have his invitation, too?" Ruth asked, serious again.

"Ruth."

"What?"

"Stop talking."

. . .

MY HOUSE
8:30 P.M.

Whyyy did my parents eat dinner so late? Why, I ask you?

Ruth's mom made dinner at six sharp every single night. Fabián's parents always gave him the login to food delivery apps so he could order whatever he wanted, whenever he wanted. My parents worked within a hundred feet of our kitchen but couldn't bother to set foot in it.

"Mom?" I called downstairs. "Dad?"

Nobody answered. They must be out.

I tried making a snack for myself but the only things in the fridge were kale, Dijon mustard, some kind of ancient grain, and yogurt soda. Thankfully, Mom and Dad walked in just then, both of them looking pretty sad.

"Who died?" I asked.

"Parvin, you've got bits of kale in your teeth," Mom said.

"We went to an immigration lawyer," Dad replied, sitting down heavily at the countertop bar.

"Why?"

"For Sara's visa," Mom replied.

"Oh." I didn't know they needed a lawyer so Sara could get a visa. "So, what'd the lawyer say?"

Dad shook his head and took a sip of water. He looked too bummed to speak. "Since Sara is only a half sister, it might be difficult getting her approved. Apparently only siblings and parents can get a visa from Iran right now because of the Muslim ban. They're not sure about half siblings."

I gave Dad a hug. He kissed the top of my head.

"Thanks, baba jaan," he said.

We sat there around the kitchen island, wondering if we'd get to see Sara soon.

"Want me to order Vietnamese food?" I asked into the silence.

"That would be great, Parvin," Mom said, putting her hand on Dad's.

It felt weird not knowing when I was going to see my aunt again. We'd always talked about her coming to visit us in the States, but this year it finally felt like it was really going to happen. Now this visa thing was standing in the way.

I had planned on spending tonight brainstorming ways for Matty to fall in love with me (and not Yessenia) for the party on Saturday.

But I didn't feel like it right now.

Wednesday

BLEACHERS
4:00 P.M.

Amir was so patient I didn't know how he hadn't exploded already.

"It's okay," he said for the millionth time as I flubbed a line of poetry from our spot on the bleachers. "Just try again."

We'd gone way past the half-hour mark on our study session this Wednesday. Because that's how much I sucked at Farsi.

"Are you sure?" I asked. "We can stop now, if you want. I don't mind." *Please let this be over,* I shouted in my head. *LET THE TORTURE STOP.*

"I'm good. So, whenever there's a و mark above an alif, or *A*, it means you pronounce it like an *O*. But only at the start of a word, though."

"Okay," I replied. Amir hunched over the poetry book with me, our knees almost touching. *Layla and Majnun* was one of Nizami's most famous poems about two star-crossed lovers, and I read a couple of lines out loud in slow Farsi:

*"While all their friends were toiling at their books
These two were trying other ways of learning.
Reading love's grammar in each other's looks.
Glances to them were marks which they were earning."*

Amir nodded along. We'd finished our translation homework a while ago, but he still insisted on making sure I got better at reading out loud for when it was my turn again in class this Sunday.

"Nice, Parvin," he said. I grinned back at him, proud that I hadn't flubbed a line. He pronounced my name the traditional way, with the hard A. I'd never had a friend say it like that. Even Ruth and Fabián said it "Pahr-VEEN," with the soft A.

"Thanks."

Amir jiggled his leg on the bleacher. "So . . . ," he started. "Want to do the next stanzas?"

Egad. No!

"Don't you have better things to do than tutor a freshman?" I asked. "Not that I'm not grateful or anything," I added. "It's just . . ."

I let the sentence hang there.

"It's just that we've been doing this for an hour already?" He laughed, finishing my sentence. "Sorry, I forgot we only said half an hour. I just don't want to go home yet."

I nodded. Talking to Amir was easy, like talking to Ruth and Fabián. I didn't have to worry about trying to be Quiet Parvin around him.

We sat there for a bit. It was starting to get chilly, one of those summer days when you could smell fall close behind it. I shivered.

"Why don't you want to go home?" I asked.

Amir shrugged. "My dad wants me to help him with patients, refill sterilized trays, schedule appointments— anything to keep me in his office. Whenever I have stuff after school, it means that I don't have to go. Like tutoring you, or track."

"You don't want to be a dentist?" I asked, though I was

pretty sure I knew the answer already.

"No." It was his turn to shiver. Even though we were done reading, we were still sitting pretty close. His dark brown eyes looked over the football field, his shaggy hair flopping over his forehead.

"What do you want to be, then?"

"I want to be a writer," Amir answered firmly. "I want to tell amazing stories. Or, put them to paper." He turned to me, eyes blazing. I wondered if my eyes ever blazed. I liked the way his eyes looked when they were almost on fire, I decided.

"That's awesome." I nodded. "I have no idea what I want to be. That's cool that you do." I figured Amir would want to become an engineer or a lawyer, something that all the Iranian moms and dads begged their kids to become. Amir saying he wanted to be a writer surprised me.

He sighed. "Sometimes it's cool. I wish we had more than one creative writing class, though, which I already took freshman year. Then I could show my parents what I can really do."

"Right," I said, chewing a nail. Ruth was in that class. "Don't we have a school journal or something?" Our middle school had one, where students could submit their poetry and short stories.

"Nah." Amir sighed. Dressed in another soccer jersey and gold chain, he definitely did not look like a writer. But then again, I'm not what people thought of when they pictured what an Iranian girl should look like. Maybe it was okay to not look the part sometimes.

"You should start your own journal," I suddenly blurted out. "You could be the first to make one at Polk."

Since school began, I'd been trying hard not to talk too much around boys, or exclaim things out loud before thinking about what I was going to say. But I could tell Amir wouldn't mind if I did. It was a huge relief, to be honest.

He laughed. "Maybe. I'm on yearbook for now. It's okay."

"Well, thanks for being my study buddy," I said, not sure what else to say.

"Khahesh mikonam," Amir replied, using the Farsi phrase for *you're welcome*.

"Your pronunciation is so good."

He waggled his eyebrows and waved his hands in the air, doing a perfect imitation of Aghayeh Khosrowshahi, "If you peh-rac-ticed FAR-see, then you could eh-sound good, too."

I snorted. Amir continued waggling his eyebrows at me. It really was uncanny.

Just then, my phone rang. "Hey." As I picked up, Amir quieted down.

"Parvin!" Mom cried into the telephone. "Sara's visa was approved."

"Really?" I squealed. "Okay, I'm coming home." I hung up, grinning like an idiot.

"Everything okay?" Amir asked.

"My ameh's visa was approved. I'll get to see her soon."

Amir grinned. "Nice."

"Thanks for helping me today," I said, hugging him. I was so happy I probably crushed him, but I didn't care. I was going to see Sara.

"Khodafez!" he shouted at me as I ran down the bleachers.

"Bye!" I shouted back.

HOME
5:30 P.M.

Mom and Dad were so ecstatic about Sara's visa that they made dinner while the sun was still out. My body didn't even know what to do with food that early. I just stared at it as they told me how Sara got a call from the US Interests Office (the US doesn't have an embassy in Iran, because . . . well . . . I don't actually know) and they said her visa was approved because she *was* a sister after all. Dad looked like he was going to cry, he was so happy.

We sat down at the dining room table (something we never did). Mom had me set the table (ditto), and it felt like we were actually one of those normal families in the frozen pizza commercials. I passed Mom salad (!) and Dad loaded my plate up with potato casserole (??!). Who were these people? And could they stay forever?

"So, when exactly does Ameh Sara come?" I asked, eating an actual vegetable.

"We're going to buy her ticket tomorrow for the last weekend in September," Mom replied. "She'll stay through Christmas. Her university's letting her take a leave of absence after midterms, and then she'll finish the courses next spring."

"Really?" That meant Sara would be here in three weeks. Which meant she'd be here for Homecoming, which was the Saturday after she got here. And she could help me with my makeup.

"Really." Mom smiled. I smiled back.

Since we ate dinner so early, Mom and Dad insisted

we watch TV together. I picked *The Great British Baking Show*, the episode where one of the contestants uses barberries, which is a berry used a lot in Iran.

Mom passed me the fluffy blanket and wrapped it around me. It was so nice being cozy in the living room with my parents for once. I remember when they first started their company how we would have random movie nights and they'd even pick me up from class before the school day ended to go into DC. But now they were so busy they didn't finish until 7:00 p.m., and I watched movies in my room by myself.

I didn't realize how much I'd missed those days.

"Wait," Dad said to the TV. "What is this kid doing? That's not how you use barberries!"

"It's too late, Dad. Paul Hollywood, the judge, already said it tasted good."

He harrumphed, then said, "The British ruin everything."

Thursday

INTRODUCTION TO VIDEO
10:00 A.M.

All week Mr. Clarke taught us how to edit videos on the school computers, and now we were screening them in class. I'd even learned a cool lighting trick that I was going to show Fabián after school today when we were supposed to film another dance video.

The classroom lights dimmed. We started with a video that Emerson Chang had made. It faded in with him walking down a street in slow motion, nodding at the camera. Then the rap music began.

"Emerson," Mr. Clarke barked. "What did I say about explicit language?"

Emerson just grinned from his desk. "My bad, Teach."

Mr. Clarke shook his head and moved to the next video, which was Sir's.

"Hello." Sir's video started in front of a small house, with him sweating in his trench coat. "My name is Sir Thompson, and this is my home."

The scene changed to Sir standing in front of a bed. "And this is my bed."

"This is my mom"—the camera cut to him pointing at a woman who looked confused as to why she was being filmed—"and this is my cat." Sir lifted a cat.

"Thank you," Sir said to the camera.

We all clapped politely. It felt more like a scavenger hunt than an introduction video, but Sir was grinning so wide I was almost happy for him.

"Good job," I whispered, trying to be nice to him after the whole where-are-you-from? debacle.

"Thanks," he said, then licked his right pinkie and index finger and used them to smooth both his eyebrows. Never mind.

I heard the music from my video play and put my head in my hands. I thought wearing a bathing suit to a birthday pool party was the most uncomfortable feeling in the world, but no, it was watching a video of yourself in front of your entire class.

"Hi, my name is Parvin Mohammadi," I said into the

computer screen. I'd been too intimidated to use one of the school's cameras, so I used my laptop camera. At least I was using natural light from my bedroom window in a way that illuminated my face, just like Mr. Clarke had taught us.

"My hobbies include—" Just then, while filming, Mom had walked into my room.

"Mom! I'm busy," I shouted at her.

"Sorry," she said, looking at the laptop. "But do you have any dirty laundry? I'm doing a load."

I sighed into the screen. "I do," I replied.

The classroom laughed. I removed my hands from my eyes, relieved. I hadn't figured out how to splice my mom out of the scene, so I had to leave her in. Thank god Wesley or Matty weren't in this class.

The camera cut again, but only because that was when I stopped recording. I hadn't learned how to actually stitch clips together from Mr. Clarke's labs, not that he didn't try to teach us. I just hated looking at my face every time we were learning about the splice tool. This time my laptop camera showed a room with a lot less dirty laundry on the floor.

"As I was saying, my hobbies include watching beauty tutorials on YouTube"—more chuckles—"eating Hot Cheetos"—some guffaws—"and playing the bassoon." Then I brought my instrument into frame, which I'd been sitting on the whole time. The classroom exploded into laughter. Hmm, that part wasn't supposed to be funny.

"Thanks for watching," I said into the camera. Then I stared at the camera for an awkwardly long time until I remembered I needed to turn it off, which made even Mr. Clarke giggle.

I nervously chewed my nails.

"Okay, class, what makes this video effective at learning who Parvin is?" Mr. Clarke asked the room. *Effective?* Did this mean I'd done a good job? A couple students raised their hands.

"She listed her hobbies," Eben Hollins said from the back row, twirling his lacrosse lanyard.

"And she kept it real," Emerson added. "Not faking it."

Mr. Clarke nodded. "The authenticity. That's what made it easy for us to get to know Parvin."

He looked at me and smiled. "Well done."

I stared back, still in shock. I hadn't learned how to use a camera or even how to edit footage together, but my teacher had said I'd done a good job. What had just happened?

We watched the rest of the class's films, but I don't think I was 100 percent there. By the time the bell rang, I was still in a daze from Mr. Clarke's compliment. After getting dumped, failing the clarinet, and botching my Farsi readings, it was tough to believe I'd done well on an assignment. Was I actually good at something for once? I started putting away my notebook when Emerson Cheng came up to my desk, his gold chains clanking loudly.

"'Sup," he said. Then he did that thing where he flicked his eyes from my shoes to my face. Was he checking me out? Is this what checking out was?

"Hello," I replied politely.

"That video you did? That was fire," he said, licking his lips. Why was he licking his lips? Were they chapped?

"Thanks."

"So, listen," he started, touching his chin as if he were stroking an invisible beard. He put his other hand in his pocket and dropped his shoulder, so he was talking to me at a slant. I tilted my head to try to align with him.

"I was thinking. You. Me. Dinner." He stood there, nodding at me, even though I hadn't said anything.

I was silent for a minute. "Um . . . can you repeat the question?" It's a good thing we were the only people left in the classroom, because I had no idea what was going on and did not need someone to witness my flustering.

Emerson laughed. "P, I'm trying to ask you out!"

I gave a nervous chuckle, my brain going into overdrive. Emerson Cheng? He was, like, a cool kid. He got suspended for setting off fireworks in the parking lot in middle school and commandeering the PA system to play old-school hip-hop. When boys pulled pranks like that, they were popular, but when I did it, I was "too much." Needless to say, he was out of my league.

"Whoa," I said out loud. Dang it. Why couldn't I just keep words in my skull?

"I know, right?" Emerson said, grinning back at me, as if he knew what a big deal asking me out was.

Emerson was cute—with his spiky black hair and bright eyes. But I had no idea what to say. All the sentences had left my brain, and I'd forgotten how to make a new one.

"It's cool, ma. I can tell Emerson has shocked you. Tell you what, you let me know next week, okay?"

I just nodded, still processing the fact that Emerson Cheng had both asked me out and referred to himself in the third person.

"Emerson out," he said, giving me an awkward fist bump and walking away with a slight, but pronounced, limp. Had he hurt himself?

But more important, what in the name of Sir's cat had just happened?

. . .

MY ROOM
9:30 P.M.

I couldn't believe Emerson asked me out after Intro to Video. Did he not think that I was too loud or too much? Or did he just not care? Or maybe the whole not-yammering-away-through-every-class-and-wearing-neutral-colors plan had worked.

It's not that I didn't want to go out with him, it's that I didn't understand why he had asked me in the first place. But what if we went out, and then he asked me to Homecoming? That would solve my problems for sure. I sat at my desk and grabbed a sheet of paper.

PROS OF GOING OUT
WITH EMERSON:

- It could turn into a Homecoming date.
- He'd make Wesley jealous.
- He's cute.
- He's a good dancer (I think).
- He's popular.
- People would think I was popular just
  for being his date.

- He would probably set something on fire
  to make me laugh.

CONS OF GOING OUT
WITH EMERSON:

- I don't know if I have a crush on him . . .
  like . . . at all?
- He'll refer to himself in the third person
  the whole time.
- He might not ask me to Homecoming,
  even if we do go out.
- I would be leading him on if I said yes.
- He would probably set something on fire
  to make me laugh.

Oh god. What was I going to do? Ruth was at a potluck
for church, and it was 6:00 a.m. on a Friday for Ameh Sara
in Tehran, where Fridays and Saturdays were the weekend.
Who knew how long she'd sleep in?

> **9:41 PM PARVIN: Fabián,
> 911 emergency! Serious
> boy conundrum!**

> **9:45 PM FABIÁN: parvin, where were you
> today? i thought you were helping me
> film my next video! i wanted to upload it
> before Yessenia's party tomorrow**

Oh no. I'd completely forgotten I was supposed to go
to Fabián's after school today to film. The Emerson thing

had thrown me off so much it had completely evacuated my brain. I could tell he was seriously annoyed.

9:51 PM PARVIN: I'm sorry!! Things got hectic and I totally spaced. Forgive me? 🙏

9:52 PM FABIÁN: 😳

9:55 PM PARVIN: Fabián?

10:00 PM PARVIN: You there?

I was just going to have to sleep on it.

Saturday

MY ROOM
10:30 A.M.

Still no clue what to do about the Emerson situation. Instead, I decided to just clear my mind and soldier on with my mission. It was already Saturday, which meant I'd be seeing Matty later today. Ameh Sara was even helping me do my makeup for Matty's party over video chat. Er, I mean, Yessenia's party. Which Matty would be at. I needed to stay focused. Besides, I probably wouldn't see Emerson until next week in class. I had time to figure it out.

"Angle your brush up, ameh," Sara said. The sun was setting there, and in the background I could hear the call to

Azane Maghreb, the last call to prayer for the day in Islam.

I tilted my eyeshadow brush higher, mimicking Sara's through the computer screen. The easiest way for her to teach me how to do makeup over video chat was if she did the same exact things to her own face. After every session we'd both walk away with the same makeover. It was our own ritual, and I loved coming up with new looks with her.

Today we were working on a look that Sara had seen in an Instagram photo. In it, a model had gold eyeshadow with dark eyeliner. There was no way I could use the same mousey brown eyeshadow I'd worn every day since hatching my plan. I had to let myself have a *little* bit of gold sparkle for today's party if I wanted to stand out from Yessenia and win over Matty.

"Blend the eyeshadow into the crease, like this," Sara said, demonstrating for me.

Because of the sanctions, Sara couldn't buy the exact same makeup as me for our makeovers, but her gold eyeshadow was close enough to mine to make it work. I focused on blending the eyeshadow in little circles like Sara, spreading it toward the edges of my eyelid. It was relaxing, getting ready with someone.

"Are you excited about the party?" she asked, still blending her eyeshadow.

"Yes!" I practically squealed. "Er, I mean, yes. Yes, I am." I remembered that I would have to be Quiet Parvin today and couldn't squeal.

"What's wrong, ameh?" Sara said, frowning. I hadn't realized I'd stopped putting my eyeshadow on.

"Oh, sorry, Ameh. It's nothing."

Sara switched eyes. "Tell me," she ordered, dabbing her makeup brush into more gold eyeshadow.

"Well, that boy I like is going to the party . . ." I paused, waiting to see if she would say anything.

Sara tilted her head, remaining silent, still listening. That was one of my favorite things about her. She always had time to listen to the dumb things going on in my life while she was probably going to cool college parties in Tehran, a city that was almost twice as big as the whole DC metro area. My life was less exciting than hers, but she never made me feel that way. For that, I loved her.

"I wanted to try something new this time around with Matty at the party. So that this time . . . this time I don't get hurt, you know?" I finished.

Sara tapped her brush against her makeup palette, thinking. "So, what do you want to do that's different?" she asked.

"Well, instead of being the one who makes jokes all the time, what if I laugh at whatever *he* says? That way he'll like me more because it shows I think he's funny." That was a key observation from the films I saw: Only the dudes cracked jokes while the women laughed.

Ameh nodded, chewing her lip. When she didn't say anything, my heart sank. Was she going to be like Ruth and tell me I was crazy?

"Azizam, do you think making jokes makes people not like you?"

I fiddled with my eyelash curler. "I mean . . . I don't know. You never see movies where the funny girl gets the guy, do you? They always laugh at whatever the man says . . ." I trailed off. "It doesn't seem to work for women who are trying to get boyfriends."

"Sometimes boys are intimidated by girls who are funny and smart," Ameh Sara replied, speaking slowly, like she was looking for the right words. "But that just means they're not sure what to do, not that it's bad."

"Exactly!" I pointed with my lip gloss. Finally, someone who understood. "So my plan is to not intimidate Matty. I'm gonna give him twenty-five percent of the Parvin Experience, and not the whole thing."

Sara's face fell. "No, khanoum, that's not what I meant. I meant that you should be a hundred percent Parvin."

I barely heard what she said. It all made sense now. *Of course* I'd intimidated Wesley. He probably felt small when standing in my "passionate" shadow. No wonder he was dating someone like Teighan now. She must make him feel like a regular old chatterbox. Even the captions on her photos were maybe three emojis. She was also not the funniest person, and as a result, Wesley probably felt like the life of the party.

"Parvin? Parvin joonam?" Sara waved at the screen. "Did you hear what I said? About how you just need to be your own person and wait for the right guy to appreciate you for who you are?"

"Yeah, yeah," I lied, still thinking about this new realization.

Sara looked unconvinced. "Hmm. I think we're ready for eyeliner now."

Oh god. Mom said eyeliner was like parallel parking— that if you messed up, you had to start all over again. And I didn't even have my learner's permit yet.

"Just hold your eyeliner pen like this, see?" I copied her hand position.

"Now bring it closer . . . ," she continued, her voice even, like she was trying to calm a skittish animal. I brought the pen nearer, its black tip looming toward my face like a missile.

"Now press onto the outside." Ameh Sara expertly applied the pen to her lash line. I brought my face toward the laptop to see, but I forgot I was holding my eyeliner pen and knocked my cheek into it.

"OW," I yelled. There was now a huge black line on my cheek. Ameh Sara's eyes went wide.

"Are you okay, azizam? What happened?"

I showed her the smudge.

She laughed. "It's okay, Parvin. That's why we have makeup remover."

. . .

IN THE CAR
2:00 P.M.

A little later, Mom drove me, Ruth, and Fabián to Yessenia's party. I started to fill them in on what had happened in Intro to Video on Thursday, swiveling around to face them from the passenger seat.

"Wait, Emerson Cheng asked you out?" Fabián cried in shock.

I crossed my arms. If Fabián had answered my 911 text, then he wouldn't have been so surprised. "Is that so hard to believe?"

"Yes," Ruth and Fabián chorused.

I sighed. "Well, he told me to think about it," I said, looking out the window. Yessenia lived in a neighborhood full of mansions with gates that opened to long driveways. This was a way fancier zip code.

"Who's Emerson Cheng?" Mom asked.

"He's in our year, Mrs. Mohammadi," Ruth piped up. "He's super popular. He was voted Most Flammable in middle school."

Mom nodded, as if that was completely normal. "So, are you gonna go out with him?" she asked me. The fact that Mom even asked me this question seemed to confirm I was allowed to date, though I probably shouldn't bring it up in front of Dad, just to be safe.

"I don't know," I moaned. "I wanted to go out with Matty."

"Emerson's hot, though. Even if he is an arsonist," Fabián said grudgingly. "He better not be here today. I'm counting on filming for my channel and do *not* need a fire marshal shutting the party down." Egad, I didn't even think about Emerson being at Yessenia's today. After all, he did not play a "cool woodwind." I pushed it out of my mind— today I had to focus on Matty.

"He's hot in a symmetrical kind of way," Ruth added thoughtfully.

"Okay then, show of hands, who thinks I should go out with Emerson Cheng?" I asked the car.

Everyone raised their hand. Even my mom, who was a big proponent of two hands on the wheel.

I guess that settled it, then.

• • •

YESSENIA'S QUINCEAÑERA
2:30 P.M.

We pulled up to Yessenia's ginormous compound. It looked bigger than our entire school.

Fabián gave a low whistle and said, *"Damn."* Mom didn't even scold him for cursing.

I stared at Yessenia's huge house and reminded myself that it was time to be Quiet Parvin. The Parvin who didn't stage elaborate pranks and just nodded and giggled at whatever boys said. The one with fantastic makeup and eyeliner (that, admittedly, had taken a couple tries). I looked down at my right hand. I'd even written the letters *NT* for "No Talking" in big Sharpie inside my palm to remind myself. It was gonna be hard.

Mom parked, then got out with us to say hello.

"You ready?" Fabián asked. I nodded. I wore a nice black dress and shoes with a wedge heel, and I'd only nicked myself twice while trying to shave my entire body. I was as ready as I was going to be.

Ruth squeezed my hand, then whispered, "This is stupid, just be yourself."

I looked away. When had being myself ever gotten me anywhere? I stared at the Sharpie letters on my hand and decided to ignore Ruth. I took a deep breath and exhaled all the "too much" out of me.

Yessenia's front lawn greeted us with two huge silver balloons for the number "15." We could hear mariachi music floating in from the backyard, and a butler opened the door when we knocked.

A freaking butler.

"Hello," Mom said, momentarily flustered in the face of a dude wearing a tuxedo and holding a silver platter. Now I knew where I got my flustering from. It must be genetic. "We're here for Yessenia?" she asked.

"Right this way," the butler said in a full-blown English accent, leading us through the marble foyer. Mom looked back at us like *Can you believe this?* We all shook our heads.

He led us from the foyer into the main part of the house, where a huge ceiling filled with skylights let in some of the September light. To the left was a gigantic marble kitchen, where parents chatted with each other, and an absolutely massive TV on the right, where some of my classmates played a really violent video game. A table with presents sat in the middle of the two spaces, practically spilling over with gifts. There must have been at least fifty guests here, plus everyone's parents. This party was no joke.

We left our presents for Yessenia on the gift table. I'd gotten her an eyeshadow palette, Ruth had made her a customized sophomore year memory book, and Fabián had regifted a skincare set that he'd gotten in the mail from some PR company.

Mom turned toward us. "Okay, I'm just going to hang out here with the adults. Just for a little bit. Then I'll come back when I pick you all up," she said, eyeing the crudité platters and fondue fountain set up just for the parents.

I rolled my eyes. "You should just stay."

"Yeah, Mrs. Mohammadi, this is kind of the event of the century. You wouldn't want to miss this," Fabián added wisely.

"All right," Mom said. "I guess I can do that." She nod-ded seriously, as if she were doing us a favor. And before I could say anything else, she waved to one of her friends and made a beeline for the fondue.

"This is amazing," Ruth said, looking up at the pink and silver balloons dotting the ceiling. I could see her eyes rov-ing over the paper straws and mason jars full of pink lemon-ade. This party was a Pinterest dream come true, and Ruth was in heaven.

"Let's go say hi to Yessenia," I said, using it as an excuse to look for Matty.

Fabián and Ruth followed me to the backyard, where a group of full-on mariachis casually strummed traditional Mexican music underneath a giant oak tree.

Fabián nodded approvingly. "That ranchera's legit."

The swimming pool had been converted into a dance floor, and a piñata in the shape of a llama hung from a tree in the yard. All around us were tables for drinks, tamales, twelve different kinds of salsa, tacos, and enchiladas.

I glanced around for Matty, but he must not have arrived yet. Instead, I saw Yessenia in a white ball gown, sitting on a pouf near the edge of the dance floor, surrounded by some girls I had seen around in band. Yessenia hadn't gone to the same middle school as us, though, so a lot of the guests here were new to me.

"Hey, Yessenia." I waved. Yessenia looked up and smiled. She wore a tiara and full makeup, and she looked like a princess.

"Oh my gosh, thank you for coming to my quince!" she said, throwing her arms around me like we were best friends. "I love your gold makeup!"

I beamed. Maybe Yessenia was nicer than I had thought.

"Hii!" Ruth squealed in the same octave as Yessenia, excited to have someone to be super girly with for once. "I love your tiara!" Ruth said. They hugged tightly as if they were long-lost BFFs.

I wasn't jealous at all.

"Hey, Fabián," Yessenia said, pronouncing it Fa-vyán.

Fabián was in peak form today—his hair was slicked back with Suavecito gel, and he had on a vintage black bowling shirt, ripped jeans, and black cowboy boots. His eyes twinkled.

"Qué bella," he said, kissing her hand like he was a prince or something. "Thanks for inviting me. This food looks amazing."

Yessenia giggled like an actual schoolgirl. "Of course." Did she not know Fabián was as gay as the day was long? Was she actually trying to flirt with him?

I gave Ruth a look. She slowly shook her head in response.

"Now, if you'll excuse me, ladies, I see a tamal with my name on it." Fabián spun away like a ballerina and headed toward a platter of tamales. We gave Yessenia a shrug as if to say *Classic Fabián* and went off to follow him. He'd already piled his plate high with every kind of tortilla, rice, bean, and meat combo known to man. I took a taco from his plate.

"Hey," he said. "I was going to eat that. After I ate everything else."

"I'll get you an horchata," I offered. Fabián glared at me, then nodded.

I left Ruth and Fabián and headed over to the corner by the piñata, where the beverage table was. Horchata was this creamy drink made from rice and spices, and almost every taco and pupusa restaurant in the DMV had their own homemade version. This horchata had the classic milky color with flecks of cinnamon. I added an extra cinnamon stick into Fabián's and sprinkled some chocolate powder on top just to be nice.

"That's my favorite way to drink horchata," a voice said next to me. I turned, then froze. It was Matty Fumero himself, looking adorable in a gray suit and tie. His dimples were out in full force today, and his green eyes were so bright he could be cast as a teen love interest, or even a boy wizard. He radiated the nice, friendly vibes I remembered from orientation.

THIS IS IT, PARVIN! my brain screamed. *IT'S WHAT YOU'VE BEEN TRAINING FOR.*

I looked at the *NT* on my hand and replaced what I was going to respond with, which was *Horchata is the most delicious drink in the world, and I'll kill you if you say otherwise* with "Ha-ha-ha-ha, right?" (Laugh at one of his "jokes," check!)

Matty smiled. He smiled! "Yeah," he replied.

Then I stood there awkwardly, not saying anything else. Part of me ached to fill the silence. The other part of me screamed to be patient and remember the steps I'd written down. According to my goals, I was right on track with having a real conversation that lasted longer than two minutes.

"So," Matty said, still smiling for some reason.

I took a gulp of Fabián's horchata just to have something to do. Oh god, there was so much cinnamon in it. It burned. I could feel it tickling my throat all the way down, threatening to make me cough. I almost spurted it in Matty's face, but I kept my cool.

"This is some party, right?" Matty said finally.

"Yeah, it's pretty amazing," I replied, my eyes wide as I nodded back at him. I pretended to look around me, as if to emphasize, *Wow, this party is amazing.*

"Totally," he said. The silence stretched on.

I pretended to take another sip this time, learning my lesson.

"I don't know if you remember my name," he finally continued. He held out his hand. "I'm Matty—I was your student ambassador for freshman orientation?"

Did I remember him? *DID I REMEMBER HIM?* "Parvin," I replied coolly, giving him a floppy, girly handshake. My dad would have been so disappointed in that handshake, but who cared? Physical contact established! And this time, it wasn't because he was helping me off the linoleum after Wesley dumped me.

"We have band together, right?" Matty asked. Did we have band together? Did a lioness stalk her prey on the Serengeti?

"Yeah, I'm in the woodwind section." I faked another sip. "You're in brass, right?" I added, guessing that was a safe, general question, even though I knew for a fact he was a trumpet player.

"Yep, I play trumpet." Matty nodded back.

I flashed him another grin, as if that info was news to me. "That's so cool."

"Not as cool as the bassoon," Matty said, laughing.

I laughed back. Was that a joke? Who cared. Chuckle-chuckle. Laugh-laugh.

Matty took a sip of his drink. "I wish my parents made this at home."

Wait, I thought Matty was Mexican like Fabián? But

then again, Fabián's skin was way darker than Matty's. If anything, Matty looked closer to Wesley's and Teighan's skin tone, with less American flag vibes.

"Do you not drink horchata with your family?" I asked.

Matty shook his head. "Nah, we're from Argentina. We drink yerba mate."

Argentina! I squirreled away that important piece of information for later, along with the realization that maybe everyone who spoke Spanish wasn't Mexican. Was Matty what Argentinians looked like? And what was yerba mate?

"It's this stewed tea thing," he explained, reading my confused expression.

"Oh." I nodded. "Cool."

We stood there awkwardly. If I hadn't been trying so hard to be quiet, I probably would have talked about how my dad sometimes made tea in a samovar, which was the most Stewed Tea Thing to have ever existed. But I didn't.

"I should get this drink back to my friend." I needed to end this conversation on a high note, before my big mouth inevitably ruined it. I had to stick to my rules. We'd definitely talked for longer than two minutes, though, and that was a win.

"Oh, totally," Matty said. "Catch you later?"

"Totally," I replied.

I gave him another smile and took the horchata back to where Fabián and Ruth had been watching us the whole time. I waggled my eyebrows, my back to Matty so he couldn't see.

Awww, yeah, I mouthed. Ruth and Fabián looked impressed.

"Daaaaamn," Fabián said for the second time today. "He looks good in a suit."

I handed him his horchata and turned around. Matty waved at me, and I waved back, a super casual smile pasted to my face.

I swiveled to Ruth, my smile morphing into a manic grin.

"I would give you a slow clap, but my hands are full of tacos," she explained.

"Why is this horchata half empty?" Fabián demanded.

Just then, the mariachis stopped playing, and the head guitarist took the mic. "Ladies and gentlemen, Yessenia and her father, Miguel Antonio López!"

The crowd whooped and cheered as Yessenia entered the dance floor with four friends, two of them girls dressed in colorful ball gowns, the other two, boys in suits. I blinked. Wait, one of the boys was Matty. What was going on? Had Yessenia already gotten her hooks into him?

I turned to Fabián. "That's her court," he explained. "Friends who shepherd you from childhood to adulthood."

It was clear that Yessenia had plans for Matty, too. But hopefully his agreeing to play a role in her special journey into womanhood didn't mean anything serious.

Matty led Yessenia onto the dance floor, bowed low, and left the stage. Then Yessenia's father approached and held out his hand. They started dancing, and everyone clapped around them. It was honestly really nice. Yessenia looked super happy, and she kept waving to friends who watched her from the sidelines. I found myself clapping, too, swaying along to the music between Ruth and Fabián. Fabián whooped loudly, and I did the same.

"See? You don't have to be quiet all the time"—Ruth poked me—"you can still have fun."

I didn't realize how loudly I'd been clapping. I'd started

to sing along to the lyrics, even though they were in Spanish and I had no idea what they meant.

I stopped swaying.

"The old Parvin probably would have spiked Fabián's tacos with a ghost pepper by now," Ruth said. "But I'll settle for the Parvin who cheers in public."

"Oh." What did that mean? I stopped clapping, too, just to be safe. Ruth sighed and looked away.

When the song ended, Yessenia's mom walked forward, carrying a pair of high heels. Someone got Yessenia a chair, and she gingerly sat down as her mom took off her ballet flats.

I turned to Fabián again to translate.

"More symbolism," he whispered knowingly.

Yessenia stood up, this time in heels. The whole backyard cheered.

Someone brought a stuffed doll to Yessenia, and she ceremoniously gave it to her younger sister, who looked exactly like a miniature version of Yessenia. She gazed up adoringly at her older sister.

"This is so beautiful," Ruth said.

"Are you crying?" I asked.

"No," she sniffed.

"Damas y caballeros," the emcee announced, "I present Yessenia Inés López Lucero."

We cheered again, though I did it softly this time. Her court joined her on the dance floor and began doing synchronized moves as the mariachi music switched over to pop. Soon, the rest of the partygoers approached the dance floor, and I started to drag Fabián and Ruth toward the middle where I could see Matty bopping away, thankfully on the other side of Yessenia. I had planned to do some dignified shuffling and bending, but suddenly, Emerson Cheng appeared, popping and locking like he was in a music video. Oh no! I thought I had until next week to see him again.

"What up!" he shouted over the music, swiveling over to me on robot legs. He was actually pretty good, and he could even do this move where he stuck his chest out and rotated it like it was a separate part of his body.

"Hi, Emerson." I still had no idea how to respond to his invitation. Did I like him? No clue. Did I want to go on a date with him? Jury was out. But Emerson could solve all my Homecoming problems, and that meant something.

I wondered whether it was a good thing that I had to ask myself if I liked him, though. Either you liked someone or you didn't, right? "You remember Fabián and Ruth?" I asked, stalling for time.

"Hey, Emerson." Ruth waved.

"Cheng," Fabián replied frostily. Clearly, Fabián was still upset about being upstaged in middle school. But the sparklers Emerson had snuck into the gymnasium had been too explosive to ignore.

Emerson nodded back. "Wanna dance?" He turned to me.

"Okay," I replied. Yeah, maybe Emerson could be my date to Homecoming! That would show Wesley, for sure. After all, there was nothing cooler than a date who set off the fire alarm. I felt this massive weight lift from my shoulders, the relief washing over me. I'd done it. I'd found someone who could hopefully take me to the dance. Yes, he kept pretending to have a limp, and he wasn't that easy to talk to, but still. Watch out Homecoming—I was dancing with Emerson "Symmetrically Hot" Cheng.

Then Emerson spun around, did a split, and jumped back up, clocking me in the face with the top of his head.

"OW!" I yelled. I had thought he was going to put his arm around my waist and dance like a normal person, not catapult into my skull.

"My bad, my bad," Emerson shouted, his deep brown eyes genuinely worried.

"What did you do this time, Cherry Bomb?" Fabián hissed, running over to me. I clutched my face, my eyes watering from where Emerson socked me with his head. My whole nose felt tender, and it had started to bleed a little bit.

Luckily, everyone was focusing on the piñata, and only Emerson and Fabián had been there to see the collision. Apparently, the piñata was filled with AirPods.

"Let me get some ice. Be right back. I'm sooo sorry!" Emerson dashed away, his limp suddenly gone. He turned around again to flash me a thumbs-up and narrowly missed decking a caterer before sprinting toward the kitchen.

Fabián handed me a napkin, and I held it to my nose. I probably deserved this from faking bloody noses at school so often, and I prayed Matty hadn't seen it. Emerson was clearly a walking safety hazard, in more ways than one.

"Are you okay?" Fabián asked. "He got you pretty good."

"Nobody else saw, right?"

Fabián craned his neck around, his eyes resting on the other side of the dance floor. "Well, Ruth *definitely* didn't see it happen." I looked over—Ruth was talking to a Black girl wearing a bedazzled NASA shirt and locs pinned up with sparkly barrettes. Ruth looked completely transfixed. The girl even had shimmery blue eyeshadow.

Ruth's *favorite* color of eyeshadow.

Wait, was Ruth . . . *flirting?* I moved my napkin down to get a better look. At least she was having fun.

"Well, looks like it's just you and me, Fabes," I said. But Fabián had already left to do crazy complicated dance moves with some cute sophomore boy with green hair, the one whose name I was pretty sure was Austin, and who had asked Fabián to Homecoming.

I waited for my ice, alone.

. . .

LATER

Emerson brought me an ice pack a good ten minutes after the assault over to where I'd been hiding out on a wicker lawn chair away from the dance floor. "Sorry," he said. "I stopped to whup Eben's butt on Xbox."

Oh my god.

"Thanks," I sniffed, snatching the ice from him. My nose no longer stung, but the ice felt good on my face.

"Listen, are you okay on your own? I gotta finish my game," he said. "I'm really sorry."

I sighed. "Fine—" I began, but Emerson was already running off toward the house. Great. Just great. What if we went on a date and I somehow got another injury?

I was happy my friends were dancing, at least. Out of the corner of my eye I saw Matty start to dance with some dude I'd never seen before. Damn it. That boy was cute, too. The competition was already stiff, and I was sleeping on the job. I just didn't know if I could rely on Emerson as a Homecoming date anymore, what with all the violence.

But before I could make a decision, someone called out, "Hey, Parvin."

My blood chilled enough to stop my nosebleed. Wesley was heading my way, and worse, Teighan was with him. What gives? Yessenia had told me she was inviting people from band—not our entire high school. I quickly threw my ice pack into a bush.

"Hey," I called out casually, as if my heart wasn't racing. It still hurt to see the two of them together. Wesley wore a navy sports coat, something I never thought I'd see in my entire life, and his arm was at Teighan's lower back, guiding her my way.

That should have been *my* lower back.

It looked like he and Teighan had coordinated outfits, judging by her navy dress. They even wore the same kind of shoes where you don't wear socks; the ones people wear on yachts, or polo fields. He grabbed two cups and poured some horchata from the table nearby.

"How's it going?" He nodded, his dark blond hair still in a tight military cut. He looked completely different from the gangly dork with braces I'd fallen for over the summer. In front of me was a blond clone of Hudson, one who now reeked of cologne instead of salt and soap.

"Fine," I lied.

Wesley handed Teighan a cup. She took a sip and promptly spit it out.

"Ugh!" she cried. "What is that stuff?"

Wesley took a sip, shrugged, and kept drinking. For some reason Teighan was looking at me for an explanation.

"Um . . . horchata?"

"I saw you talking to Emerson Cheng," Wesley said. I

prayed he wasn't referring to Emerson attacking me on the dance floor.

"Yep."

"Is he your date to Homecoming?" Wesley was looking me in the eyes for once, and it was so easy to dive deep into them and pretend we were back on the beach. I could practically get a phantom whiff of sunscreen just from that look.

"Why do you care?" Teighan interrupted. I snapped out of it. *Yeah, Wesley, why* do *you care? You dumped me, remember?*

"No reason," he said, and laughed nervously, shifting his feet back and forth. "Well, time to dance." He turned to Teighan and led her back to the dance floor.

I grabbed my ice and brushed mulch off it as I watched them walk away, the wheels in my head turning.

Was Wesley *jealous*?

Just then, Ruth came over. She must have seen the whole thing.

"Was that . . . ?" Ruth asked.

"Yep," I replied.

"Do you want me to kill him for you?" she asked, deadly serious.

"With what?" I replied. "A glue gun?"

Ruth shrugged. "It's how I'd want to go."

Suddenly, I felt super tired. I had put on a good front with Wesley and Teighan, but the truth was, what he did to me at orientation still hurt. He made me feel amazing when he'd kissed me at the beach, but now I felt ashamed I let it happen in the first place. I thought today would be fun and important, but now I felt sad all over again.

"You sure you're okay?" Ruth wheedled. "I feel like . . . I feel like you don't really talk about it. Maybe talking about it would be good?"

I bit my lip. Having a meltdown at Yessenia's party wasn't a part of the plan.

"Who were *you* talking to?" I changed the subject. "She's cute."

Ruth's pale skin went full crimson. "Parvin, Naomi is sooo cool! She's a sophomore, and she's already got an internship at Jet Propulsion Labs in California, where they make spaceships and stuff."

Whoa. This girl sounded almost as ambitious as Ruth Song. Just then, I noticed Matty head to the dessert station (a chocolate fountain where you could dip fancy French macarons). Even though I'd shaken Matty's hand, I knew I should try for another moment of physical contact.

"She asked for my number," Ruth continued, gushing.

"Cool." I got up and tracked Matty's trajectory, then walked into him right as he got to the chocolate fountain, pretending to reach for the same macaron. Lightning went up my arm from where our hands grazed each other.

"Oops, sorry!" I smiled.

Matty smiled back, his eyes as green as the pistachio macaron. "No worries. Did you want this one?"

"You have it," I said with a shy smile, pretending to be one of those bashful, clumsy women in the movies who knocked into things and were perpetually mortified.

He placed the macaron on a plate and handed it to me. "I insist." What a gentleman! He gave me a small wave, then went to fill his own plate. I chewed the macaron slowly. There was no denying it: Pistachio tasted like success.

"Parvin? Did you listen to anything I said?" Ruth huffed behind me.

"Huh?"

. . .

MY BEDROOM
11:00 P.M.

11:03 PM FABIÁN: matty thinks you're cute

11:03 PM PARVIN: !!!!! Really?

11:03 PM RUTH: Wait, really??

11:05 PM FABIÁN: yeah, I was texting him about play tryouts and he asked if we were friends.

11:05 PM PARVIN: And???

11:07 PM FABIÁN: and I said yes and he said he thought you were cute

11:07 PM PARVIN: OH MY GOD. IT'S REALLY WORKING!

11:08 PM RUTH: Just to clarify, he was referring to Parvin, right?

I shrieked into my phone. Matty thought I was cute! It was too late to grill Fabián on the specifics, but it was never too late for me to do some more social media stalking.

Matty hadn't posted anything useful to Instagram in a while, though, as he only had pictures of random stuff, like a guitar in its case, or a sunset. There were barely any new photos of him at all.

Still . . . Matty thought I was cute. Visions of the two of us at Homecoming flooded my brain. Matty could wear that gray suit he had on today at the party while I appeared in a tame dress and nude lip and we danced all night. Wesley's jaw would drop at how gorgeous I looked, and he'd feel like a complete idiot for dumping me at orientation. Meanwhile, Matty and I would probably be voted Homecoming royalty. But most important: A boy liked me. One who didn't make my nose bleed.

I finished scrolling through all of Matty's socials, but I was too awake to go to sleep now. I typed in another name instead, just to have something to do: Amir Shirazi. I scrolled through his profile—most of his feed was pictures of him with friends, although there were a couple with his family. I wondered what he was doing tonight.

I went deeper into his grid. It looked like in the summer between middle school and high school he went on a family trip to Iran. It was amazing to see him next to his mom and dad, how you could place every feature on Amir's face with a corresponding one from his parents'. Looking at them, he made sense. I stared at that photo for a while. What did people think when they looked at my family?

Sunday

FARSI SCHOOL
11:00 A.M.

I did it! When it came time for me to read a verse of poetry out loud in Farsi class this morning, I actually did it without stumbling over every word. Sure, there was the odd flub or two, but I read pretty well if I do say so myself.

"Nice," Amir whispered to me afterward.

He looked so happy for me I couldn't help giving him a high five. I'd washed the "No Talking" *NT* off after yesterday's success at Yessenia's quince. I didn't need it for Farsi class.

After we read poetry, Aghayeh Khosrowshahi gave us classwork to do with our partners, and I used it as an opportunity to catch up with Amir.

"Were you at Yessenia López's party?" I asked. "I didn't see you there."

Amir laughed. "No, I was definitely not invited to Yessenia's party."

I frowned. "But aren't you a sophomore?"

"Yep. Guess I'm not cool enough to go to a quince," Amir said sarcastically.

"*I'm* not cool enough. I probably only got invited because of my friend," I replied, thinking of Fabián. "Is Yessenia cool?"

Amir shrugged. "She's fine—she's just a little stuck-up. She must like you because you're in band."

I nodded. Sometimes it felt like Ruth and I were insulated from everything because of Fabián, who was so hip no one dared mess with us. I didn't realize Amir and Yessenia weren't in the same sophomore social level.

"Well, what did you do this weekend?" I asked him. I didn't know why I was suddenly so desperate to find a topic we both wanted to talk about. I guess I wanted it to feel like we were on the bleachers again.

"I had a track meet," Amir said.

My eyes went wide. "Like . . . throwing javelins and sprinting and stuff?"

He nodded. I had never met someone who ran around voluntarily. I was impressed.

. . .

CANTEEN
1:00 P.M.

After class, we went to the little café in the basement where they served food, tea, and pastries. I got a bowl of asheh reshteh, which was a soup of herbs, lentils, and noodles that was somehow creamy yet healthy tasting at the same time. Amir got a tea and baklava.

"Soup? It's eighty degrees!" Amir exclaimed.

I shoved the soup in his face. "Hello? Don't you smell this delicious smell? I only get to eat ash if I make it myself. Which means never. This is my only chance."

Amir was shocked. "What? That's awful! You have to come over—my mom makes the best ash." He looked so serious about me having proper ash that I just nodded.

"Okay," I said. "That would be cool."

Dad was waiting for me at the parking lot, as usual. Amir walked up with me this time, sipping his tea. Allah help me.

"Hey, Dad, this is Amir," I said. "And this is my dad." *Please don't embarrass me in front of a sophomore, Dad!* I shouted telepathically.

"Hi, Mr. Mohammadi." Amir extended his hand and gave my dad a firm handshake. I could see Dad's mustache twitch in approval.

"What's your last name?" Dad asked, cutting to the chase.

"Shirazi," Amir replied.

Dad nodded, looking thoughtful. "The dentist?"

"Yep."

It was like all Iranians in the DC area knew each other, and my dad had a mental database.

We stood around in the parking lot—me sipping my soup, Amir nibbling his baklava—as Dad peppered him with the routine questions all Iranian Americans ask each other:

- What year did your family come over? (Hint: It was probably during the revolution.)
- Where in Iran is your family from?
- Which mosque do you go to? (Trick question: Not all Iranians are Muslim, but this was a sneaky way of finding out which religion you were.)

I rolled my eyes at the last one. Dad left Iran when he was eight, and barely fasted at Ramadan. The most Muslim thing about him was the tasbih he kept in the car, and it looked a lot like the rosary in Fabián's dance studio. Did he really have to ask which mosque Amir went to? We barely went to ours.

"We're Zoroastrian," Amir replied, which was the original religion of Iran before Islam came over. Dad nodded.

"Parvin says you own your own advertising studio?" Amir ventured.

My mouth flopped open. I never told him that. Did Amir Shirazi *google me*?

Dad nodded. "Yeah, my wife and I own a small company. She handles most of the art direction, while I do most of the writing."

"So, you're a writer?" Amir asked. I could see his eyes get wide with excitement.

Dad laughed. "Well, I'm a *copy*writer. I don't write novels or anything. It's mostly just slogans or headlines for whatever Daphne's designed," Dad explained.

Amir nodded, still impressed. "That's so cool. I don't know any Iranians with . . . with . . ." He struggled to find the right word.

"A super cool job?" Dad gloated. I groaned.

"Yeah, exactly." Amir laughed. Then he checked his phone. "Sorry, guys, I have to get going. My mom's making abgoosht and wants me home early." Amir was already looking for somewhere to throw away his cup.

"Abgoosht," Dad said wistfully. "Your mom must be a great cook."

Amir grinned. "She is."

"What's abgoosht?" I asked.

"What?" Dad and Amir cried at the same time. Dad looked shaken.

"Okay, that's it," Amir announced, getting out his phone to send off a quick text. It buzzed back instantly. "My mom says Parvin has to come over and eat abgoosht.

Is that okay, Aghayeh Mohammadi? My dad can drop her off after."

Dad practically fainted at someone addressing him so traditionally. He nodded.

"Wait," I whined. "What actually *is* abgoosht, though?" Why was everyone so obsessed with it?

"You'll see," Dad said. "Go with Amir. It'll be good for you to eat some Persian food that isn't kabob."

"Okay," I replied.

"Shirazi . . . Shirazi . . . ," Dad said to himself. "Hmmm . . . Nope, don't think we're related."

I said nothing. I knew Dad was teasing me.

Still. That was good to know.

. . .

AMIR'S HOUSE
1:30 P.M.

Amir's house looked *exactly* like the houses of Dad's friends we visit for Iranian New Year. The second I walked in, the rosewater scent that reminded me of Amir hit me like a wave.

Everything seemed to be made out of glass, gold, or shiny white fabric. Not only that, but when we took our shoes off at the front door we were met by random bowls of fruit everywhere. A bowl of fruit on the entry table. A bowl of fruit on the glass coffee table. A bowl of fruit on the gold tablecloth in the dining room. Why were there so many bowls of fruit? And were cucumbers a fruit? Because those seemed to be sticking out of them, too.

"Parvin joonam!" A short woman I recognized from Amir's Insta feed bustled over. Amir's mom was dressed entirely in black and had dyed blond hair. Could Iranians go blond? Must remember to ask Mom if I could dye my hair blond like hers.

"Salaam, Khanoumeh Shirazi!" I returned, kissing her three times on the cheeks. She had Amir's dark brown eyes and the same long eyelashes.

"Bah-bah-bah"—she flapped her hands—"call me Farah."

Behind her came Mr. Shirazi, with the same tall, lanky frame as Amir. They both had big noses with a sharp crook in the bridge. It felt good to not have the biggest nose in the room for once.

"This must be Parvin," he called out, shaking my hand. I noticed his English was better than Farah's. "Call me Hoshang," he added, pumping my arm enthusiastically. "Farsi baladi?" he asked. *Do you speak Farsi?*

"Umm . . ." I panicked, looking between him and Amir. Amir nodded at me encouragingly. "Baleh, man kami Farsi midaanam."

Hoshang and Farah exploded into laughter. Kill me now.

"Sorry, sorry, Parvin jaan—it's just that you speak so formally. I haven't heard that since I got my visa in Tehran." Hoshang guffawed, trying to catch his breath. "You sound like a cleric!"

Farah added something else in Farsi that was too quick for me to catch. Even Amir chuckled at that one. I felt my face go red. Fantastic. Laugh at my expense, why don't you. It wasn't my fault I was learning formal Farsi and sounded like a medieval knight. I didn't grow up with parents like Hoshang and Farah who spoke Farsi at home and who could teach me the spoken stuff.

"Don't worry." Amir led me toward the dining room. "My mom says your Farsi sounds very good."

Hmm.

"Parvin, are you hungry, azizam?" Farah asked.

I nodded, and she led me over to the dining room table and sat me down right in front of the fruit bowl. Amir sat next to me, and Hoshang moved the fruit to the kitchen island (which also had gold flecks in the marble countertop). I looked back at my chair, and yes, even the chairs were painted gold.

"Amir says you have never eaten abgoosht?" Farah asked, looking concerned. "Do you know what it is?"

I shook my head. Finally, was someone going to explain it to me?

"Khob . . ." She clapped her hands. *Well*. "It is a lamb shank that has been cooked in a pressure cooker, then you add potato and dried lemon and some tomato to make a good stew. Yes?"

"That sounds amazing." My mouth was officially watering. I could smell the lamb cooking in a sealed pot on the stove. Suddenly, the pot began to shriek like a teakettle. I jumped a mile high.

"That's the pressure cooker," Amir explained. I had no idea what that was, and I'd never heard a soup pot scream before, but I was learning a lot today.

Hoshang sat down and filled my fancy crystal glass with water.

"So, Parvin—what do you want to be when you grow up?"

Oh god. Classic immigrant parent question. I was lucky Dad rarely asked me. So far the only things I had an aptitude for were being dumped, contouring my face, and cackling so loudly an usher once asked me to leave a movie theater. "Umm . . ." I fished around, hoping a brilliant answer would come to me, "I'm not sure yet."

Hoshang laughed. "That's okay. You're a year younger than Amir, yes? He only just figured out what he wants to be."

I smiled at Amir, remembering how he wanted to be a writer, but he looked incredibly uncomfortable.

Hoshang filled the rest of the water glasses. "Yes, after Amir goes to dental school he can take over the family dental practice. And we can call it 'Shirazi and Sons.' Like the Americans!"

Wait . . . did Amir's parents not know about his dream of being a writer? I opened my mouth, but Amir suddenly shouted, "Aaaand here's the abgoosht."

Farah held a big bowl of orange-and-brown stew and placed it on the table. "It's nothing fancy," she explained. "This is very simple Persian food." Her accent made it sound like *eh-simple*.

Amir ladled some of the stew on top of a bowl of basmati rice for me and passed me a spoon. It smelled delicious and tangy, the dried lemon smell cutting through the meatiness of the lamb. There was no way my parents could pull this off.

I smiled at Amir, glad he'd invited me even though I'd almost outed his writing goals. He took a bite of stew and grinned back.

"Bokhor!" Farah commanded, waving at the food. *Eat!*

I stuck my spoon in, scooping up a bit of potato, lamb, and broth. The tomato and potato dissolved deliciously the second they hit my mouth. It was so good I wanted to shout *WHERE HAS THIS BEEN ALL MY LIFE?*

I didn't realize everyone was staring at me until I finished the first bite.

"So?" Amir prodded. "What do you think?"

I swallowed my stew, trying to downplay how jealous I was that Amir got to eat this kind of food every day. "This is the most incredible thing I've ever eaten."

"I knew it," Amir shouted. "I knew she'd love it!"

Farah looked near tears. "She likes my abgoosht!" she shouted to no one in particular, followed by some lightning-fast Farsi. "She likes my abgoosht!"

Hoshang just smiled. "We're glad you enjoy it."

I turned back to my bowl of abgoosht and began to attack it for real.

. . .

AMIR'S ROOM
3:00 P.M.

"I think my parents are obsessed with you now," he said from his desk. I had flopped onto his bed, too full of abgoosht to even sit up straight.

"I'm going to burst," I moaned. "Why did they make me eat so much pistachio ice cream?"

Amir laughed. "You've never had to deal with a Persian mom shoving food down your throat before, huh?"

I shook my head gently. If I moved too much, I'd pop a rib. "Thanks for inviting me." I'd never eaten home-cooked Iranian food, since all the New Year parties we went to were catered. Not only that, but I'd been able to shut off my brain from dissecting how my interactions with Matty had gone yesterday. I'd forgotten how nice it was to not be obsessed with getting a Homecoming date. The past couple of hours at Amir's house had felt like a vacation.

"Thanks for coming," Amir replied. He looked at me, holding my gaze.

"What? Do I still have ice cream on my face?" I shot up, wiping my hand across my mouth.

"No, no, you're fine." Amir swiveled around in his chair, turning back toward his desk. He was quiet for a moment. The silence suddenly felt heavy.

"Why didn't you tell your dad about your writing, Amir?"

"Oh. Um . . . I guess I don't want to disappoint him. He asked me to help out at the dental office this year, and I said I would. I think he assumed that meant I wanted to be a dentist, too. He worked really hard to build his business, and I don't think he wants me to struggle like they did. It was really hard for a while."

I looked around Amir's giant bedroom, with its big mahogany desk, full-size bed, and bookshelf stuffed with track trophies. If they had been struggling before, they definitely weren't now.

"I think he'd be okay with it," I replied. Hoshang had been so nice and welcoming at dinner. I couldn't imagine him flipping out at his son for wanting to become a writer. But then again, he wasn't my dad. "Maybe he won't be thrilled, but you shouldn't lie to him, either. He seriously thinks you're going to become a dentist."

"I know, I know. It's just that he'll want me to have a plan. A plan for how to make money as a writer so I don't struggle. But I don't have one yet."

I looked away, relieved I didn't have to decide my own career path for a while. Amir looked so tortured at the thought of telling his dad that it made me grateful my parents would probably support whatever random thing I wanted to do with my life. They might not be great cooks, but they would be encouraging with whatever I chose.

"That's tough." I didn't know what else to say.

Amir sighed. "Thanks for listening."

"Anytime." I rubbed my belly. It gurgled painfully. "Amir?"

"Yeah?"

"Do you have any ginger ale?"

. . .

MY ROOM
10:00 P.M.

> **10:03 PM SARA MOHAMMADI:** So? How did the party go?

> **10:05 PM PARVIN MOHAMMADI:** Matty talked to me! I got a bloody nose, and I was worried he'd be with Yessenia because he was in her quince court, but he wanted to drink horchata with me instead!

> **10:06 PM SARA MOHAMMADI:** What??

> **10:06 PM PARVIN MOHAMMADI:** I'll video chat you tomorrow.

Tuesday

LUNCH
12:00 P.M.

"Naomi texted me!" Ruth squealed for the zillionth time in the courtyard on Tuesday. "She says she wants to go out! Want to come over after school? We can make posters for Fabián's dance showcase tonight and strategize how I should respond."

"Of course, Ruth. I can even show you how to properly stalk someone online."

Ruth beamed. Naomi and Ruth really hit it off at the quince. I knew for a fact that Ruth had already created a wedding Pinterest board for the two of them.

"What about you?" I asked Fabián. "Are you gonna see green-hair guy again?"

Fabián shrugged. "Austin? Maybe. I've got theater with him today."

He had a toothpick in his mouth and wore his leather jacket, the one with all the buckles and snaps. He didn't fool me, though. I knew he only wore that leather jacket when he wanted to impress someone. Probably Austin.

"And you have theater with Matty, right?" I pressed. "Maybe you could find out if he's dating anyone?"

"Maybe." Fabián shrugged. "I have tryouts against him this weekend."

I'd told Ameh Sara about the party on Saturday, but she asked so many questions about how a quinceañera worked (she'd never been to one, either), I barely had time to tell her about how Matty talked to me before she rushed off to class. She'd mentioned how her schedule was going to be more intense since she was leaving in the middle of the semester to see us, but I didn't realize that meant she'd have less time to talk to me. I wished she was here already.

Ruth's mom had packed her seolleongtang for lunch today, and the milky ox-bone soup smelled like heaven. I took a spoonful, trying to get a bunch of cellophane noodles in each bite. If I couldn't talk about my feelings, at least I could eat through them.

"Ew," a girl said as she walked past. "What *is* that?"

I narrowed my eyes. I recognized that girl from the party—she was one of Yessenia's friends and played flute in band. Her shampoo was so fruity I could practically taste it, and her brown hair had been highlighted to within an inch of its life.

Ruth had gone very still next to me, her eyes looking down.

"It's seolleongtang." I rolled my eyes. "And what's that? A sad sandwich?" I pointed to the crustless PB&J in her ziplock bag. Who cut the crust off bread? It was literally the best part.

The girl rolled her eyes back. "At least my lunch doesn't smell."

"Yeah, or provide probiotics," I scoffed loudly. She looked at me like I was crazy. The courtyard, I noticed, had suddenly gone very quiet as people watched our standoff.

"Whatever," the girl said, stalking away in a cloud of

mango and coconut. Fabián hissed at her retreating back. Ruth looked like she was going to cry. She wordlessly passed her thermos of soup my way, suddenly ashamed of it.

"Don't worry, Ruth. That girl's probably just constipated—her lunch had zero vegetables or fiber." I glared at her across the courtyard as she opened a diet (shiver) soda.

Fabián took his boots off our picnic table and leaned forward. "That was Amanda Michaels," Fabián began. "She is a *terrible* dancer," he added, as if that settled what a bad person she was.

"It's fine," Ruth said, looking miserable. "I just haven't had someone make fun of my lunch since middle school. I thought we were over that stuff here."

"Of course we are, Ruth. And anyone who doesn't like seolleongtang isn't worth getting upset over."

Ruth nodded. "I wonder if Naomi likes seolleongtang?"

"She better," I replied. "Or heads will roll."

Ruth gave me a small smile.

"So, can I finish this . . . ?" I gestured to the rest of her lunch. I'd already inhaled my portion, and I wasn't about to let good soup go to waste.

"Parvin!"

"What?"

...

BAND
1:00 P.M.

Amanda Michaels thinks she's so great. What she doesn't know is that I left lunch early to head to the band room and dump Cheeto dust into her flute. The extra-spicy kind.

The second she played her instrument, she was going to spray herself with 100 percent pure orange. Served her right for messing with my friends.

We started playing arpeggios, and I kept Amanda in the corner of my eye. After the first note, she recoiled from her flute, wondering what was going on with it. She clasped the open end of the woodwind and started to blow into it, trying to dislodge whatever was stuck in there and failing. I watched her shrug and keep playing, but I doubted any sound was coming out. We came up to the arpeggio run, and *thunk*, the Cheeto dust shot out of the mouthpiece, spraying her chin with orange powder.

"AHHH!" she screamed. Ms. Kaiser stopped conducting and blinked down at Amanda, who was now covered in orange dust. I tried really hard not to laugh. It was an Oscar-worthy performance.

"Oh my GOD!" Amanda shouted. "What the HELL?!"

Her entire face was orange. She looked like she had a spray tan gone wrong. All she needed was a red baseball hat and she could run for president.

I watched Matty laugh along with the rest of the back row. What would happen if he found out I was responsible? Would he think it was cool? Or would he be grossed out that I had crushed an entire bag of Cheetos under my shoe to make the perfect powder to slip into a flute? I swiveled back around. Better to have nobody find out I'd done it.

"Ew!" Yessenia shuddered, sitting next to Amanda. "Did you eat Cheetos before you played?"

Amanda looked near tears as she ran out of the room, still clutching her flute.

"That"—Ms. Kaiser frowned to the rest of the class—"was distracting."

She tapped her music stand, raised her arms, and resumed conducting us through our arpeggios as if nothing had happened. I innocently blew on my bassoon, my embouchure hiding my grin. I turned my head slightly to look at Ruth, and she looked right back, also trying hard not to smile as she realized what I'd done.

Nobody messed with my friends.

Except me.

. . .

GYMNASIUM
8:00 P.M.

Later that night was one of Fabián's dance showcases, and Ruth and I promised we would go to support him. At least I thought that's what the showcase was for. Fabián took dance, step, theater, and gymnastics at school. He had so many extracurriculars that involved performing in front of other people I'd lost count.

We were sitting on the top row of bleachers in the gymnasium, and Ruth handed me one of the posters she'd made for the occasion.

¡FABIÁN ES FUEGO! her poster read in sparkling blue and red letters (our school colors). She also made one for me that said **GO FABIÁN!** in neon orange. I think neon orange may be my new power color.

"You're welcome," Ruth sniffed. She seemed in a huffy mood despite my excellent band prank. You'd think she'd be more grateful. As soon as the bell rang after band, I'd followed Matty to the auditorium to see if he would say hi to me again, but he stayed in deep conversation with someone who was also in the fall play.

"Parvin, you were supposed to come over and help me make posters today, remember?" Ruth asked. "And help me strategize how to respond to Naomi!"

Oh no. I'd completely spaced. "I'm sorry. I was just trying to get Matty to talk to me again. I only have, like, three weeks until Homecoming."

Ruth snatched back the poster she'd made for me. "So? I like someone now, too, but you don't see me ditching you."

"I know, I know." I hung my head. Balancing boys and friends was tougher than I'd realized. "Forgive me? I promise I'll make it up to you somehow."

Ruth eyed the candy in my open backpack. "You can make it up to me right now, if you want."

I handed her my bag of peanut butter cups. She gave me back the poster. Just then, the lights in the gymnasium dimmed.

I lifted the poster as Fabián sauntered onto the dance floor sporting a baseball jersey, black pants, and a baseball cap. The rest of the dance team followed close behind him in similar outfits.

"WHOOO!" We cheered like complete fangirls. Luckily, I'd already cased the joint to make sure Matty wasn't here. I could scream my head off and he'd never know.

The music started, and the whole group pounded the air with their fists as they began their routine. They moved like one organism, their hips swaying in time to the music, their feet slamming on the floor.

I noticed green-haired Austin sitting in the front row. The

team formed a V, with Fabián at the front of the formation. He broke his serious concentration to give Austin a wink.

"Oh my gosh!" Ruth exclaimed. "Did you see that?"

Just then, the music changed to a faster song. Suddenly, Fabián's wrists were whirling above him, each hand like a flag that was moving in fast circles.

"This is called voguing," Ruth whispered to me.

"I know what voguing is," I snapped back. I had no idea what voguing was.

The dancing reached a fever pitch, the moves quicker without losing control. It was honestly mesmerizing. I held my poster up higher. Fabián was so good I couldn't believe he sat at the same lunch table as us. We were not worthy.

With a giant boom, the song finished, and Fabián did a move where he tucked his right leg under himself like he was doing a quad stretch, then fell backward onto the floor. "Nice death drop!" a nearby parent shouted to another dad. Ruth and I went nuts.

"WOOOOO-HOOOOO!" we screamed, not caring that we were making a scene. How could I pretend to be Quiet Parvin now? My friend was going to win a Golden Globe, or whatever they gave to dancers.

"Fabián, WILL YOU MARRY ME!" I shouted.

"I WANT YOUR BABIES!" Ruth shrieked back.

"Thank you, freshman dance team!" an announcer said, ushering them offstage. Fabián blew us a kiss, and we pretended to melt in our seats. Austin looked up at us from the bottom bleacher and frowned.

That's right, Austin, Fabián's a hot commodity. You wanna get to him? You have to make it through us.

Just kidding.

But seriously, though, Austin. If you hurt him, I'll kill you.

. . .

MY ROOM
9:30 P.M.

I felt bad about ditching Ruth this afternoon, but it was a necessary sacrifice in the name of Homecoming. Yessenia's party had gone well, yet my mission to get Matty had stalled. With less than three weeks to get a date, it was time to make a progress report so I could see what the next steps were. Waiting around for him after school wasn't going to cut it anymore.

ACTIONABLE
MATTY FUMERO STEPS:

- Have him initiate a conversation with me **(This has happened twice now—thanks to Yessenia's party last weekend.)**
- Talk for longer than two minutes **(Done!)**
- Laugh at one of his jokes **(Done . . . though I'm not sure they were jokes.)**
- Compliment him on something **(Shoot—I forgot to compliment him on his suit at the party! Will do next time.)**
- Make physical contact **(Check!)**
- Have sustained eye contact **(Need to work on this.)**
- ?? **(Maybe this should be something like, "Give a Mysterious Smile," like all the women in the movies.)**

- ??? **(I'll add "Go on a date with Matty" here. People go on dates before they go to dances together, right? We need a date first.)**
- Go to Homecoming together, make Wesley jealous, etc., etc.

Wednesday

HALLWAY
9:45 A.M.

"Naomi asked me to hang out this Saturday," Ruth said, eyes panicked.

"But . . . that's a good thing, Ruth. She wants to spend time with you. You only met her a couple days ago, right?"

"But what if we run out of things to talk about? Or she realizes I'm not cool or . . . or . . ."

"Or what?"

Ruth dropped her voice. "Or not gay enough."

"What?" I shouted. "What do you mean, not gay enough?"

"SHHH!" Ruth spluttered furiously. Somehow Ruth's *shhh* carried through the entire freshman hallway in that way that whispers sometimes do. People stopped talking to look at us.

"Nothing to see here, folks," I said, waving them on like a traffic cop. "Move along."

I turned back to Ruth. "What do you mean, not gay enough?" I murmured. "You don't need a thermometer to show people how gay you are."

Ruth hung her head. "But I like girls, guys, and non-binary people," she said. "Naomi is full-on gay. She identifies as a lesbian. What if she thinks it's stupid that I like boys and masculine people, too?"

I was a little out of my depth here. Did people really dump on folks who identified as pan? That seemed pretty messed up. Fabián and Ruth usually talked more about their queer identities with each other, and they went to GSA meetings every week and Pride every June in DC without me. Maybe it was time I started coming with them to GSA meetings, too, if only to support my friends and understand what Ruth was talking about.

"Ruth, you are amazing. You are my best friend. And anyone would be lucky to go on a date with you. If you being attracted to masculine people is a deal breaker for Naomi, then she is not worth it." I wished I had a beard to stroke in this moment, like a wise old man. It would have been very fitting. Too bad I had waxed it off.

Ruth emerged from her meltdown. "Yeah," she said slowly. "You're right. I *am* pretty amazing."

"Atta girl, Ruth."

"And she would be *lucky* to go on a date with me," Ruth said, puffing herself up.

"Yasss, queen," I replied sagely.

"Honestly? It's kind of a miracle that I'm even *letting* her go on a date with me," she added, her eyes alight.

"Okay, let's not get carried away here."

"Right, right," she said, snapping out of it. "Sorry."

"It's okay." I patted her shoulder. "Do you feel better?"

She bit her lip. "Yeah. Thanks, P." She hugged me, and I smelled cotton candy and watermelon, her two favorite scents.

"Aww, of course, Ruthie." I hugged her back.

"By the way," she said, "I told Naomi it'd be a group date, since I'm technically not allowed to go out with anyone yet. And that you're coming apple picking with us. With a date."

I un-hugged Ruth.

"You what?"

Being on Ruth's awkward date sounded terrible. Never mind everything I said before. It was going to be uncomfortable as hell.

The bell rang.

"Don't forget to find a date." She waved cheerily as she headed to class.

I stood in the hallway, dumbfounded. How had I gotten roped into this?

Ruth better be careful on this apple-picking trip. Or she might find herself tumbling down a ladder.

. . .

INTRODUCTION TO VIDEO
10:00 A.M.

> 10:03 AM PARVIN: Fabián—are you free this Saturday? Want to go apple picking with me and Ruth and Naomi?

10:05 AM FABIÁN: can't—i've got play tryouts. i'm up against Matty, remember? parvin you know how important this is to me!

I replied by sending him a bunch of sobbing emojis, but he didn't respond. Now what was I gonna do? I couldn't leave Ruth in the lurch, but I also didn't want to be a third wheel on her date. My progress with Matty was nowhere close enough to ask him to go apple picking, plus he'd clearly be at the audition. Who was gonna go apple picking with me now?

The bell rang. I had sat in the very back of Intro to Video all this time so Emerson wouldn't have a chance to talk to me yet. I can't go out with him. It just wouldn't work. I'd be in the ER by the end of the night, and Wesley would know that Emerson wasn't boyfriend material. Emerson should go out with some other girl who actually liked him, especially when I really wanted to go out with Matty.

I would have to break it to Emerson gently.

"Today we're going to be working on commercials!" Mr. Clarke smiled from the front of the classroom.

I swear, it was like he actually rolled out of bed in the mornings, fully clothed, excited to teach us. I'd never seen Mr. Clarke not hyperventilating with joy.

"Now, class, I used to work in animation before I became a teacher. And I'm particularly thrilled to teach you about the wild world of commercials."

Sir neighed. Like a horse. Mr. Clarke beamed at him.

"First we're going to watch a couple commercials and talk about what makes them so good. Then I'd like you all to make your *own* commercial, or 'spot' as we say in the biz. I'll go around the classroom with a hat full of brands, and it'll be your job to make a thirty-second spot for the brand you pick out. Got it?"

Everyone mumbled some affirmative noise.

"Great!" Mr. Clarke exclaimed. He turned on the TV and queued up the first commercial.

It was for fungal cream.

"I animated this one a long time ago," he panted enthusiastically. I blinked, surprised he'd show it in public.

The animation started by zooming in on a graphic of a foot, then cutting to an animation of fungus cells being obliterated by the cream. It was the worst commercial I had ever seen. Mr. Clarke looked so happy to be sharing it with us it honestly broke my heart.

After the fungal cream cartoon, we watched commercials for frozen pizza, laundry detergent, and a luxury car. I'd actually seen some of them before. The luxury car one was even pretty cool.

When the commercials finished, Mr. Clarke went around the room with a baseball hat full of different brand names. I prayed I'd get a cool makeup brand or even a car brand if I was lucky.

I reached in.

"Tuna!" Mr. Clarke yelled, reading my slip of paper before I could. "Canned tuna!"

I looked at the slip. It said, "Tongola Tuna."

"That's a really good one." Mr. Clarke nodded confidently at me. "Lots to work with."

I gave him the fakest smile I had ever pasted on my face.

I had to make a tuna commercial. Great.

"Your parents work in advertising, right?" Mr. Clarke followed up. "This should be a breeze for you!" he squealed. He actually squealed.

"Oh yeah." I had almost forgotten how Mom and Dad had worked on commercials before. Sometimes they freelanced for other ad agencies that were too swamped, and I'm pretty sure they'd helped write TV scripts for them.

I smiled. He was right. This was going to be a cinch.

. . .

INTRODUCTION TO VIDEO
LATER

All throughout our lesson on commercials I'd been avoiding Emerson's eye. Sir had even passed me a note from him. I didn't read it, though. We just weren't at the notes stage in our relationship yet. The bell rang, and I walked to his desk, ready to rip off the Band-Aid.

"Hey, Emerson," I said quietly.

"Yo, P. What's up? Did you read my note?"

I handed him back the letter. It felt like we were already breaking up. But had we even dated? God, high school was so confusing. I was too young to break a heart. Too young to become a woman made of unfeeling stone.

"How's your nose?" he asked.

I winced. Time to cut to the chase. "Emerson, thank you so much for asking me out, but my answer is no."

Emerson nodded. "I feel you." He was wearing a T-shirt three times his size today, and I could barely see his cargo shorts underneath.

"I just think you should go out with someone who is more . . . um . . . adventurous."

Emerson nodded again. He was taking this pretty well.

"Aight, well, dang. Thanks for keeping it one hundred with me, P."

I gave him a sad smile, trying to be nice about the whole thing.

Emerson handed me the note. "Well, you might as well keep this," he said. He chucked a peace sign at me. "Hasta la vista."

I waved the somber kind of wave you give to people when they're looking at you through the back of a car window, never to be seen again. In retrospect, it did feel like a weird thing to do when the person was two feet away from you.

When he left the classroom, I opened the note. It was a hangman game that had been half finished. There were five blanks, with the middle two filled in with the letter *O*.

"Parvin, do you know the answer?" Emerson had scrawled out at the bottom.

I squinted at the paper, then sighed.

Boobs.

The answer was boobs.

. . .

BLEACHERS
3:00 P.M.

Ruth asked me to come over after school to help her with her Creative Writing essay, but she forgot I had Farsi tutoring with Amir. When I reminded her, she just raised her eyebrows in that smug Ruth way.

"What?" I asked.

"Nothing," she replied in a singsong voice. I swear, if

she wasn't my BFF, I would have probably strangled her by now.

Amir had a hot chocolate waiting for me when I got to the bleachers. That was really nice. I sat down next to him and flinched—the aluminum metal slats were chilly now that September was almost over. Being outside didn't feel like swimming in swamp water anymore.

"Thanks," I said, clutching the warm hot chocolate.

"No problem." He smiled.

Amir looked different today. His wavy hair was combed to the side, and he wore a sweater instead of his normal soccer jersey. He already had his book open to our homework, but he didn't seem in any rush to go through it.

"How's your week been?" he asked.

I thought for a second, remembering Fabián's dance showcase, Amanda's face full of Cheeto dust, and the relief I felt when I turned Emerson down.

"Pretty good, actually," I said. "How about yours?"

Amir frowned. "It's okay. I tried to start a journal through the school, actually."

"That's great!"

"Yeah . . . but they don't have the budget for it this year." Amir shrugged. I could tell it meant more to him than he was letting on, though.

"What do they need the money for?" I asked, taking a sip of hot chocolate. He had even put extra marshmallows into it. Amazing.

"For the paper, getting the layout software, that kind of stuff. I think schools usually get sponsors to pay for it, but we don't have any." Amir sighed.

"But why a physical journal?" I asked. I hadn't even thought of the publication being printed when Amir first mentioned it. "It should be a digital one. Then you wouldn't need a huge budget for paper or anything."

Amir's eyes widened. "Parvin! You're a genius."

"I know," I replied modestly, though the truth was, our middle's school's journal had been digital, too. "Here, I asked my dad if you could borrow these." I handed him some books about writing from my parents' office. I figured Amir needed them more than Dad did, considering he rarely looked at them now.

"Whoa!" His eyes lit up as he read the titles. "Thank you." He started flipping through the pages, already excited.

"Do you mind if we cut our study session short?" he asked, still looking through the books. "I want to go try out your idea. Mock up an online journal to share with Principal Saulk."

I was about to say sure when I remembered Ruth's date.

"Actually, before you go . . . um . . . would you want to go apple picking with me and some friends on Saturday?" I asked. "It'll be really casual," I added, making it clear I wasn't asking him on a date or anything. Amir was a safe bet. We'd have a nice time, and I knew it wouldn't be awkward. Plus, he was so easy to talk to, it might even be fun.

"Apple picking? Like . . . with real apples?" Amir asked, bewildered.

"You've never gone apple picking before?" It was my turn to look baffled. "It's the best. You pick some apples, go on a hayride, carve pumpkins, and then they give you apple-cider doughnuts with fresh-pressed cider."

"Wow. Is this from your white side?" he said, laughing.

I actually didn't know if our family's love of apple picking was from my mom's side. I was flummoxed. Didn't they pick apples in Iran? I stayed quiet, though it would have been nice to ask what he meant by that question. I'd never had someone ask about my white side before. Most days it felt like I wasn't white enough, but when I hung out with Iranians, it was like I wasn't Iranian enough, either. Sometimes, being with Amir and everyone in Farsi class made me feel like I'd never be enough in general.

"Sure, that sounds fun," he finally said.

"Okay, great. I'll see you Saturday." I smiled. "Thanks for the hot chocolate."

"No problem." Amir grinned.

He leaped off the bleachers and jogged away, waving goodbye. I sat for a while, thinking about apple picking this weekend. Amir had left his Farsi notebook with me, this week's Nizami poetry already translated to English. I read through.

Layla was a lute, Majnun a viola.
All the radiance of this morning was Layla,
yet a candle was burning in front of her,
consuming itself with desire.
She was the most beautiful garden
and Majnun was a torch of longing.
She planted the rose-bush;
he watered it with his tears.

I closed the book. Were women lutes, and men violas? What was a lute?

I googled a lute. It looked like a baby guitar. I was definitely not a lute. I was a bassoon, and nobody wrote poems about us.

Friday
BAND ROOM
3:15 P.M.

After band, I hovered around the classroom, returning to my please-talk-to-me strategy with Matty. I hadn't seen him in the hallways so I could bump into him, and I was growing desperate. After all, I still needed to compliment him. And somehow stare at him long enough to indicate that I wanted him to ask me out.

"What are you doing?" Ruth asked suspiciously as I pretended to read my sheet music.

"I'm just studying my parts."

"Uh-huh," Ruth said, unconvinced.

Just then, Matty walked up with his trumpet case. *PLEASE LOOK AT ME!* I screamed inside my heart.

"Hey, y'all," he said. "It was cool seeing you two at Yessenia's last weekend."

"Hey, Matty," I said calmly as Ruth looked on. "Yeah, that was cool." *Ha-ha-ha-ha-ha!*

"Are you reading the concert piece?" he asked. I almost blurted out that, yes, I was reading it, and that I was nervous about the bassoon solo in it, but I held back. I simply nodded.

"I love the trumpet parts," Matty said. "They're so, like, raw, you know?"

"Totally." I had no clue what he meant. "So raw."

He laughed. Had I even made a joke? Every time I talked to Matty I never knew why we were laughing. But still, he looked super cute in his green sweater and jeans today. Perfect Homecoming material, for sure.

I gave Ruth my nonverbal signal to leave so Matty could ask me out, but she just mouthed, *What?*

Ugh, Ruth! A boy who thinks I'm cute is talking to me! I gave her my furious eyes, but she just shrugged.

I turned back to Matty. "I like your . . . um . . ." I cast around, quickly looking for something to compliment him on. "Your shoes," I finally said.

Matty looked down. They were plain white sneakers that, if anything, looked a little worse for wear. He laughed, holding my gaze. "Thanks, Parvin. Gotta find beauty in the unexpected, right?"

I nodded, though I had no idea what he was talking about. But who cared? The compliment seemed to have worked. I stared deep into his eyes, hoping my dateability would come across. It was uncomfortable, and all I wanted to do was blink.

"See ya later," he said, breaking our eye contact with a smile. He headed toward the exit.

"See ya." Ruth waved goodbye, and Matty walked out the door, clutching his trumpet case. How I wished my bassoon were as small and as light as that case.

"Ruth! Why did you stand there like a gaping fish? I was hoping he'd ask me out."

Ruth rolled her eyes. But who cared what she thought? Matty just went out of his way to speak to me. Soon he'd be asking me to hang out. Ha-ha-ha-ha!

Whether Ruth wanted to admit it or not, my plan was working.

"Parvin?" she said with a smirk.

"What, Ruth? Are you going to tell me what a bad idea this whole plan is again?"

"Your sheet music is upside down."

Dang it.

· · ·

PRACTICE ROOMS
LATER

Ruth left to go to her church group, and Fabián wasn't replying to any of my texts. He must be at practice, or talking to his zillion fans online. I headed to one of the practice rooms to figure out how I was going to play a bassoon solo in front of a whole auditorium in three months. The solo was only two notes, but still.

I opened the door to what was really just a glorified closet, but someone was already in there.

"Oh, sorry." It was Azar, the girl from Farsi school who spoke twelve languages.

"No worries," she replied, her voice still husky. She turned back to her guitar. I didn't know she played an instrument, and I hadn't seen her around in band. There were a few students who rented instruments and practiced for fun. I guess Azar was one of them.

"See you in Farsi class?" I asked.

She nodded, giving me a small smile.

I grabbed the next room over, and I could still hear Azar

practicing her guitar through the thin walls. I began running through my solo piece. My fingers were starting to automatically go to the right keys without having to look down now, which felt like a big step, and I could sit on the instrument easily. I ran through the solo a couple times, the long, sustained notes making it boring but at least easy. I'd been playing for only three weeks, but the bassoon was finally starting to feel familiar.

"Knock-knock," a voice said before the door opened. It was Ms. Kaiser, her hard-to-read face smiling for once. "That's sounding pretty good, Parvin."

"Really?" I'd been practicing at home and watching the tutorial videos she gave me the login for. I was relieved I sounded okay.

She nodded, her huge eyes blinking back at mine through circular glasses. "You'll be ready for our concert in no time." She gave me a small wave, her straight black hair swishing as she closed the door.

"Yessss!" I said to myself. "You are a bassoon queen, Parvin!" which rhymed. "Yes! Yes! Yes!" I continued pumping my fists until a voice interrupted my solo celebration.

"Um, congratulations?" Azar's voice called out through the wall.

Oh my god. "Please tell me you didn't just hear me do that," I moaned.

"Yep," she called out through the thin partition. "Every word."

Kill me now.

Saturday

By Saturday afternoon, the temperature was brisk—the perfect weather for apple picking. The whole farm's cornfield had been converted into a huge maze, while the barn had been outfitted with an apple-pressing station, an apple-cider-doughnut truck, a face painting stand, and a pumpkin-carving station. There was even a hayride ferrying people to different parts of the farm.

Ruth, Naomi, Amir, and I were in the orchard, dropping apples into rustic wooden baskets straight out of Ruth's fantasies. I even wore my hair curly and had a colorful dress and leggings on. I'd been on my best behavior at school. I could take a day off.

Ruth looked like a fall princess with her sparkly eyeshadow, flouncy skirt, and big cable-knit cardigan. Naomi wore skinny jeans that hugged her tall frame and some sort of shimmery highlighter on her cheeks that made her dark skin glow gold. Even Amir had worn a nice button-down shirt and autumnal corduroy pants. We might just be the best-dressed apple pickers here.

We'd already picked a dozen apples each, though I had no idea what I was going to do with all of them. We barely ate fruits and vegetables at our house, much less fresh ones. Amir was excited, though, climbing up ladders and shaking branches that had clusters of apples as Naomi caught them in her basket.

"It's just like picking mulberries!" he cried before

scampering back up a ladder. Naomi laughed. I hadn't really talked to her yet, so today was the perfect opportunity to make sure she was good enough for my BFF. I had forgotten that Amir and Naomi were both sophomores, and that they already knew each other. I think that made Ruth less anxious.

"Here, try one," Naomi said, holding an apple out for Ruth. Ruth took a bite, the apple still in Naomi's hand.

Amir raised his eyebrows at me. The moment was undeniably steamy for a "casual hang" with friends.

Oh boy.

"So, Parvin, are you in band, too?" Naomi asked as Ruth chewed her bite of sexy apple.

"Yeah, I play the bassoon."

Naomi's brown eyes lit up. "That's so cool. It's a double-reed, right?"

"Yeah." I nodded. Dang, Naomi knew her stuff. It was nice meeting someone who'd actually heard of my instrument for once.

"Do you play an instrument?" I asked. I could feel Ruth staring at me, probably praying I wouldn't mess this up for her.

"No way." Naomi shook her head. "I do not have a musical bone in my body. I'm head of Astronomy Club, though."

Ruth gasped. "So you can tell which constellation is which?"

Naomi nodded. "That's a small part of it, but yeah. I want to be an astrophysicist," she said proudly. "And eventually an astronaut."

Amir gave a low whistle. "You could be the next Mae Jemison."

"Hopefully," she replied. I could practically see the heart eyes Ruth was beaming at her from across the orchard. I think it was safe to say Naomi was definitely good enough for Ruth, if not a bit overqualified.

"Oh yeah, we had English together, right?" Amir asked. "You wrote about wanting to work at NASA."

"Yeah," Naomi said. "I almost forgot."

I smiled. See? We were all getting along great. Ruth and Naomi were having an epic first date, and Amir and I were having a good time, too. I still didn't have anyone taking me to Homecoming, but at least I could distract myself from my dateless existence today.

"Let's go get doughnuts," I shouted. I had forgotten to eat lunch (not that we had anything to eat at home, anyway) and my stomach was starting to gurgle. Amir grabbed the basket we'd both been dumping apples into, and we headed over to the barn, where families carved pumpkins and drank cider.

Up ahead, Naomi held out her hand. Ruth took it.

Amir's eyebrows surged.

"Hey," he whispered to me. "Are they together?"

I gave a vague nod-shrug combo. "Nnnyeeah."

"So is this, like . . . a date?" he asked.

I could feel my face go red.

"Um . . . sort of? Ruth isn't allowed to date, so she asked me to go with her—"

"Like . . . a double date," Amir clarified.

"I mean—" I started, feeling flustered. "I asked Fabián if he wanted to come, but he had auditions today. I thought you would like apple picking?"

Amir frowned. "Fabián Castor? Isn't he gay?"

"He's my friend," I huffed. Why was I being so defensive? "I'm sorry. I should have told you Naomi and Ruth were dating. I just wanted a friend to come with me . . ." I trailed off. How had things suddenly gotten so weird?

"Oh . . . so . . . as friends," Amir said flatly. Was he mad at me? "We're here as friends," he repeated.

What was I supposed to say?

"I *thought* we were friends . . . ," I started uncertainly. "Are we not?"

Amir sighed, running his hands through his hair. "Yeah, we are. Sorry. Never mind."

I must have still looked confused, because Amir gave me a sad smile.

"Let's go get those doughnuts," he said. He trudged ahead through the hay, and I followed him, not sure what had just happened.

• • •

BARN O' PUMPKINS
LATER

By the time we'd picked which pumpkins we wanted to carve, things were back on track. Ruth and Naomi were carving a pumpkin into a scaredy-cat. Ruth concentrated hard as she made each cut with the carving knife while Naomi provided moral support. Amir was deep into a grinning jack-o'-lantern while I sipped cider and ate doughnuts, supervising.

"Is that a smile?" I asked Amir, peering at his pumpkin carving.

"It's a mischievous grin," he replied defensively. It looked more like a jagged gash, but I didn't say anything.

"I can feel you judging Mr. Jack," Amir said to me, his hands on his hips.

"Mr. Jack?"

Amir gestured with his knife to the jack-o'-lantern. "Now you've upset him."

Ruth walked over. "Abstract pumpkin carving," she said, eyeing Amir's pumpkin. "Nice."

Amir sighed, exasperated. "None of you deserve my gifts."

"Hey, it's getting dark soon," Naomi said. "Want to do the corn maze?"

Ruth squealed. "Oooh, yes! We can take the hayride over."

Amir shook his head. "What are we? Ten years old?"

"Who doesn't like hayrides?" I asked at the same time Naomi said, "Hayrides are awesome," and Ruth said, "We don't have to—"

Amir laughed. "Guys, there's no way I'm going on a hayride with a bunch of kids."

. . .

HAYRIDE
LATER

A toddler crawled into Amir's lap and decided to stay there. Amir gave me a look that told me I seriously owed him as the kid's parents cooed over how "forthright" their child was with their "intentions."

"Smile," I said, taking a photo on my phone. Amir grimaced, but then the kid gave him a kiss on the cheek, and he broke out into a genuine grin. It was adorable.

We rode along a dirt road on the way to the corn maze, passing rows and rows of pumpkins. It was a lot of fun, bumping away on a trailer as the sun set. It was almost romantic, even though there was way too much denim happening in the back of this truck to be attractive.

"Here we go," a man in overalls, flannel, and a straw hat shouted from the tractor. He looked like he got his outfit off one of the scarecrows in the pumpkin patch. I did a double take.

It was the *exact same outfit*.

Naomi helped Ruth down from the trailer bed, holding out her hand. Amir bowed and did the same for me.

"Thank ye, kind sir."

"M'lady." He tipped his imaginary hat.

It was getting dark now, the sun setting past the fields, and I could hear the swish of hay and dried corn husks below our feet. It felt like the perfect place for a first date. I hoped Ruth was having a good time.

Just then, Ruth giggled into Naomi's shoulder. They'd been whispering to each other the whole ride and seemed to have forgotten Amir and I existed.

"We're gonna go ahead," Ruth announced, still laughing. Naomi grabbed her hand, and the two skipped away into the first ring of the corn maze. It was the biggest one in the DC metro area, but I'd never been through it before.

I turned to Amir and shrugged. "Ready?"

He gave me a long look. "Sure."

The sun's fading rays made his brown eyes look almost gold. I shivered. Amir had never looked at me like that before. Was he still upset I didn't tell him we were tagging along on Ruth and Naomi's date?

"Watch out for ticks!" the hayride operator shouted before hopping back on his tractor. Delightful.

We walked into the maze, and it instantly got darker, the rows of corn blocking out some of the sunset. It seemed like everyone had gone ahead of us by now, and the only sound was the crunch of our sneakers as they cracked brittle leaves.

The maze was easy at first, but then we came to our first fork. The sun had now set, and whatever light was left over didn't reach inside the maze.

"What do you think?" Amir whispered, the maze suddenly quiet and spooky. "Left or right?"

I shrugged. "I don't know. Flip a coin?"

Amir got out a quarter. "Heads we go right," he said as he tossed it in the air. It landed with a tiny *thunk* on the dirt. "Tails." We headed left.

Up ahead, I could hear laughter, probably from a family outside that was still picking pumpkins. Were we the only people left in here? Had Ruth and Naomi already made it through?

"Ow!" I shouted, slamming into a hard wall of hay bales. We'd come upon a dead end in the maze, but it had been too dark to see properly.

"Are you okay?" Amir jogged up, concerned. "You really went for it."

I spit out some hay. "Ugh, I hit my head." Was I seeing stars? I couldn't tell, it was so dim in here.

"You've got some hay in your hair." He picked it out. I looked away, embarrassed. It was a good thing he probably couldn't make out my burning cheeks. There weren't even any lights to help us see which way to go.

"You're a good friend," I assured him as he picked the last piece out.

Amir cleared his throat. "Um . . . Parvin," he said, his eyes going dark. He gave me that same look he'd given me when I suggested we go into this stupid maze in the first place. "I don't think I want to be friends."

"I thought . . . you just said we were!" I hated how childish my voice sounded then. Was I not Iranian enough? Or did Amir want something more? We'd had so much fun in Farsi class and that day we ate abgoosht at his house. I thought I could be myself around Amir. But now I felt like I was misreading the situation, like I had with Wesley.

He stepped toward me, closing the distance between us. And then he kissed me.

His lips were soft but firm, not chapped and salt-crusted like Wesley's. He wrapped his arms around me, bringing me closer, pushing me against the wall of hay.

I was so surprised by the kiss that I only remembered to close my eyes just as he let go.

"Whoa," I said. Why did I say that out loud? What was wrong with me?

"Whoa," Amir agreed. "So—" Just then, Ruth's voice cut through the cocoon of corn we'd been in.

"PARVIN! PARVIN!" she cried. "Where are you guys?"

"We're over here!" I shouted. Oh my god. There was literally no light left. How long had we been kissing for? What was going on?

"Amir"—I turned to his general direction in the dark, suddenly panicking—"do you know how to get out of here?"

"Crap," he said. "I wasn't paying attention."

I was going to rot away here. In a corn maze. With a boy who I thought was my friend but turned out is a really good kisser.

This was the most confusing way to die.

Sunday

BED
10:00 A.M.

> 10:03 AM PARVIN MOHAMMADI: Ameh, are you there? Do you have time to talk?

> 10:10 AM SARA MOHAMMADI: Sorry, ameh! This is my last week of class before I see you and things are a bit busy. Maybe tomorrow?

> 10:10 AM PARVIN MOHAMMADI: Sure, of course. Good luck with class!

I tossed my phone back onto my quilt. I needed Ameh Sara to help me make sense of everything that happened last night. Until then, I had no idea how to face Amir at Farsi school today.

I was being a bad person and skipping class this Sunday. But to my credit, I actually did look pretty pale, and my throat was hoarse from shouting our location to the pumpkin patch manager from the maze for twenty minutes with Amir. In the end, I think Mom felt bad for me. She tucked me into bed and made me a cup of tea with honey this morning.

My phone had been blowing up all night with our group text. Apparently, Fabián had beaten Matty for the lead role in the play, and Ruth couldn't shut up about her first kiss with Naomi. She'd even walked Ruth to her front steps, risking a serious smooch despite her mom being able to fling the door open at any moment. I was super happy for both of them, but my brain just felt dead after last night.

> 10:07 AM FABIÁN: so you brought your friend from Farsi school to apple picking

> 10:15 AM PARVIN: Amir? Yeah, he's helping me with my reading

> 10:15 AM FABIÁN: uh-huh

> 10:16 AM RUTH: Why were you acting so weird after the corn maze?

> 10:16 AM FABIÁN: [shares a photo from Amir's Instagram] pretty cute, for a friend

10:20 AM PARVIN: Um. Because Amir kissed me last night.

10:20 AM FABIÁN: HAHAHA! ruth, you owe me $10!

I had no idea how to feel about Amir kissing me. How had I missed that he liked me like that? We were just Farsi friends—I didn't think guys like Amir dated watered-down Iranians like me.

I liked Amir a lot—he was funny, nice, and easy to talk to—but part of me felt a little weirded out that he liked me that way at all.

I replayed the way I acted around Matty and the way I acted with Amir. The two Parvins could not be more different. When I was around Matty, I acted like the Quiet Parvin I wanted to be. The one who didn't talk so much and laughed without snorting. When I hung out with Amir, though, I felt like the Parvin that I already was, the one who was "passionate," and who cracked jokes and slurped soup even if that wasn't what women did in the movies.

It was almost like I found Amir less attractive for liking the version I was now. Even *I* knew the Parvin of this moment wasn't that great. I had let my heart get stomped on over the summer, been uninvited from the clarinet, and couldn't even speak the language that matched up with my face. The Parvin that Amir had seen was the same Parvin who didn't get asked out in middle school, the one who'd spent every school dance on the sidelines. And just when

I was working on making sure that never happened again, Amir made it clear he liked that version of me.

Wasn't your significant other supposed to make you a better person? To help you be the best version of yourself that you could possibly be? I was still updating my software. Only someone demented would choose Parvin 1.0 when they could wait and get the latest model.

I reached toward my laptop to email Ameh Sara since I couldn't call her, then stopped. There was something I'd been afraid to think about when it came to Amir—a deeper, ickier dread that I had never said out loud, much less dared to drag to the front of my brain. It was a feeling that was hard to put into words, and one that I knew would seriously upset Ameh Sara.

I opened my phone and stared at Amir's photo feed. He had the same crick in his nose as me, and the same thick, curly hair. His skin was a bit tanner than mine, but the arm hair was just as present. He practically looked like a member of the Melli soccer team, he was so Iranian.

Meanwhile, I'd spent the past few weeks waxing my body, shaving my arms, and straightening my hair. It was like I was trying not to look Iranian at all. And here was Amir, liking me on the days I hadn't bothered to do those things, accepting me for who I was.

I thought back to our sleepover: None of the women in the movies looked like me. There were no ads in magazines of girls with big noses or commercials with women who could definitely grow a unibrow. The more I tried to look like those models and actors, the closer I looked to my mom . . . and the more beautiful I felt.

Now I knew Amir thought I was pretty. You didn't kiss

someone you found ugly. So what did that mean for the things I'd always thought were beautiful? Were the movies and TV shows wrong? Or maybe it was wrong of me to try to change myself to look like them in the first place.

This was the kind of thing I couldn't ask Ameh Sara about over email without her getting super upset. Just mentioning that I didn't feel beautiful would probably send her reeling into a long lecture about self-esteem and how society was always trying to bring women down. No, this weird feeling was something moms helped their daughters with, because most moms looked like their daughters. Too many freckles, knobby knees, big teeth—those were the kinds of things where moms could say, "I had those when I was your age, but look at me now. I grew to love those features." But my mom didn't have oily skin or ingrowns or frizzy hair that puffed up the second it rained. I didn't have a mom who could help me understand how I felt. My stomach was in knots just replaying the kiss and what that meant for everything I thought I knew. And I didn't have anyone who could walk me through this.

I'd shown Amir the true me simply because I never figured he'd like me that way, so there hadn't been any point in pretending to be someone else. But now he had kissed me, and that made me feel more scared than anything. At least Matty knew absolutely nothing about me, so he could never hurt me that badly if things didn't work out. But if things went wrong with Amir, it would be like Wesley all over again: getting dumped for being "too much" and "loud" and being *me*.

More than anything, I was confused. My stomach didn't give me butterflies when I saw Amir, not the way it did whenever I spotted Matty.

I pulled up the Actionable-Matty-Steps list I had printed

out and put under my pillow. I was pretty sure getting kissed meant I could have a Homecoming date if I wanted it. But what would people say if I dated a full Iranian?

Deep down, I doubted Wesley would be impressed if Amir and I went to Homecoming together. I thought back to the bumper stickers on the cars outside of Teighan's Labor Day BBQ. I had a hunch the crowd Wesley ran with was not very pro-Iranian. He'd probably think we were having an arranged marriage or something, even though few Iranians did that in the first place these days.

Seeing Amir in Farsi school would have just been too much today. I couldn't handle a reunion after such a crazy night and an even crazier kiss.

Someone knocked on my door. "Come in," I said, my voice scratchy.

"Hi, baba jaan." Dad leaned over to feel my forehead. "Khoobi?" *You good?*

"I'm okay," I replied. Which was true. I was fine. I was just wallowing.

Dad sat down on the edge of the bed. Why did parents always just assume they could sit on the edge of your bed? He sighed. I think he missed being in the parking lot with all the other Iranian parents today. I felt bad that I'd made him miss it.

"Hey, Dad?" I said, my voice pathetic and feeble. "Was it hard marrying someone who wasn't Iranian?" Dad had always hinted that his family wasn't exactly supportive, but I'd never gotten the full story.

Dad turned to me, surprised. "Why do you ask?"

I shrugged. This whole Amir thing was throwing me off. I needed answers.

He laughed, stroking his mustache.

"It wasn't hard," Dad began. "But . . . there were things that definitely could have been easier."

"Like what?" I sat up.

"I don't know . . . basic stuff. Like Taarof."

I nodded. Taarof is a complex Iranian hospitality ritual where everyone tries to out-kindness each other. It drove Mom crazy when Dad offered to pay for dinner whenever they went out with friends. One time he even offered to pay for his own birthday meal. Then Dad got upset that Mom was upset and said that if he didn't offer to be hospitable, the evil eye would look upon our family and curse us all.

It came up a lot.

"It's big in Iran, you know? Guests are important. We don't really do that here," Dad said, his shoulders sagging. "But then there are other things that your mom makes easier. Like calming me down when I get angry. Or thinking of the best concepts for our campaigns. There are few people I could own a business with and also be married to," he said firmly.

I drank in every word. Were Amir and I like that? There weren't many guys that I knew who could both tutor me in Farsi *and* make me not want to murder them.

"Was your family happy you married a non-Iranian?"

Dad laughed, a harsh, barking sound. "No. They were not. Did your mother never tell you about the time she first met my father? He had brought another Iranian woman to the dinner to set us up in front of your mom. And we'd already been engaged for a year!"

My eyes widened in horror. Who set up a blind date for someone who was engaged? "That sounds awful."

"Oh, it was terrible. They referred to her as a khareji—an *outsider*—and wouldn't speak in English in front of her," Dad said. "But it's funny now, looking back at it."

How she didn't dump him then and there, I will never know.

"But . . . what about Iranian women? You didn't want to date them?" I pressed.

Dad shrugged. "I met your mom at the Corcoran. There weren't a ton of Iranians in design school. Actually, I think I was the only one."

I nodded, digesting that information. I wondered what it must have been like being the only Iranian in your entire school. At least I had Amir, and Azar, and a handful of other Iranians I'd seen around. Not having people from your culture in college sounded pretty lonely.

"It didn't matter that she wasn't Muslim? Or that she couldn't speak Farsi?"

Dad gave me a long look. "Baba jaan," he said. "The Iran I am from no longer exists. It wasn't even called the Islamic Republic of Iran then—it was just Iran. When I was growing up, women could wear miniskirts and makeup and you didn't have to be Muslim. Coming to the US felt normal. We all listened to the same music. We all learned English at school. I worked hard to assimilate, but it wasn't like it is now." Dad swallowed, thinking of how to continue.

"The Iran your ameh Sara is from is very different. She grew up always wearing a chador. She always had to be Muslim. I have more in common with the people I see here every day in this country than with someone who just flew in from Tehran."

"So, are you Iranian? Or a khareji outsider or whatever?" It felt like the most important question I'd ever asked him. I didn't realize how badly I needed to know.

"I'm American, baba jaan," Dad said. "And that means I can be anything."

He got up and kissed me on the forehead. "That's enough for now, okay, Parvin joon? You need to rest."

"Hey, Dad?" I asked him again.

"Yeah?"

"What if I dated someone who was Iranian? Would that be weird?"

Dad gave me another look. What did all these looks mean? I needed to know.

"Nope." Dad smiled. "Not weird at all."

He gently closed the door.

• • •

GUEST ROOM
6:00 P.M.

By the end of the day, I was feeling a lot better. My voice even sounded normal again. And, to top it off, Mom had made me chicken soup. And it was edible.

It was a miracle.

I was helping Mom get Sara's room ready, making sure we had all the right sheets and linens and stuff since she was going to be here next week.

"Hand towel?" Mom called to me from the guest bathroom. I dug through the clean laundry hamper until I found it.

"Comin' in hot!" I shouted, throwing the towel to her.

Mom folded it the special way, like we were in the Hotel Mohammadi.

"Fancy soap?" she asked. I dug around in the dresser where Mom also stored our bougie soap and extra sheets. It helped make the linens smell really good.

"Honeysuckle," I said, tossing the soap to her. She put it in the soap dish. "And a bath towel."

I threw her an extra fluffy one. Hopefully, Ameh Sara would like the honeysuckle smell.

"I think this looks pretty good, wouldn't you say?" Mom put her hands on her hips and surveyed the room. It was definitely the cleanest room in our house now.

"We should buy fresh flowers when she comes," I said, pointing to an empty vase on the nightstand.

"Great idea." Mom was the super creative one in the family, but it felt nice to come up with a good idea for once.

"Now, Parvin, there's something I want to show you."

Oh no. Was she going to try to make me use organic tampons again? Was nothing sacred?

Mom laughed at my expression. "It's not bad. I just think you're old enough to handle this now." She motioned for me to follow her. She was leading me to the basement.

Oh god.

· · ·

BASEMENT
7:00 P.M.

Mom stood next to the washing machine, tapping the lid. My stomach growled. Normal families would be eating dinner now.

"When was the last time I washed that shirt for you?" Mom asked, pointing at my favorite long-sleeved pajama top. It was flannel and made me feel like it was really autumn.

"Umm?" I couldn't remember the last time it had been washed. Usually, Mom and Dad switched off doing the laundry, but they haven't had time to lately. Why were we having this conversation in the basement? Was Mom going to give me a talk about boys or birth control or something?

"We're getting so busy with work, I want to make sure you can do your own laundry if we can't, okay?" Mom said.

"You want me to do my own laundry?" I repeated, horrified.

Mom pursed her lips. "You're a big girl now. You can handle it."

I nodded. But what if I messed it up? What if I turned everything pink? Or accidentally bleached something?

Mom put her hand on my shoulder. "It's gonna be okay, Parvin. It's just clothing."

Monday

HOMEROOM
7:30 A.M.

I was wearing my only clean T-shirt to school this morning. Which also happened to be stained pink.

The laundry lesson did not go well.

Amir texted me a zillion times already asking me how I was feeling, whether I wanted to meet up, or if I was okay.

I had no idea what to say.

> **10:00 PM AMIR: Parvin? You there? I'm starting to get worried.**

> **7:42 AM PARVIN: Sorry! I was super sick yesterday and am just catching up now.**

Ruth shot me a dirty look for sending a text during class, but it promptly morphed back to the dumb grin she's had pasted on her face all day. I wondered why I didn't look like that. If I liked Amir, I should have been floating on cloud nine, like Ruth was at the thought of Naomi. Instead, I just felt anxious and a little queasy.

I needed to snap out of it. I didn't get upset with myself for not jumping for joy over Emerson, even though he had asked me out. So why was Amir making me feel so strange?

> **7:43 AM AMIR: That's OK. I'm glad you're feeling better. I'll see you on Wednesday? I can catch you up on everything you missed in class?**

> **7:50 AM PARVIN: 10-4.**

There. I sent the least sexy reply known to man so I wouldn't confuse things even more.

. . .

LUNCH
12:00 P.M.

I was surrounded by smiling idiots in the courtyard today. Fabián couldn't stop recounting his epic audition and how he nailed his monologue as he inhaled another plate of fries. Ruth was just grinning and nodding along on her own daydream of bliss. Good god, was I the only one steering this ship? It was like that book we were reading in English, about the Greek dude and the sirens who kept tempting him to make out with them on dangerous rocks or something. Was I the only one who remembered to put wax in my ears and not succumb to love?

• • •

FABIÁN'S ROOM
3:00 P.M.

Fabián wanted us to come over and help him film another video after school. His parents were home for once—I couldn't remember the last time I'd seen them.

"Fabián!" Señora Castor called out from downstairs, pronouncing it *Fa-vyán*. "Could you come here a minute?"

Ruth and I turned back to Fabián's laptop, where we answered social media questions pretending to be him. "Don't use so many exclamation points," he said to Ruth.

He headed downstairs, but we could still hear them talking.

"Again?" Fabián cried, his voice echoing up the stairs. "But you've been gone all month."

"I know, mi amor, but things are getting worse. Children

are in the camps at the Mexican border. We have to help them."

"I know, but . . . I can't just wave at you through the living room cam and pretend like we're one big happy family," Fabián said, sounding upset.

"Maybe we should close the door," Ruth said, clearly feeling awkward for eavesdropping.

I tried not to listen, but it was hard to ignore the pain in his voice. I didn't realize how much he missed his parents. I thought he liked the freedom of being home alone all the time.

"Fabián, it's only until Christmas—" I heard Señora Castor say.

"That's what you said last year!" Fabián yelled.

A door slammed, followed by the sounds of stomping up the stairs. Ruth and I busied ourselves at Fabián's laptop. I threw in two heart emojis to someone on Twitter.

Fabián stormed back into his room. His face was red and his carefully combed hair had come undone, a big strand flopping onto his forehead.

"Are you okay?" I asked. Ruth handed him some peanut butter cups.

"No, I am not okay!" he shouted.

I flinched—Fabián rarely got upset like this.

"My parents said they have to go to Texas again for another trip! That means they'll be missing my step performance *and* the fall play!"

Oh no. I knew how hard Fabián had been working after school. And he'd been uploading snippets of his performances to social media, too.

"I'm so sorry, Fabián." I reached to give him a hug. He looked away.

"Are you, Parvin? Because ever since we started high school, you haven't asked about my parents once. You haven't helped me put outfits together or film routines like Ruth has. You didn't even ask me how play rehearsals were going!"

Fabián breathed heavily. I had no idea he was this upset with me.

"Fabián . . . I . . ."

"All you care about is Homecoming!" he continued. "But news flash, Parvin, there are more important things than Homecoming happening in the world right now. Really bad and awful things. And none of them will be solved by making Matty like some pretend version of you, okay?"

"What?" I was stunned. We'd been friends since elementary school, but we'd never said stuff like this to each other. I looked to Ruth for backup, hoping maybe she could explain what was going on, but she just looked down. My face felt hot, and the corners of my eyes started to itch.

"Ruth?" I whispered. "Is this how you feel, too?"

Ruth tipped forward and let her curtain of black hair hide her face. She shrugged. "You missed our crafting day before Fabián's showcase. And you haven't even asked me about Naomi. It's like you don't care."

"That's not fair!" I balked. "You know that once Homecoming's over things will go back to normal, right?"

"That's not how it works." Ruth shook her head. "You can't just ignore us for a whole month, then still expect to be BFFs after the dance. That's not real friendship."

"I know, I know, but we only have one more week. I'm so close, and I've got these steps in my plan—"

"For someone who's supposed to be quiet these days, you sure haven't shut up about yourself and your stupid plan," Fabián spat.

The room went very still. Ruth looked away, like she didn't want to stick up for me. I had no idea what to say. So I grabbed my things and left.

. . .

SCHOOL
5:00 P.M.

Fabián's house was too far for me to walk home from with my bassoon, so I walked to school to wait for Mom or Dad to pick me up instead.

I couldn't believe Ruth and Fabián had said those things to me. Had this whole Homecoming debacle really made me so self-absorbed? Maybe a little. But did that make me a bad friend?

I thought through the past month since school started, trying to pinpoint places where I'd been a shabby pal. If anything, I struggled to find moments where we'd spent time together in the first place. We were all so busy with either Farsi or church group or dance that we'd hung out less than we had in middle school. Back then we'd gone to Fabián's house almost every day after class and helped him record livestreams for his account. I hadn't recorded a single livestream for him since school started or gone to Ruth's to help her with crafting. If anything, I hadn't really seen them outside of school at all.

Oh no. My friends were on to something. Fabián had been so excited to sign up for extracurriculars, but maybe he took that many to distract himself from the fact that his parents weren't home. And I knew how much Ruth liked company for making posters for school events. I thought about how we used to work together on her memory books all through middle school. Besides the emergency sleepover at the start of school, I hadn't made any effort to hang out with them. Being at Fabián's today was the first time the three of us had hung out since school started, and it was practically October.

I walked up to Polk's main entrance and sat down on the low brick wall by the flagpole. They were right. I hadn't been a great friend.

"Hey," a voice said behind me. I turned around, hoping my face hadn't gone all splotchy and red from my fight. It was Matty, holding his trumpet case.

"You waiting for a ride?" he asked, sitting down next to me.

I nodded. "Yeah." I was too sad to feel triumphant over Matty talking to me. This stupid Homecoming plan was spiraling out of control. I wondered how I could make it up to my friends.

"Are you okay?" Matty asked.

"Oh, sorry." I had almost forgotten he was there. "Just thinking."

He had on what looked like a Shakespearean outfit, the kind of shirt with ruffles and stuff. His shaggy brown haircut looked at odds with his Elizabethan collar.

"I'm trying on my costume for the play, making sure it fits and everything," he explained.

"That's cool," I said. "The costume looks good on you." The green and gold accents brought out the color of his eyes. I bet Fabián's looked even better, though. Maybe I'd help him accessorize it, if he'd let me.

"You think so?" he asked.

"All you need is a horse and you'll be set."

Matty laughed. "I'll see what the props department can do."

Just then, my mom pulled up. *Is that him?* she mouthed through the window, pointing furiously at Matty. Clearly my mother wanted me to die of embarrassment.

"There's my ride, gotta go!" I said, practically sprinting toward the car so she couldn't humiliate me further.

"Oh, okay, bye," Matty said. I waved to him from the passenger seat.

"What's he wearing?" Mom asked, pulling out of the parking lot. "Is that what all the cool people wear these days?"

"Yes, Mom." I was too tired to explain.

She got excited. "Should I get you something like that for Homecoming? With the high collar and everything? Won't you need a corset?"

I thunked my head against the window. *To sleep, perchance, to scream.* Or however it went.

Tuesday

BAND
2:00 P.M.

Matty came in late to band today. Ms. Kaiser raised an eyebrow and said, "So nice of you to join us, Mr. Fumero."

I felt butterflies go crazy in my stomach, almost making it ache. Matty walked toward us as if there were a fan machine blasting his perfect hair in slow motion. That's how a *true* Homecoming date was supposed to feel. Even Wesley had never given me butterflies like that.

To top it off, Matty caught me looking at him and smiled. Somebody hold my bassoon—I think I might faint.

My reputation for pranks must have preceded me, because when we went through arpeggios, Amanda was giving me the stink-eye. But I just played on, my cheeks puffing with each note. Amanda had zero proof; I was already in the getaway car, on the other side of the country. Good luck trying to pin your gross Cheeto habits on me, Amanda.

I'd been trying to talk to Ruth all day, but it was like I was invisible. She'd switched seats in homeroom and eaten lunch with Naomi and the sophomores instead. As soon as band finished, she rushed home, even though we had to play at the football game later tonight. Her mom had signed her up for something called "cram school," and it sounded worse than Farsi school, to be honest.

I still hadn't patched up things with either her or Fabián since our fight yesterday. Besides, Fabián had clubs and rehearsals every day after school from now on. I had no idea how I'd even get them alone to apologize, they were both so busy. And I didn't think a text message was going to cut it this time.

I took a while to put my bassoon away. I wasn't looking forward to walking home alone with my thoughts.

Just then, I felt someone hover over me as I put the pieces in their case. It honestly seemed like I was dismantling a gun, the bassoon was so big. I looked up.

Matty Fumero was standing right next to me. "Hey," he said.

I smiled back, remembering that opening my mouth to speak was probably not the best idea when butterflies were in there.

"How's it going?" he asked, nodding to me. Gosh, his eyes were so beautiful. It was like staring at a closeup of an actor on TV, and not a real person. What was he saying?

"Oh, good. Just packing up." I smiled again. I could see Yessenia staring at us as she put her flute away. Why was she taking so long? A flute was, like, three pieces, tops. Amanda was right next to her, glaring harshly at us.

"So," Matty said.

I gave another smile, just standing there, waiting for him to continue. *It isn't your job to fill the silence, Parvin,* I reminded myself. *He's the one who wanted to talk.*

"I was wondering . . . do you want to go out this weekend?" he asked. My hammering heart went quiet all of a sudden, as if it had forgotten to beat at all. I swear you could hear a pin drop in the band room at that moment—that's how many people were listening in on our conversation.

"Sure," I replied, in a very chill way. *OH MY GOD, MATTY FUMERO JUST ASKED ME OUT!*

"Cool," he said, and smiled. Ah, he had the cutest teeth! They weren't as white as Amir's, though. Probably because Amir's dad was a dentist. *Shut up, Parvin. Shut up!*

"What's your number?" he asked, handing me his phone. "I'll text you, and we can figure out what we want to do."

I entered my phone number, floating above myself as I watched the whole scene unfold. It felt surreal. Was it really that easy? Just smile and laugh and nod? I couldn't believe it. I needed to write a book or something to enlighten all girl-kind.

"Cool, I'll text you soon." Matty grinned, taking his phone back. I watched him walk away, ignoring Yessenia's raised eyebrows.

I had said two full sentences to Matty Fumero today.

And it worked.

. . .

FOOTBALL GAME
7:00 P.M.

Brr. It was actually chilly tonight on the football field. The entire band had taken over a section of the bleachers where we'd play fight songs whenever something happened, which was tough to know, as I had no clue how football worked. Our team just scored something called a safety, but it didn't look very safe. The worst part was that my bassoon was so fragile I couldn't play it outside, so Ms. Kaiser gave me some cymbals and told me to hit them "whenever felt best." I accidentally clanged them before the team arrived, and they were so loud my ears hadn't stopped ringing.

I stared longingly at Ruth in her section of clarinets, but she was still kind of ignoring me. At least when a clarinet messed up, you didn't hear it ricochet across the bleachers.

Matty sat with the rest of the trumpets in the last row. He smiled and gave me a small wave. I gave him a tiny wave back, trying hard not to upset the cymbals.

I still couldn't believe he had asked me out this afternoon. Probably because most things didn't feel real until I told Ruth or Fabián about them. Homecoming was already next weekend. I needed my date with Matty to go really well, or I doubted he'd ask me to the dance. Good thing

Mom helped me French braid my hair today, so I could at least look cute in this sad-sack band outfit.

This was our first football game of the year, but the actual Homecoming one with floats and everything was before the dance. Dear god, I hoped band didn't have to march or do anything then. Me and my cymbals were not ready. Plus I needed that whole day for Ameh Sara to help me with my makeup and outfit in person. I couldn't wait to do a make-over that didn't involve a computer screen when she came this weekend.

Our football team did something again, and the band started up another song. Ms. Kaiser gave me a death glare, probably because I hadn't figured out how to hit the cymbals in time to the beat. She should have just given me a clarinet. To feel like I was doing something, I crashed the cymbals . . . right as the song ended.

Everyone was looking at me now. I hit them a couple more times and shouted, "GO TEAM!" to cover up my mistake.

Amanda smirked.

. . .

LATER

After the first quarter, everyone from band could go home if they wanted to. I tried to catch up to Ruth, but she just hopped into her mom's car and left without so much as a backward glance.

I still hadn't called Fabián. And I'd pushed back my tutoring with Amir to later this week since I had no idea what to say to him, either. I wished Ameh Sara was free to talk tonight. So many thoughts swirled around in my head that I needed help figuring them out.

"Do you need a ride home?"

I turned around, forgetting I was holding my cymbals. It was Wesley. They slammed together in my hands before I could stop them.

"Oh . . . um, no thanks. I should be okay."

He sat down next to me on the bleachers. Why was he here? Where were his pale friends? He must have been here to see the game, even though he never mentioned liking football before. I guess that was one more thing Wesley had changed about himself that I didn't understand.

Most of the other kids from band had left now, and we were the only ones in our row.

"So, how's it going?"

"Why do you keep talking to me?" I suddenly asked. "Didn't you dump me?"

Wesley's blue eyes flickered for a second. His military-style haircut was already growing out. He'd have to get it cut again soon if he wanted to keep it up.

"What do you mean?" he asked, his face red. But I knew he understood.

"If I'm so 'loud' and 'too much,' then why do you keep talking to me?"

"Parvin, come on, that's not what I meant—" Wesley sighed, making it sound like I was crazy for even suggesting that's why he broke up with me.

"So why, then?" I stared him down, waiting for a response.

He squirmed in his slacks. "Listen, Parvin—it wasn't you. It was just, I was starting a new school, you know? And my friends aren't exactly, um, into this kind of stuff," Wesley said, gesturing vaguely at me again. But I wasn't letting him off the hook that easily.

"Excuse me?"

"You know! Everyone at my church . . . they aren't really big fans of Iran right now. And can you blame them? I mean, look what your government is doing with their sharia law and everything. And your last name—I mean, it's pretty Muslim, right?"

I could feel the blood rushing to my face. Was this really happening? Was this what it had been about all along? The second Wesley was back from the beach, he had an image to project to his church friends. And I was clearly hurting his brand. After all, you couldn't be a different person depending on who you were talking to. Unless . . . well . . . it was me trying to be a different person.

"So let me get this straight"—my voice cracked—"even if I had been this super quiet, mousey, boring girl, you still would have broken up with me?"

"Mousey? Huh?" Wesley asked, looking confused.

I could feel the anger boiling inside me, my voice getting stronger. "Yeah. You said I was too loud, remember? As in noisy? Conspicuous? Garish?"

"Well, whatever I said, I'm sorry. I really am. I didn't mean to hurt you. I just don't think our families would get along, you know?"

I laughed. It was a manic, loud cackle that echoed off the bleachers. It felt so, so good to laugh like that. "So it had *nothing* to do with me! I could have changed myself completely and it wouldn't have mattered. I'd still be Iranian, and my last name would still be Mohammadi!" Wesley looked terrified, and he glanced around to make sure I wasn't causing a scene, but I didn't care.

I wanted to scream. To tell him how the stuff he'd said about Iran was completely wrong. I wanted to dunk my head into a shower and let my curls finally be free because this straight hair made my scalp itch. But most important, I wanted the old Parvin back—the person I'd been before I changed myself to get a date and make Wesley jealous. I shook my head, sad that I hadn't listened to my friends when they'd warned me how bad my plan was. "Wesley, you are a butt and a bad kisser. May all your ketchup be replaced with hot sauce, and may every passing seagull poop on your khakis! KHODAFEZ!" I howled. *BUH-BYE!*

"Wait, what—?" he asked, still confused.

And then I crashed the cymbals right in his face and walked away.

Wednesday

MY ROOM
6:00 A.M.

I Skyped Ameh Sara as soon as I woke up, even though there was a chance she might still be at school. I was desperate to talk to her. Luckily, she picked up.

"Ameh!" I wailed.

Sara threw a chador over her hair and peered into her laptop screen. "What is it, ameh? What's wrong? Is everything okay?"

"I thought I had to change who I was to make Wesley jealous, but now Fabián and Ruth are mad, and I think I really screwed things up with Amir, and now it turns out Wesley never would have been with me no matter how much I changed!"

Sara held up her hands, confused beyond belief (and who could blame her?). "Wait, who is Amir? And why were you changing? Slow down, azizam. Start from the beginning."

So I did. I told her how I lied about having a Homecoming date after Wesley dumped me, and how I'd ignored Ruth and Fabián, and how Amir kissed me last Saturday but we hadn't really talked because I didn't know what to do. And now I had a date with Matty this weekend despite what Wesley had said to me last night.

"Oh, ameh," she said when I finished, shaking her head. "That is a lot."

"So what do I do?" I whimpered.

She chewed her lip. "Well, first off, I think you need to apologize to your friends, no? Maybe start there. And, Parvin joonam, you need to forgive yourself, too. Why are you so hard on yourself? Why did you think changing would be worth it? Look at what happens when you aren't true to who you are."

"Parvin! Hurry up or you'll be late for school!" Mom called up to my room.

"Coming!" I shouted back. "I gotta go, Ameh. But I'll apologize to my friends first thing. Thanks for the advice."

She blew a kiss through the screen. "Don't worry, azizam—I'll be there on Sunday and we can talk in person, okay? I think we have a lot to go over."

I blew her a kiss back. "I know. I wish you were here already. Bye, Ameh!"

She waved, and I hung up.

INTRODUCTION TO VIDEO
10:00 A.M.

We were working on our commercials in class today, but I was pretty sure I was the only one doing stop-motion animation, which is when you take a photo of an object, move it a little bit, then take another photo. When you stitch them all together, it looks like the object is moving on its own.

Mr. Clarke was beside himself with excitement.

"Is this a stop-motion commercial?" he asked, pointing to my cardboard ocean diorama, complete with a little tuna fish made out of construction paper that I nudged between shots.

I shrugged. "Yes?"

Mr. Clarke nodded. "Right, right, okay. I can see what you're doing here. You've got a consistent source of light—very good. And you're moving the fish over an equal amount every time, to make it look smooth—very good." His head snapped up suddenly. "Will you have music in the background of your commercial?"

"Er, yes," I replied. Crap. I had forgotten about music.

He nodded to himself again. "Good, good, carry on."

Who was he? A reality-TV-show judge? I pushed my little tuna fish over a bit more and took another photo. I'd already done some test shots, and it actually looked like a real spot. It was a lot easier than editing footage because with stop motion, there was no splicing or fade-ins or whatever, just assembling all the photos in order. It was way more my speed.

I looked at everyone else in class. Almost our entire group was already editing their videos at the computer bank in the back of the room, using the skills Mr. Clarke had taught us.

Sir had drawn a cat food brand out of the hat and was monologuing in a corner in front of a camera, holding up a metal tin. Because that's what was gonna sell cat food: Sir's monologues.

Suddenly, he looked at me. Oh no.

"Hey, Parvin!"

I looked back at my diorama. "Hey, Sir."

"I just realized!" he shouted across the classroom. "We're both making commercials for cat food."

I looked back at my tuna tin.

He was right.

. . .

GAY-STRAIGHT ALLIANCE
3:00 P.M.

It had been almost two whole days since our fight on Monday, and I had no idea where Ruth and Fabián had been hanging out. I hadn't seen them in the courtyard for lunch, so I'd been spending it in the practice rooms. But I knew there was a Gay-Straight Alliance meeting today, and they never missed a meeting. I had a plan forming in my mind on how I could make up everything to my friends, but before I could set it into motion, I needed to apologize.

I grabbed a seat in the back of the theater just as Ms. Kaiser called the meeting to order. I'd forgotten she was the GSA sponsor.

"Hello, everyone," she called out. She wore a floral dress today, and her long black hair was in a bun at the top of her head. I could see Fabián and Ruth sitting near her in the front row, along with—wait, was that Matty Fumero? And why was he sitting next to Fabián? I thought they were theater rivals or whatever.

"Today we'll be talking about our plans for Transgender Day of Remembrance. It's a little over a month away now, so any and all suggestions are welcome for how we can honor those lives."

I looked over. Shocker—Ruth was already scribbling a bunch of ideas down. I didn't know these issues were so important to her. But then again, I was realizing that a lot of things were important to my friends—I'd just never bothered to ask them.

"Now it's time for announcements." Ms. Kaiser sat down and opened the floor as different students got up and talked about activities, fundraisers, and resources. Scary Becca from orientation even stood up, saying that anyone who wasn't comfortable going to Homecoming could go to her house for an "Anti-Homecoming Homecoming." That was nice, even if she was still terrifying. Once the announcements were done, everyone kind of milled around and caught up with one another. I waited for Fabián and Ruth to spot me.

"Parvin, hey," Matty said, beating them to it. "I didn't know you came to these."

Ooof. He really was *so cute*. "I'm trying to be a more supportive friend," I replied.

"So, about our date. I was thinking this weekend—" Matty began. In that moment, Fabián and Ruth saw me. Fabián gave me a dark look.

"Sorry—would you excuse me?" I asked Matty. Friends were more important than dates. I knew that now.

"Sure. I'll text you?"

I nodded and headed toward my friends.

"Fancy seeing you here," I said, smiling pathetically. God, I hoped I hadn't messed things up too badly.

Fabián crossed his arms. "What are you doing here, Parvin?"

Ruth crossed hers a second later. "Yeah." She scowled.

I led them over to an empty corner of the auditorium. "I came to apologize. Y'all were right. I was being dumb and didn't even know it. I'm really, really sorry for how obsessed I got with this whole Homecoming thing."

"*And?*" Ruth asked.

"And . . . um . . . I owe you Hot Cheetos for a month?"

"*And you'll make an effort to be a better friend?*" she asked again.

"Yes, of course!"

"*And—*"

"Okay, Ruth, stop before you make Parvin promise to cross-stich a laptop cover or something." Fabián sighed.

"First off, it's an iPad cover, and it took three weeks without help! Also, my mom wants you to come over for dinner tomorrow night, and since you're trying to be a better friend, you have to."

I nodded, even though Mrs. Song always made me feel on edge.

Fabián faced me. "Parvin, I accept your apology, but you're not off the hook that easily."

I hung my head. "I know—I'll go to Costco and get some Cheetos and—"

"Not that." Fabián shook his head. "You gotta stop this

whole Homecoming mission thing, okay? I hate it. It's stupid. And it probably won't even work."

"Well," I began. And then I told them everything. How Matty had asked me out, how Wesley had revealed that there was nothing I could have done to stop him from dumping me, and how I still hadn't talked to Amir.

"So your plan *did* work," Ruth pointed out. "Even though you didn't need it in the first place."

"Parvin, what are you gonna do?" Fabián asked.

I shrugged. Good question.

• • •

OBSERVATORY
5:00 P.M.

"Knock-knock?" I called out from the bottom of the stairs. Our observatory was in a deserted courtyard toward the back of the school. I'd never seen anyone go inside it.

"Come in," Naomi called out. I climbed up the steep ladder leading to the main part of the observatory where the telescope was. When I reached the top, Naomi was sitting there, her books spread out by the base. Her locs were twisted up and secured into place with a colorful scarf, and she wore round glasses I'd never seen on her before. On her shirt were the words **BLACK GIRL MAGIC** in silver letters.

"Parvin! Hey!"

"Hey, Naomi." I gave a small wave. "Hope you don't mind me stopping by."

"Not at all." She pushed some of her books aside so I could sit down.

I looked around the observatory. It wasn't that big—maybe about the size of my bedroom. I could still hear kids talking at picnic tables nearby through the metal frame and the crunch of leaves as students walked home.

"This is pretty awesome," I said. It felt like the inside of a metal treehouse.

"I know, right?" Naomi said. "I was just prepping for the PSATs. What's up?"

I guessed I'd have to take that test next year, too. I was not looking forward to it.

"Well . . . I wanted to run something past you," I said, staring down at my feet. I'd only come up with the idea this morning. I had to make sure I could even pull it off. No matter how much I planned and schemed for people to notice me, I couldn't forget the people I already had, like Ruth and Fabián.

"Okay, what is it?" she asked, closing her book.

"Can I look through the telescope?" I asked, stalling for time. I still didn't know how to word my request properly just yet.

She laughed. "Sure, though you're not going to be able to see anything until it's dark."

"That's okay," I said. I'd never looked through a telescope before.

Naomi peered into the scope and started adjusting some wheels and dials. I could see the color-coded notes she'd been taking next to her books, complete with flash cards. No wonder Ruth was smitten.

"Here," she said, stepping away from the telescope. "You can at least see the moon right now."

I bent over the telescope and peered in. The craters and

crags on the moon's surface looked huge, all the details I'd seen from afar suddenly magnified.

"Pretty cool, right?" Naomi said behind me.

"It's amazing," I breathed.

I unglued my eye and turned to Naomi. "Do you know what the Pleiades are?" I blurted out.

"The Pleiades? Like, the constellation?" she asked, surprised by my question.

I nodded. "That's what my name means in Farsi. The Pleiades." I'd never told anyone that before. I could barely get non-Iranians to pronounce my name properly, much less spell it right. People always got so hung up on where my name came from that no one ever thought to ask what it meant.

"That's so unique!" Naomi lit up. "I wish I had a constellation for a name."

"Thanks." I smiled.

Our conversation stalled, and we sat there in the quiet, only it didn't feel awkward.

"Do you have Homecoming plans?" I finally asked. I was scheming again. Oh, how I missed scheming!

"Well . . . ," Naomi began, folding her long legs underneath her. "I was hoping to ask Ruth. Do you think she'd go with me?"

"She would love to go with you."

"Cool," she replied, looking hopeful.

Excellent. Phase one of the plan was already in motion, so I could give my friends the best Homecoming entrance ever.

Naomi held up her flash cards. "Want to help me study?"

"I have never helped anyone study in my entire life," I confessed. It was usually Ruth or Fabián who helped me study. Or, I thought with a pang, Amir.

She handed me the cards. "Don't worry—I'm a flash-card genius."

I smiled. That was probably true.

Ruth would be so happy to have a date to a school dance where she could wear the pink dress of her dreams. I couldn't wait for her to text me after Naomi asked her out. All I needed to do was double check that Fabián and Austin were going together. I'd noticed Austin commenting on Fabián's livestreams—it was just a matter of time. Right now, my plan was to make sure everyone's outfits and makeup were on point, and yes, even prep Ruth's memory book for this special night. We could all head to the dance together, and Ameh Sara could help, too. My plan to make sure my friends had an incredible Homecoming was already off to a strong start.

. . .

HOME
9:00 P.M.

9:03 PM UNKNOWN: Hey, Parvin, it's Matty. Are you free this Saturday?

9:05 PM PARVIN: Hi, Matty. Yes I'm free.

My heart was hammering in my chest. Matty texted me! I sent him my response and screenshotted the text to my group chat. It felt good to be able to text them again.

9:06 PM FABIÁN: what? no emojis?

9:06 PM RUTH: Are you mad at him?

9:07 PM PARVIN: No, I just don't know him well enough for emojis yet!

9:07 PM FABIÁN: 🫣

9:07 PM MATTY: Great. Want to see my improv group at the community center? We can grab dinner afterward.

9:09 PM PARVIN: 😄👋🔥💥

9:10 PM MATTY: What?

9:10 PM PARVIN: Sorry wrong text that sounds great.

I flopped back onto my bed. That was a close call. Was dating always going to be this exhausting? Was this what I had to look forward to? Having butterflies was fun, but it required a lot more deodorant than I anticipated. Still. It was nice to have my friends back.

In that moment, I thought back to Amir and how we still hadn't really talked about what happened at the corn maze last weekend. I squirmed in front of my phone, wondering if I should text him, too. I settled for Ameh Sara.

9:15 PM PARVIN: I apologized to my friends, Ameh. We're better now (hopefully)

9:18 PM SARA: See, azizam? You're doing just fine 😊 💐

Friday

BLEACHERS
3:00 P.M.

Amir was already waiting at the bleachers, our Farsi books spread out on his lap. It was pretty chilly out this afternoon. Soon it would be too cold for us to have our study sessions outside.

I sat down next to him, my curly hair flying all over my face in the wind. His cheeks looked red, and he had big bags under his eyes. He looked miserable, and I prayed I had no part in making him feel that way. *Maybe he just had a rough day,* I thought to myself. *Yeah, that's it.*

"Hey," he said, his voice different from the happy tone he used last week at the pumpkin patch. This voice sounded metallic, like Robot Amir.

"Hey," I replied.

"Are you feeling better?" he asked. His voice cracked on the word *better*, but he didn't look away.

"Um, yeah. Thanks." I nodded. He smelled so good. And he looked really cute in his navy peacoat. Crap, despite my date with Matty, I could feel butterflies creep into my stomach with Amir, too. I had seriously underestimated how awkward today would be.

I took in Amir's messy curly hair, huge eyelashes, and big nose, just like mine. On me, I thought those qualities held me back. But on Amir, they just made him look even more handsome. He thought I was cute just the way I was. If I allowed myself to like him, did that mean he was right? That I was fine just the way I was?

I sucked on a strand of my hair. Before my conversation with Wesley at the football game, I'd straightened my hair, plucked my eyebrows, and shaved my arms every day for school. Now I let my hair be curly, encouraged my eyebrows to grow out, and wore bright and colorful clothes. All that straightening and plucking took too long, anyway. I still had that painful ingrown hair on my thigh, though. But there was nothing I could do about that.

"So, about last Saturday . . . ," Amir started. I stayed silent, letting him finish, like I had with Matty.

"Aren't you gonna say anything?" he cut in.

"What do you want me to say?"

"You're being weird," Amir countered.

"I'm not being weird! *You're* being weird," I said, even though I knew I was definitely being weird.

Amir ran his hands through his hair, stretching out its waves. "This isn't how I wanted today to go."

I nodded. Me neither.

"Can we just go back to normal?" I asked. I didn't know how to deal with all the emotions swirling around. And Amir dramatically sighing and tossing his hair wasn't helping.

"I thought . . . ," Amir began. "Is that what you want? To go back to how it was before?"

Now that I didn't care about impressing Wesley, I could feel myself looking at Amir differently. He was cute, and smart, and easy to talk to. But what about Matty? I shrugged. I didn't know what I wanted.

"Sure," I said. Going back to normal was better than whatever this awkward conversation was.

Amir nodded, his jaw set. "Okay." He turned back to the Farsi book and tried to find the page we needed. His eyebrows were still slanted down.

"Are you all right?" I asked.

"I'm fine," he replied gruffly, his throat hoarse. I knew he was lying. It definitely didn't feel like we were going back to the way things were.

He turned a page. "We finished the Nizami poem last class and switched to Rumi." He tried to keep his voice normal. "These are the next stanzas we have to translate."

My eyes scanned the page Amir held out. He sniffed, and I saw him dab at his eyes. "I need to go to the bathroom," he announced suddenly, running off before I could say anything.

Had I just made Amir cry? The small sliver of guilt I felt over how I reacted to last weekend's kiss grew. It had been almost a week since I'd seen him, and I hadn't really bothered to text or call him after the corn maze. He must have been feeling really low right now. And after everything Wesley had done to me, I felt awful knowing I'd made someone just as sad.

I read the poem in Farsi, trying hard to translate it into English. Rumi was a famous poet from Iran who was also a Sufi, or an Islamic mystic. People always forgot that he was Muslim. It drove Dad crazy.

It took me twenty minutes to translate the three lines.

Your task is not to seek for love,
but merely to seek and find all the barriers within
*   yourself*
that you have built against it.

Amir never came back.

• • •

RUTH'S HOUSE
DINNER

As promised, I headed to Ruth's for dinner. Mrs. Song had prepared a feast. Scallion pancakes, purple sticky rice, and a big pot of doenjang jjigae, or soybean stew, greeted me from their dining room table. She flitted in and out of the room, in a cool asymmetrical dress and high heels. I couldn't remember the last time I'd seen my own mom wear heels, much less a dress.

"Eat all you want, okay? I made enough to take to church tomorrow."

"Thanks, Ellen!" Fabián smiled. I was still too intimidated to call Mrs. Song by her first name. She beamed at him, then clicked out of the room and back to her office. Her book on data science stared down at me from the mantel, the words ELLEN SONG, PHD, in bright red letters.

"I think Naomi might ask me to Homecoming," Ruth whispered. Fabián looked down the hall to make sure Mrs. Song was still gone.

"Ruth, that's amazing," I said, keeping my mouth shut about my conversation with Naomi. I wasn't about to ruin this moment and spill the beans on how Naomi was definitely going to ask her. Besides, I was still putting together makeover looks that Ameh Sara and I could give them for the dance.

"I know! I've never had a date to a dance before. I need to get a dress and stuff."

Knowing Ruth, she'd probably end up making her dress from raw fabric. She was talented like that.

"I'm really happy for you," I said, but I felt my smile falter, still thinking of how I had no clue whether I had a date to the dance myself. Matty had asked me out for tomorrow night, sure, though that didn't guarantee a Homecoming date. But after my talk with Wesley, it didn't seem like going to Homecoming alone was a life-or-death situation anymore. Still, I felt terrible after my study session with Amir today. I'd upset him. It wasn't a good feeling.

I took a sad slurp of my soup.

Fabián squinted at me. "Why are you acting so glum? Aren't you excited for your aunt to come on Sunday? She's going to do your makeup for Homecoming, right?" he asked, lasering his eyes into mine. Little did he know Sara was going to help with his makeup, too.

I exhaled, opened my mouth, then closed it again. "What about you?" I tried switching the subject. "Are you going to go to Homecoming with Austin?"

Fabián shook his head. "I'm not sure yet, but he's a good backup option, for sure. And don't change the subject!"

Drats.

"Here," Ruth said, sliding the scallion pancakes over. "Pajeon makes everything better." I took a bite, then told them about my disastrous Farsi session with Amir.

Fabián leaned back as he listened. Tonight, he was sporting an olive-green military sweater with shoulder patches and Doc Martens. He looked like a runway model for the army.

"So, what's the problem?" he asked once I finished telling them everything.

"Fabián," Ruth chided. "She's clearly torn between Amir and Matty."

"Amir's hot." Fabián shrugged. "And he's obviously a good kisser."

I chewed my pancake, not sure how to answer. "The way Amir and I hang out feels more natural than anything Wesley and I ever did. Amir's funny and smart and he understands my Iranian side. He sees the real me. It's one thing if Matty doesn't like a fake version of myself, but what if Amir breaks up with me after seeing who I really am?" After all of our study sessions, I was finally crushing on Amir, too, but after making him cry, the Amir ship had probably sailed.

Fabián shook his head. "You can't start dating someone while worrying about how things will end."

"But Matty sees only the best parts of myself. That's a way safer bet."

Ruth squeezed my hand. "There are no safe bets in the game of love. Trust me." And then she went all misty-eyed again, probably thinking of Naomi.

I took a sip of water and set it back down on their spotless wooden table.

"Parvin!" Mrs. Song shouted from the other room. "Use a coaster."

"Sorry," I squeaked.

"Do you think Matty will be a good kisser?" Ruth whispered, wide-eyed.

I shrugged. How was I supposed to know?

Fabián winked. "Want me to find out for you?"

"Fabián!" I whined. He cackled. It was great to have him back.

"Well, now we know why you've been so blue," Ruth said.

"What are you going to wear on your date with Matty tomorrow night? Are you going to make an effort and not wear the same jeans?" Fabián asked.

I gasped. "How could you tell? Who even keeps track of other people's jeans?" I exclaimed. I had skipped laundry this week after my epic failure with the pink shirt.

"Parvin"—Fabián gently placed his hand on mine— "everyone can tell."

. . .

Saturday

HOME
7:00 A.M.

I woke up like I was in a horror film where the corpse suddenly sits up in bed. Today was my date with Matty. My butterflies had morphed into full-on pterodactyls, zooming through my stomach. It was time to bust out the big guns.

It took a while for her to pick up the video chat, but when I saw Ameh Sara's face, I instantly felt better.

"Parvin joon! Why are you calling me? I'm going to see you tomorrow!" Sara laughed. She wore a sweatshirt and a small scarf covering her hair. Behind her, I could see a bunch of open suitcases.

"Are you done packing?" I asked.

"Almost," Sara said with a little frown. "My flight to London doesn't leave for four and a half hours. So I have some time." She sat down in front of the screen and leaned in. "What's up?"

"I have that date tonight," I said.

Sara squealed. She and Ruth were going to get along really well. "With who? That Amir boy?"

"With Matty Fumero! The boy I had a crush on, from that party." I tried not to think about Amir and how he and Ameh Sara would get along really well, too.

Sara's eyes went wide. "Wow, that's so exciting!" She leaned toward me. "Why do you not look excited?"

"I'm excited," I said. "I'm just really nervous."

Sara nodded. "Parvin joon, it's okay to be nervous. Just be yourself, right?"

"That's the plan." And for once, it was. Instead of scheming or writing things on my hand so I could make sure I wasn't "loud" or "too much," I was going to throw all my little steps out the window. Wesley hadn't really wanted me to change; he'd wanted to change himself. Better to be who I was instead of pretending to be someone else for other people's sake.

"Don't worry, khanoum, once I'm there I can help you get ready for your next date, and the dance," she said. "You should wear your purple eyeshadow tonight. That one looks very nice."

"Actually, Ameh, do you think you could help Ruth and Fabián with their Homecoming makeup, too?"

Sara beamed. "Of course, joonam, I am honored!"

Yes! Homecoming was going to be awesome. Just then, my thigh gave a painful twinge.

"Er . . . Ameh, do you know how to get rid of ingrown hairs?" I asked suddenly.

Sara nodded. "Can you show it to me? It depends on where it is, and how deep it's in your skin."

I tilted my laptop screen toward the front of my thigh. There was the angry red ingrown hair, pulsing. It was tender to the touch.

"Oh, wow," Sara said, sucking in air. "Parvin, that looks infected."

"Infected?" I wailed. "What do you mean infected?" I couldn't go on my date with a gaping thigh infection. How could my own body hair infect me?

"It's okay, it's okay! I'm going to run to the store and get a lotion we have here for you, all right? When I arrive tomorrow I can help you get it out."

I took a deep breath. Having a plan always made me feel better.

"Okay, that would be great. Thank you, Ameh," I said.

Sara shook her head. "Of course, Parvin joon, just don't touch it until I get there, okay? It just looks like you picked at it too much."

I looked down at my thigh. The circle around the follicle had turned a weird purplish color.

"I can't wait to see you, Ameh!" I cheered up at the thought of having *someone* in this house who knew how my body worked.

"Me too, joonam. Now I have to finish packing, all right? I'll see you tomorrow!"

"Bye, Ameh. I love you." I blew a kiss through the screen.

"Manam hamintor," Sara replied. *Me too.*

MATTY'S IMPROV SHOW
6:00 P.M.

I met Matty at the community center where his improv group was setting up. I had tried to wear my most theatrical outfit, which really just translated into wearing all black. Black jeans. A black turtleneck. I almost wore a black beret, but Mom told me it was overkill. My eyeliner, though, was silver, paired with the shimmery purple eyeshadow that Ameh Sara had recommended. It was my most ambitious makeup look to date, even better than the gold eyeshadow I'd worn for Yessenia's quince. I wasn't going to pretend to be someone I wasn't tonight. I hadn't even written *NT* for "No Talking" on my hand. There was no holding back.

"Hey!" Matty said, waving me over to the stage where his troupe was doing weird mouth exercises and stretching. Did improv require stretching?

"Hey!"

"Thanks for coming," he said. "It's really cool that you're here."

"Thanks for inviting me." I looked down at his outfit. Matty was also wearing all black. I couldn't believe I accidentally matched with my date.

Just then, the lights in the small auditorium dimmed, and Matty's troupe took their places onstage as everyone else went to go find their seats.

"I'll see you after the show, okay?"

I nodded. "Cool."

I found a seat a couple rows in as the group got started. Matty, I noticed, was the youngest performer there by far. The leader of the group got up and started talking about how improvisation was all about "Yes, and . . ." It meant that whenever someone started doing something new onstage, it was your job as a performer to go along with it and add to it, saying something like "Yes, and what a mighty fine gown you are wearing, O Queen of England." Which meant the person you were performing with was now the Queen of England. Which was exactly what happened to Matty when his partner called him a queen.

The whole auditorium laughed, and I felt a surge of pride when Matty took the curveball in stride and switched to a British accent. But that was the only time I genuinely chuckled the whole night. From that point on, I just felt awkward for the people onstage as they tried to come up with jokes.

The troupe switched gears and started bringing in props and costumes, but my mind had already begun to wander. Matty Fumero, the most desired sophomore at James K. Polk High (at least to me), was here *with me. I was on a date!* It was the first real date of my life. I'd gone from nobody crushing on me to an actual dinner date. After everything that had happened, that was a pretty big deal.

One of the actors asked for audience participation. Nearly everyone around me raised their hand. But I just sank lower into my seat. Needless to say, the theater was not for me.

6:25 PM FABIÁN: how's improv night?

6:28 PM PARVIN: It's cool.

6:29 PM FABIÁN: translation=it's boring as hell

6:30 PM PARVIN: I can't hear you over the sound of me being on an amazing date with a cute boy.

I turned my phone off, determined to have a good time. I wondered what Amir was doing. Dad was still gonna make me go to Farsi school after we picked Ameh Sara up from the airport tomorrow, and I hoped I'd see him there. I should have called him to make sure he was all right after he rushed off the other day. I didn't feel good about how we'd left things.

After the improv show, Matty met me in the lobby in a different outfit. Thank god. I didn't want to go to dinner dressed as a sad mime couple.

"What did you think?" he asked.

"It was great!" I lied, trying to be nice.

"Really?" Matty asked, smiling back. What was this, twenty questions? I already said it was great.

"Totally," I replied, using his favorite word. What were Fabián and Ruth doing? Probably watching something funny at Fabián's. I'd tried so hard to get this date set up, but after pretending to politely laugh for the last hour, I was already exhausted. Maybe dinner would be better.

"All right, let's go get some food. I'm starving," Matty said, taking my hand.

He took my hand.

I was holding hands with a guy in public! It made me feel

like I was walking on air, especially since Wesley and I had never really gotten to that moment, except for that one day on the beach.

I tried hard to hold in the huge smile on my face, but since Matty was walking in front, I let some of it slip out. I would take my victories wherever I could.

. . .

DINNER
LATER

Horror of horrors, I forgot that dinner was the part of the date where there were no distractions and it was up to the two of us to make conversation. Normally, talking was really easy for me, but for some reason our conversation at the restaurant kept stalling. Probably because I'd never said more than a handful of words to Matty before.

Things we discussed:

- The weather
- Classes at school
- Band
- The shape of the saltshaker on the table
- Whether the burger was a good bet, or maybe the grilled cheese?

By the time our food came, I was desperate for real conversation.

"Grilled cheese," I said out loud. "Yum."

"Totally," Matty replied. He ate his burger easily, not thinking about whether bits of the sesame bun would get in his teeth, or whether it would be weird to be eating so much food on a first date. Even the way he tore into his burger was adorable. Dang it.

I picked up my grilled cheese. It came with a side of tomato soup, and I dunked bits of the sandwich into the bowl before taking a bite. I had considered getting a salad, something all women in the movies seemed to eat in every date scene, but then I remembered I didn't need to try that hard anymore. I could order the most garish and obnoxious thing I wanted.

"Whoa," Matty said, commenting on my submerged sandwich. "Does that taste good?"

"Yes!" I beamed, glad to have something to talk about. "My mom used to make this for me since it's pretty easy. But it tastes better if you use sound effects."

Matty gave me a look like, *Huh?*

"Oh no! Don't drown me!" I demonstrated in a high-pitched voice, soaking the grilled cheese in the soup. Then, in a lower voice, I replied to myself, "'It's too late, Captain! She's gone too far! She's fifty percent tomato now!' 'Ack, we've lost another one to the soup!'" I switched between the different voices of what must have been a very panicked crew aboard the SS *Grilled Cheese*, who for some reason sounded Scottish. And then I took a huge bite. "Nooo!" I whimpered, pretending to be the innocent passengers on board.

I grinned at Matty, waiting for my applause. Instead, he stared at me like I'd grown another head. Huh, Fabián and Ruth always thought that was funny.

We ate quietly for a little bit, Matty not commenting on my excellent interpretation of the *Titanic*. Lord help me, this was so awkward.

"So . . . ," Matty began again. "What do you want to be when you graduate?"

Oh god, I was only fourteen! How was I supposed to know? I wasn't like Amir who was probably already drafting his first novel, or Fabián who was going to sign with a manager soon.

I swallowed a spoonful. "Um. I don't know yet."

Matty nodded like I'd said something really interesting. "Totally."

"How about you?"

He stared thoughtfully at the wall next to me, thinking of an answer. I considered stealing a fry from his plate, then wondered whether he'd laugh like a normal person or just stare at me like I was weird again. "I'm not sure either yet, but I'd love to be an actor, or a singer-songwriter, if I could."

I nodded. "That's cool. Is that what you want to study in college?"

Then Matty launched into this big spiel about how he was going to apply to liberal arts universities, then from there try to make it in New York or LA with his music or his acting, but I wasn't really paying attention. Suddenly, I wished my friends, and not Matty, were sitting across from me, and we were talking like it was the easiest thing in the world and they had laughed at my soup escapade. We could have been brainstorming our Halloween costumes, or deciding what we wanted to do after Homecoming. It had been a while since the three of us had hung out on our own outside of school or our houses. And then I wondered what Amir was doing again, and I wished it was him sitting with me, too.

"So, yeah," Matty continued. "It's been cool working with Fabián. He has an interesting process."

"Hmm?" I had zoned out. My ears perked up at the mention of Fabián's name.

"For the school play? We're doing *Twelfth Night*. Fabián got Orsino, which I wanted, but playing Sebastian is going to be cool, too."

"Yeah," I replied. "That'll be cool." How many times was I going to use the word *cool*?

"And we get to make our own set designs, which will also be rad," he added.

Rad? Were we saying rad now?

"Totally rad." I winced. I didn't really care about theater, I realized. Matty must have cared about it a lot, though. If Fabián had been here, he could have provided conversation topics.

Matty took a bite of his burger. Just then, a woman at the table next to us leaned over. She smelled like baby powder and expensive perfume and wore head-to-toe beige. Mom called people like her "Old Money."

"You two make a very cute couple," the lady said, beaming.

"Thanks!" Matty grinned, surprised.

The woman went back to her husband, who seemed like even older money, and they both looked at us approvingly. Matty smiled at me and went back to his food.

Wasn't this what I wanted? To be a part of a cute couple? To like, and be liked?

My dream of finally being good enough to go on a date had come true.

But it didn't feel that great.

· · ·

MY ROOM
10:00 P.M.

> **10:04 PM PARVIN:** Hey, Amir, I hope you are feeling OK.

> **11:00 PM PARVIN:** OK, well, see you in Farsi class tomorrow.

> **11:23 PM PARVIN:** Good night.

> **11:31 PM PARVIN:** I mean, shab bekheir.

I had a bunch of missed calls from Ruth, but when I called her back, she didn't pick up since it was so late. She probably wanted to know how tonight went, but the truth was, I had no idea what to tell her. I stared at my bedroom ceiling, going over the evening.

Matty was a kind, polite date, but there wasn't really any connection between us. Just trying to get through dinner had been excruciating. How could I handle another date, or even a whole dance? At least with Amir, time flew by every Wednesday as we went over our dry, difficult Farsi homework. With Matty, there just didn't seem to be the same chemistry. And the more I thought about it, the more I was pretty sure I'd never had the same sparks with Wesley, either.

I couldn't wait to see Ameh Sara tomorrow. As soon as she arrived, she could help me figure out everything.

She'd know what to do.

Sunday

DULLES AIRPORT
8:00 A.M.

Normally I would protest having to wake up this early on a Sunday, but I hadn't seen Ameh Sara in so long I didn't mind heading to the airport at the crack of dawn.

I made a sign for her and everything, using some of Ruth's glitter glue and fancy markers. It read **WELCOME, AMEH SARA!** in Farsi. Dad helped me spell it out, and I used my best Farsi handwriting.

Mom and Dad clutched the coffees they'd bought in the domestic baggage claim area, which doubled as the reception lounge for international flights. Both of them had been working like crazy lately, but today they actually looked well rested and happy to be away from their computers.

We glanced up at the TV with the arrival times. Ameh Sara's connecting flight from London had just landed. She'd been traveling for a while at this point, taking a flight from Tehran to London, and then London to DC. She must have been exhausted.

Dad checked the time. "She has to grab her bags and go through Customs and Immigration first," he said, pointing to the double doors we couldn't pass through. "That usually takes a while."

I put my poster down, ready to wait.

AIRPORT
9:30 A.M.

Ameh Sara should have been out by now. We asked an English family who had just arrived in the waiting area which flight they'd been on, and they'd been on the same one as her. They said they were the last people to get their bags from the customs carousel.

Dad was starting to look nervous. Airports always made him a little jumpy.

"It's fine, Mahmoud," Mom said, patting his arm. "She should be out any second."

Dad frowned and shook his head. "No, something is wrong."

I checked my phone. Ameh Sara had texted us the second her plane landed in London, using the airport Wi-Fi to respond. She hadn't replied to any of our texts here, though.

"I'm gonna go ask," Dad said, his face set. Mom put her hand on his arm again.

"I can do it, okay?" she said.

"Daphne, let me—" Dad started, but Mom's blue eyes bored into his brown ones, and I could see them fight some kind of invisible battle.

Somehow, Mom won.

"Excuse me?" she asked a young security officer by the arrivals door, the one who made sure people didn't reenter the airport gates. "My sister-in-law was supposed to arrive on a flight, but she hasn't made it out yet. I wanted to make sure everything is okay."

The officer waved us closer, her nails sparkling with pink polish. She had on flashy pink eyeshadow that matched, and looked like she should be working behind a makeup counter, not Dulles International Airport. "What's her flight number?"

"UA 989, coming from London."

The officer got out her walkie-talkie and asked about the flight. "What's her name?"

"Sara Mohammadi," Mom replied.

The officer said some more stuff into the walkie-talkie and grimaced. "She's being detained."

Detained? What did that mean? I thought she had everything she needed to enter the country.

Mom gasped. "Do you know why?"

The woman shook her head.

"Can you ask?" Mom tried.

"They're not allowed to disclose the nature of detainment." The officer frowned. "I'm really sorry."

Dad stood very still, his whole body waiting for the officer to say something else, to offer any more information. Mom started getting upset.

"But this is unbelievable!" she shouted at the officer. "We have the right to know when we can see our sister."

"Daphne, come on," Dad said, trying to drag Mom away.

"But why is she being detained?" Mom asked again. "She has a visa!"

The officer remained silent.

"You're causing a scene, Daph," Dad muttered.

"I don't care!" Mom shouted. "This is ridiculous." I'd never seen Mom get so upset. Usually Dad was the one who got hotheaded. I could feel my stomach start to twist into knots. Why was this happening?

"Daphne," Dad said, his voice low and urgent. "If you make a scene with me in it, it's not the same, okay? You know why they're detaining her. We need to call our immigration lawyer. This officer doesn't know what's happening and did nothing wrong. You need to calm down." I could tell Dad was trying to hold it together. His eyes were glassy, and his words were coming out choked. Mom nodded.

"Okay. You're right. I'm sorry," she apologized to the TSA officer.

Dad called the immigration lawyer while Mom got out her phone. Iran didn't have an embassy in the United States. I wondered who else Mom could turn to.

I sank down to the floor. I still didn't understand what was going on. Sara had done nothing illegal; she had her passport and her visa. Why would they have let her on the plane in Iran if she couldn't get out of the airport in the US?

> 9:52 AM PARVIN: My aunt's being detained at the airport.

> 9:53 AM RUTH: OMG, Parvin! I'm so sorry! Did they say why?

> 9:53 AM FABIÁN: calling you

My phone buzzed. "Hey, Fabián." My voice sounded all warbly like it did when I tried hard not to cry.

"My mom wants to talk to your mom," he replied. A tiny part of my throat unsqueezed itself. I had forgotten that Fabián's parents worked for the Mexican embassy. They dealt with detained visitors all the time at their jobs.

"One sec." I handed Mom the phone. "Fabián's mom wants to talk to you."

Mom put her hand on my shoulder. "Good thinking, Parvin." She took the phone.

"Hi, Celeste. Yep, yep. Exactly." Mom hunched over my phone, already nodding and taking notes in her sketchbook as Fabián's mom told her what to do.

I grabbed a chair off to the side and curled up in it, my stomach aching. It looked like we would be here awhile.

• • •

AIRPORT
10:30 A.M.

I made a list to try to calm down. Here is what we know:

- Ameh Sara still hasn't been let out.
- Apparently there was an issue with her visa.
- The security officers don't know when she'll be released.
- They won't let us see her.

I felt numb and helpless. Every time I thought of Ameh Sara all alone in the airport's detention center, I wanted to cry. Why was this happening? She'd done nothing wrong. Were they giving her food and water? Would they let her use the bathroom? My mind swirled, and my racing thoughts made me feel worse. There was nothing we could do, and no one would tell us what was going on.

According to Fabián's mom, they probably confiscated her cell phone. That was why she wasn't answering our texts. Mrs. Castor had been calling all her colleagues at the Pakistani embassy to see if anyone from the Iranian Interest Section there could help.

The immigration attorney my parents were working with, Ms. Jordan, drove to the airport the second Dad called. She was talking to the immigration officers in the airport's detention center.

The tea Mom had bought me at the coffee kiosk had grown cold in my hands. I was not going to make it to Farsi class today.

. . .

AIRPORT
LATER

Ms. Jordan got back to the coffee kiosk where we'd been camped out. She had to be escorted by ICE and everything through the main doors. I thought most lawyers wore suits and stuff, but Ms. Jordan had on black leggings, a sweatshirt, and bright red hair up in a messy bun. I doubted she thought this was how she'd be spending her Sunday morning. She didn't look very hopeful.

"I wish I had better news," she said. Dad's face crumpled when she said that. I saw Mom grip his arm more tightly.

Ms. Jordan made a pained expression. "According to ICE, she has an incorrect visa. Your sister is being deported."

· · ·

HOME
12:00 P.M.

I remembered getting into the car, and then somehow, we were back at home. Without Ameh Sara. Without any real explanation.

There'd be no hugs today. No getting to shout "SARA!" and showing her my poster as she walked through those double doors from Customs and Immigration. The excitement I'd had was gone, and instead I felt empty and hollow. This was so much worse than Wesley dumping me. So much worse than being nervous about Homecoming. My ameh was being deported, and my thoughts raced between sadness, anxiety, and fear for my aunt.

I looked at my phone. Sara was boarding her deportation flight to London now, where she'd spend another five hours back in the air. Then they'll make her wait in a detention center in London Heathrow Airport until her second flight home to Tehran. In Iran, Ms. Jordan explained, they would finally give her phone back.

I couldn't believe this was happening. It seemed like a nightmare.

When we got home, Mom and Dad went to their bedroom to discuss what to do in low voices, and I went to mine to cry my eyes out. I still couldn't process that I wouldn't be seeing my aunt today, and every time I remembered she was being sent back, the tears started flowing again.

My phone buzzed.

And then I burst into fresh sobs.

. . .

HOME
5:00 P.M.

Mission success. Woo-hoo. Here it was: the goal I'd been working so hard toward. Matty Fumero had asked me to Homecoming. I'd finally gotten my wish. But I was too numb to care.

I knew now that I didn't like Matty that way. I didn't feel a single butterfly in my stomach. Good looks and green eyes could only go so far. The second we'd gotten home, I'd just collapsed into bed, exhausted after everything that had happened. I still hadn't responded to him.

If Ameh Sara were here, we'd be poring over the text message and strategizing how to let him down gently. Instead of stressing about a date, she'd help me research dresses and test out different eyeshadow combinations. But now the thought of going to Homecoming seemed impossible. I just wanted my aunt.

Someone knocked on my door.

"Parvin?" Mom called up the stairs. "Ruth's here."

My door opened a crack. Ruth stood in the doorway, looking as miserable as I felt.

"Hey," Ruth sniffed.

"Hi." She gave me a big hug. I could feel her trembling.

"I'm so sorry," Ruth said, wiping at tears. "That's so awful that your aunt wasn't allowed in."

I didn't even know how to respond. Ruth's eyes looked even puffier than mine from crying. Why was that?

"Ruth," I said, patting the bed next to me. "What's wrong?"

As Ruth took off her shoes and climbed onto my quilt, she sniffled. "Parvin! It's been so awful. Last night, Naomi asked me to Homecoming—"

"But that's great," I interrupted. Ruth nodded, the first smile of our conversation peeking out. "Yeah, it was really romantic. She had planned a picnic at the observatory and everything."

That was just the kind of thing Ruth would appreciate.

"But when I asked my mom if I could go with her, she flipped out. She said I was too young to be dating, and that I can't have a girlfriend at this age."

"Wait—you came out to your mom?" I asked.

Ruth grimaced. "Yeah. I did."

"But . . . so . . . wait . . . What did she say about you being pan?"

Ruth shrugged. "She said it didn't matter if I was going out with a guy, girl, nonbinary person, or anyone else. I just can't date until I'm sixteen."

She burrowed into the covers. I patted her back.

"At least your mom was cool with you being into a girl, right?" I said. "That was one of your four goals for the year, wasn't it? To come out?"

Ruth nodded. "I know . . . but I never thought someone like Naomi would ever like me. And now that I finally find an amazing person, I can't go out with them."

"I'm sorry you can't date yet, Ruthie"—I hugged her again—"but at least your mom is just really strict . . . and not close-minded?" It was a small win. But after today, I'd take any wins we could get.

Ruth flopped onto her back and stared at the ceiling. "She said that God doesn't make mistakes, so me not being straight is a sign of God's love. But she says I'm still too young to date. She wants me to take my PSATs first before I 'get serious,'" she said, using air quotes.

That made sense. After all, Mrs. Song had gone to college her junior year of high school. The PSATs were a big deal for the Song family.

"I just wish I could go with Naomi. She showed me her dress. It's so pretty . . ." She trailed off. "I'm glad my mom's okay with me being pan. It just really sucks that I can't date."

"Did you get a dress yet?"

Ruth's eyes lit up a tiny bit. "I made it." She showed me a picture on her phone, the skirt full of pink tulle and topped with a shiny pink crop top. It was perfect.

"But now my aunt can't do the makeup," I croaked. It still hurt so much that I wasn't going to see her. That I didn't even know *when* I could see her again.

"You're already good at doing your own makeup. It'll be great," Ruth insisted, not knowing Ameh Sara had been planning to do hers, too.

"Thanks, Ruth," I said, forcing a smile. But then the tears burst through when I realized Sara wouldn't be here to see me off before the dance. I'd have no one to help me find a dress or figure out how to style my hair.

Ruth handed me a tissue. "I guess there's nothing I can say right now that's going to make you feel better," she said slowly. "But I love you a lot. And I'm glad you're my friend."

"Thanks, Ruth. I love you, too."

Then she handed me a peanut butter cup she'd squirreled away in her dress pocket.

And that was why Ruth Song was the absolute best.

• • •

DINNER
7:00 P.M.

We all sat on the couch, eating pizza and watching *The Great British Baking Show*. Dad hadn't spoken that much today. His face was still purple from all the crying. Mom's nose was pink from where she'd been blowing into tissues.

"Ms. Jordan texted me just now," Mom said between episodes. "She said Sara was deported because she told the immigration officials she'd be learning 3D graphics from me. They asked her if she was learning at an accredited university, and she said no, that I was just going to teach her in my spare time. Apparently, that was the wrong thing to say, since Immigration said her visa wasn't a student visa, even though Sara never said she'd be a student or anything like that. They blew it all out of proportion."

Dad nodded, his pizza untouched.

"Why did they give her a visa in the first place, then?" I asked, confused.

Mom shrugged. "Because Sara coming to visit us is one hundred percent legal. Ms. Jordan says they made up a reason to deport her at the airport, something ICE has done in the past for other Iranians who also had valid visas. We had hoped they were done with lying, though. It's stricter for Muslim-ban countries."

I took a bite of my pizza. It tasted like cardboard in my mouth.

"This is bullshit," I said to no one in particular.

Usually Mom and Dad didn't like it when I cursed, but this time neither of them scolded me.

"Yeah," Dad said weakly. "It is."

. . .

MY ROOM
8:00 P.M.

It was too depressing hanging out downstairs. Dad was so sad he didn't even touch the cup of black tea I'd made him. Ameh Sara's flight wouldn't arrive in Iran until after midnight, which was when we could finally talk to her. I couldn't believe we had to wait that long just to make sure she was okay.

"Baba jaan?" Mom and Dad stood at my door. Mom was wringing her hands.

"Come in," I said. I was lying on the floor, listening to Rostam Batmanglij. He was a member of Vampire Weekend and was one of the most famous Iranian American musicians in the US, next to the guy who made the *Game of Thrones* theme song. It seemed appropriate to wallow to his music.

Mom and Dad sat down on my bed.

"We know how hard this is for you," Mom said. "We know how close you are to your aunt."

Dad nodded, his skin dull like copper that hadn't been

polished in a while. It was as if weeks had passed since the awful news this morning and he hadn't slept since.

"Baba jaan, we wanted your ameh to come because we love her and miss her, of course, but . . ." Dad trailed off awkwardly.

"But there are things she can teach you that we can't. That I can't, really." Mom gave a hollow laugh.

"You're becoming a young woman now," Dad continued. "You're growing up . . . and your ameh was going to help with some of that."

Mom smiled sadly at me. Was this because of the eyebrow fiasco?

I turned off the music. "I didn't realize that was why she was coming."

"Well, it was one of the reasons. And so I could teach her some graphic design programs. Waxing, dressing for your skin color, styling your hair . . . those are just some of the things I have no clue how to help you with," Mom said, biting her lip. She looked like she was going to tear up all over again.

I stared at Mom. It was wild how little we resembled each other. Her skin was so pale I could see the blue veins underneath. Once, in elementary school, a teacher had asked to see her driver's license before she picked me up, not believing we were related. I didn't realize how much it bothered her. Her blue eyes blinked back at my brown ones, searching for a reaction.

"It's okay, Mom," I said with a shrug. "I have YouTube." They laughed.

"That's true," she said, looking thoughtful. "But you still need female role models who look like you. And I can't be that for you."

Dad nodded. "We're going to figure something out, okay? You'll get to see her again, I promise."

"Okay."

Mom crouched down and gripped my shoulders.

"I'm so proud of you, you know that? You're dealing with things I couldn't have fathomed when I was your age." She started sniffing again.

"Thanks, Mom."

She got up to leave. "Mahmoud, you coming?"

He waved her on. "I'll be there in a second."

Mom nodded and closed the door. Dad played with a loose thread on my quilt.

"Dad?" I asked. He took a shaky breath.

"I just want to say one thing, okay? And then you can say whatever you want." He opened his mouth, closed it, then opened it again. Whatever he had to say, it seemed to make him incredibly uncomfortable.

"You had asked me about not marrying an Iranian woman, and I think I missed the point of why you were asking that question."

I looked up at him. I remembered that conversation.

"I married your mother because I love her. But it's not because I thought she was more beautiful because she's white, or because she looks the way women do in magazines here. I married her because she has the same kind of soul as me, even though we were born on opposite sides of the planet."

Dad's lips trembled, like he was going to start crying again. "Your full name is Sa'adateh Parvin Veronica Mohammadi. You are Sa'adateh Parvin, a descendant of the third Imam of Shiites. You come from the empire that invented math, astronomy, and poetry while the people who decided that your aunt can't come to the United States were still living in caves." Dad's face was wet now, his skin stained with tears.

"We named you Parvin after the brightest stars in our sky. After the most beautiful constellation in the galaxy. Never forget that you are beautiful, too, baba jaan. And that the things people try to shame you for are what make you stronger."

I gulped. My mind flickered back to that moment when Wesley had called me "too much" and "loud"; how he'd tried to shame me for who I was. There would be more Wesleys in my life, for sure. The next time I watched a movie or opened a magazine, there would be superstars who'd make me feel ugly or obnoxious, and I had to be prepared. But I came from a long line of people who had stood strong. For the first time in a while, I felt proud of who I was. I just wished Ameh Sara were here to share this moment with me.

Dad gave me a hug. I didn't know which of us needed it more.

"I'm sorry, baba jaan," he said into my hair. "I'm so sorry."

• • •

PLAYGROUND
9:30 P.M.

The air in the house felt too heavy to breathe. Everything seemed harder than normal, even drinking water or chewing food. Just looking at my phone made my eyes swim.

Mom and Dad were on the phone with relatives in Iran to tell them what had happened, and it felt too raw and real. I missed when the biggest problem I had was trying to make a boy like me. It seemed so silly now.

The swing sets by our house were perfect for moping. My feet had already made deep trenches in the mulch where I pushed back and forth in the seat. The swinging motion helped me calm down.

Someone's feet crunched in the wood chips behind me. I turned around.

"Hey," Amir said. "Your dad said you were out here." He wore a Team Melli hoodie and clutched an envelope in his hand.

"Hi." I wiped my face on the back of my sleeve. No matter how hard I tried, I couldn't stop tearing up at the thought of Ameh Sara scared and helpless in a detention center. Just the idea of it made my eyes swell up again.

"Aghayeh Khosrowshahi told us what happened in class," Amir explained, sitting down on the swing next to me. He kicked a piece of mulch. "We were all pretty upset, so we made you this."

He handed me the envelope. It was bright red, with an angry emoji cut out and pasted to the front.

I flipped it open, reading the first message:

THIS IS BS! Call me if you need to talk. My maman makes the best zereshk polo and said you have to come over and have some. —Hanna

The same thing happened to my uncle—I'm here for you if you want to vent. —Bobak

The notes ranged from pissed off to sympathetic, many of them offering dinner at their house or asking me if I needed anything.

I clutched the card to my chest. I forgot that I had a whole group of kids who, though we looked a little different, could understand what I was going through. Some of the sadness in my heart lifted.

I got up from my swing and embraced Amir, glad he'd stopped by despite not answering my texts. "Thank you," I said, my throat choking up for the millionth time today. I smelled his rosewater scent, and it smelled like the best cologne in the world.

"I'm so sorry, Parvin," he whispered. I sniffled again. Why wouldn't the crying stop? "I'm so sorry," he repeated, gripping me tighter. I turned my face toward him, and before I knew what was happening, we were kissing.

"I'm all gross." I pulled away in protest, wiping my eyes. They just wouldn't stay dry.

Amir's brown eyes blazed gold. "I don't care."

He kissed me again. Amir liked me just the way I was, even though I was loud, talked a lot, and was "too much." I wasn't a full Iranian who drove a BMW and wore Armani and had a nose job, but that didn't matter to him. That feeling didn't give me butterflies exactly, but it made me feel confident. And that confidence made me feel like maybe my personality didn't need a complete makeover.

I stood up on my tippy toes to kiss him back. By the time he pulled away, my tears had dried, replaced by my burning cheeks. Amir's face was red, his eyes locked on to mine.

I smiled back at him, but he looked away.

"I still can't tell if you like me," he said finally.

My heart stopped. Where was this going?

He grabbed my hands and held them in his own. "I really like you, okay? Like, a lot. I want to take you on dates and be your boyfriend and brainstorm ideas for the new school journal with you. I want to make you laugh and I want to drink hot chocolate with you on the bleachers. And . . . the next time you swap out Principal Saulk's spot and give him a panic attack in the parking lot, I want to help."

I snorted. I'd almost forgotten about the parking spot prank. "Is that why you haven't been answering my texts?"

Amir nodded, his eyes still glued to mine. "I know you've been through a lot today, but I needed to tell you how I feel."

"Amir—" I started.

But he shook his head. "You're really cool, Parvin. And judging from that kiss, I know you like me. But I want to be with someone who wants to be with me. And I can't tell if you do."

The last time I'd really thought about my feelings for Amir, they'd turned into dread and shame. But this time, it felt like something else. It was *fear*. I was afraid of going out with Amir Shirazi. He knew the Real Parvin, and that left me nothing to hide behind. I could barely handle Matty not laughing at my tomato soup skit. What if Amir eventually decided he couldn't handle me, either?

"You don't have to say anything, okay? Just think about it. Please."

I nodded. It was a lot to process. For the first time today, I thought about Matty asking me to Homecoming and how I hadn't texted him back. What was I going to do?

"Bye, Parvin," Amir said, walking away.

"Khodafez," I replied, still stunned.

Monday

HOME
9:00 A.M.

Mom let me skip school today. She said I've been through enough trauma to warrant a day off. I woke up to the sound of Sara video chatting me.

"Ameh!" I shouted, jumping out of bed toward my desk.

Sara looked tired. She didn't have her makeup on like she normally did, and she wasn't wearing her veil. Her hair was up in a messy ponytail, and she blinked back at me in a University of Tehran sweatshirt.

"Hi, ameh." Sara gave me a sad smile.

"Are you okay? What happened?" I asked. I must have looked wild with my smeared eyeliner and bedhead, but I didn't care. I hoped she was all right.

"I'm fine, azizam," she said, waving me off. "I'm sorry I can't be there with you right now, though."

I squinted at the room she was calling me from. It looked like her whole family was in there behind her.

"Is that your mom?" I asked. Sara nodded.

"Yeah, she came over when I . . . when I came back." Sara gulped. I wished I could go through the screen and be there for her in person.

"So . . . what happened?" I asked quietly.

Sara pushed her hair out of her face and sighed.

"I told your parents already, but I think it's important for you to hear, too, azizam." I nodded, pulling my arms around my legs as I braced myself for the full story.

"When I got off the plane, Immigration asked me a couple of questions, like why I was coming and what I planned to do here. I told them I was going to be visiting my family and sightseeing. They double-checked the visa and said it's suspicious that it's a five-year visa just to sightsee, but I wasn't in charge of the visa length—that's just what the US gave me. Then they said they'd have to search my personal belongings."

Sara swallowed. I could tell she was holding back tears. Her face looked so pinched and sad.

"It's okay, Ameh. We don't have to talk about it," I said.

"No." Sara shook her head. "Mahmoud and I agree, you need to know what happened."

I stayed quiet.

"After that, they escorted me to a detention center in the airport. They put me in a room and confiscated my phone. They made me unlock it for them, too, so they could scroll through it. They wanted to see if I was a terrorist and followed radical social media accounts. It was for national security, they kept telling me. I think I waited for two hours, then your attorney came, the woman, as they were going through my bags."

I nodded, not wanting to interrupt.

"She started disagreeing with the officers, the ICE and USCIS people. And then they said I was going to have to go back."

I didn't jump in even though I had a million questions. I could tell it took everything in her to repeat this story for me after repeating it a hundred times already to her other family.

"They put me on a plane back to Heathrow in London with an air marshal next to me on the flight, and then I had to wait in the detention center there. They let me get a sandwich in the airport, but they had the air marshal with me the whole time, even for the bathroom, where she waited outside my stall. From there I went to Iran, and the air marshal couldn't follow me onto the plane, so she gave me my phone back. And now . . . now I'm here."

"I'm so sorry, Ameh. I'm so sorry," I said, choking up.

My aunt, who was normally so happy and cheerful, looked like a shadow of the person I knew. I couldn't believe I'd only met her in real life once. She was such a big part of me, but I hadn't seen her in forever. Why did it have to be so hard?

"It's not your fault, azizam," Sara said, wiping her eyes with a tissue. "Maybe we can meet in another country next year."

I'd heard of families doing that—meeting in Canada or Europe, where they had better immigration policies with the Iranian government. That would be nice.

"They did let me do one thing, though," Sara said with a smile.

"What?" I asked. Let her watch a movie on the plane?

"Go check your front door. It should be there by now. Then come back."

I nodded and headed downstairs, wondering what could be out front. I opened the door, sunlight hitting my face for the first time that day. On the porch was a package covered in airline barcodes like a checked bag. I brought it back upstairs.

"Is this it?" I asked, holding up the box.

Sara nodded. "Open it."

I cut through the tape and opened the box. Inside was a bunch of makeup and stuff I'd never seen before. I sorted through the tinier boxes inside.

"Ameh, this is awesome! How did you get it here?"

"Ms. Jordan helped me. They wouldn't let her carry it back to you in the terminal, but she helped me send it from the airport after they searched it."

Inside the box was a vial of 100 percent kohl charcoal, a wax kit, eyelash curlers, facial oils, and all kinds of things I had no idea what to do with.

"Thank you so much, Ameh!" I smiled for the first time in a while. It wasn't the same as having my aunt here, but it made me feel a bit better. "Can you show me how to use them?" I asked, holding up the glass vial of kohl. It looked like something out of a medieval apothecary.

Sara shook her head. "It's too complicated to show you over video, but don't worry, I got a good replacement." She gave another sad smile.

I nodded, though I wasn't sure what she meant. It didn't matter. "Nobody can ever replace you, Ameh. I love you."

Sara tilted her eyes up so the tears didn't spill over her cheeks. "I love you, too, azizam."

. . .

NATIONAL MALL
LUNCH

Mom decided that even though I wasn't going to school today, I still had to learn something. She dragged me to the mall, where we ate in the cafeteria between the East and

West Buildings of the National Gallery. An indoor waterfall cascaded into the bright dining area, and all around us were field trips and tourists visiting DC.

"Parvin?" Mom asked, edging my sandwich closer. I had forgotten it was there. I took a bite, suddenly starving. In that moment, I was so hungry I just wanted to fill myself up. I finished half of my sandwich lightning fast, then reached for the chocolate cake Mom had bought at the dessert station.

"Slow down! Chew, please."

I sighed and finished the rest of my sandwich.

"It's nice in here," I said between bites. "I forgot it was so . . . normal."

Mom kept quiet, sipping her coffee. She had a cup with every meal, that's how addicted she was. Her hands were stained with ink, probably from frantically making notes yesterday at the airport with her illustration pens.

"It's hard to see the world move on when it feels like your own is falling apart," Mom said in a soft voice. She made as if to run her fingers through my hair but I squirmed away.

"That hurts!" I whined. Mom always forgot that I had curly hair, the kind you couldn't just run your hands through, while hers was stick straight.

"Oh, right, sorry, sweetie." She patted my arm instead. "I used to bring you here when you were in your stroller. Your dad was working at an agency downtown, and I missed designing so much I would bring you to the museums and just look at all the work."

I vaguely remembered those days. The National Gallery had huge mobiles hanging from the ceiling, and I would look up at them as a toddler, soaking it all in.

"Come on, let's go see some art." She held out her hand. I hadn't needed to hold my mom's hand since elementary school. But today, I didn't care.

"Which museum are we going to?" I asked. The National Gallery cafeteria was a hub for all eleven museums on the mall, but Mom had never said which one she wanted us to visit.

She smiled. "We're gonna go see your ancestors."

. . .

FREER GALLERY
1:00 P.M.

Mom led us to one of the smaller brick buildings on the mall, near the carousel. I didn't think I'd ever noticed this museum before, much less been inside. The galleries inside were dimly lit and had works from Korea, Japan, China, India, and other Asian countries that didn't normally get featured in the bigger museums. It was practically empty.

"This way." Mom led me down the stairs.

There, in the basement of the museum, was an exhibition on Ancient Persia. I'd never seen anything from Iran in a museum before, much less a whole exhibition.

All around us were stone sculptures of men with curly beards, their eyes hollow circles as they faced right or left like the kings in hieroglyphics. A stone tablet next to them had little lines etched into it, with slashes and crosses.

"That's cuneiform," Mom said, pointing to the description. "It's the first written language of the world. And it comes from the same place you do." She put both hands on my shoulders as I peered at the strange marks.

I never knew that.

"But I come from you, too, right?" I turned to Mom.

She nodded. "You do. Especially your creativity. And your compassion. But my culture . . . my ancestors . . ." She trailed off. "My heritage hasn't been as big a deal because everywhere you look, you see it. Your grandparents grew up speaking English, and so did theirs. There isn't a museum for Scotch-Irish-English bloodlines because pretty much every museum in this country already *is* one. I've never had to defend my culture to anyone before. For better or for worse, I'm not as in tune with it. And that means I have nothing to pass on to you. Besides green chicken chili."

I laughed. Mom laughed, too. "That's okay. I understand."

She squeezed my shoulders as the empty eyes of Persian kings looked back at us. Could they have known Persia would be what it is today? What would they think of the fact that so many of their people had to leave and live in other countries?

I squinted at one of the kings engraved in stone as he clutched a scepter. He probably wasn't even Muslim, the carving of him was so old. He was older than the Quran, than Customs and Immigration enforcement and the Muslim ban. He was older than borders and passports and visas. I studied his smooth face, wondering what he'd think of how our family worked hard to keep our culture strong on a completely different continent. From Farsi school to Iranian New Year parties, to chelo kabob takeout and abgoosht outings, we were doing our best.

I think he would have been proud of us.

. . .

COURTYARD
3:00 P.M.

School was out by now. I wondered if anyone had noticed I was absent. I know Mom called the main office and said I was feeling sick, but she didn't elaborate.

We wandered through the gardens of the Freer Gallery, bending over to smell flowers and look at the fountain in the courtyard. Despite everything that had happened yesterday, I knew we'd be okay. My family had been through something horrible and survived. It made me wonder what else I could handle.

"Hey, Mom? I'm gonna go for a walk." She just nodded, already getting out her sketchbook. I knew I had a good twenty minutes once she got out her drawing pens.

I grabbed my phone and sent off a text. The reply came back immediately.

It looked like I wouldn't be going to Homecoming alone after all.

From there, I googled makeup looks that I knew would match my date's and ordered a corsage. It wasn't the date I was expecting for myself, but it was the one I owed someone.

Finally, it was time to text Matty.

> **3:13 PM PARVIN:** Hey, Matty, I'm really sorry but I'm going through some family stuff right now. I don't think I can go to Homecoming with you.

He texted me back right away.

I didn't respond, but it felt good that Fabián had my back. I hadn't seen him since Friday. I didn't realize how much I missed him already. Even if I couldn't have my whole family here, at least I had my friends with me. Nobody could take them away.

. . .

HOME
LATER

Mom helped me put the finishing touches on the animation for my TV commercial assignment. It was nice getting to hang with her today. I felt like Dad and I always had our little talks, but Mom was better for activities like this.

"Are you ready?" she asked. I nodded. We had our whole animation set finished now. All we needed to do was record it. Between every click of the camera, Mom and I would move my tuna-shaped piece of paper, yank our hands out of the frame, then take a photo. When we put the photos all together, it looked like the little tuna fish was moving on its own. We even had blue waves rocking across the top of the video. It took forever to move each wave back and forth, but it was worth it.

"Ready?"

"Shoot," I'd say, and Mom would take a photo.

By the time we finished, it was already nine. Five pens were stuck into Mom's topknot, and I had a paper cut on almost every finger, but we were happy.

"Let's watch it together," Mom said, pressing play on the video after I stitched all the photos together. She clapped once the commercial finished. It was pretty good, if I did say so myself.

"Thanks for helping me, Mom," I said, squeezing her hand.

"Thanks for letting me help you." She squeezed back.

OCTOBER

• • •

THINGS I HAVE GOING FOR ME:

- Family
- Friends
- Good health

And that's all that matters.

Tuesday

INTRODUCTION TO VIDEO
10:00 A.M.

Mr. Clarke was practically exploding with anticipation, he was so excited to see our videos in class today.

I was actually eager to share my spot, too. Animating even a single second took forever, so the full thirty seconds was nothing short of a masterpiece.

"Who wants to go first?"

Sir's hand shot straight up. He was wearing his "dress" trench coat today and had even put gel in his hair. I didn't think he knew what he was doing, though, as his hair was shoulder-length and he only applied gel to the top. It looked like someone had smashed an egg on his head and let it dry there.

"Excellent!" Mr. Clarke loaded Sir's video onto the projector, and I chewed the inside of my cheek, thinking, *Don't laugh don't laugh don't laugh.*

The video blinked on. Sir stood in the middle of at least twenty cats, all of them clawing at his jeans as he held a can of cat food toward the screen. It was complete pandemonium.

"I'm here at the local animal shelter to see if cats love Compañera Cat Food. These are *real* cats. Accept no imitations!"

One cat started climbing up Sir's leg. "Ouch, your claws!"

Soon, more cats began crawling all over him as he screamed in pain. You could barely see Sir, he was so covered with felines. It looked like all the cats were part of a single organism now, and Sir was buried somewhere inside.

"See how much they love it?" he screamed frantically through the mountain of fur. "COMPAÑERA CAT FOOOOOOD!" Just then, a cat must have knocked over the tripod, because the camera fell over and cut to black.

Emerson caught my eye and slowly shook his head, then mimed a sad explosion going off between his fingers. I nodded. This was painful to watch.

Only Mr. Clarke clapped.

"Thank you, Sir. That was . . . disturbing."

"This commercial's an homage to classic cinema."

Mr. Clarke nodded kindly. "I can see that." Sir smirked, pleased with himself.

"Parvin?" Mr. Clarke gestured toward me because I was dumb enough to make eye contact with him. "Want to go next?"

I nodded and handed Mr. Clarke my USB stick. The music started up, and my voice filled the classroom.

"Need help planning your next meal? Look no further than Tongola Tuna." On screen, my little tuna fish swam in the sea as a paper boat bobbed above it on the waves.

"Low in fat, high in protein, it's perfect for snacks, salads, or sandwiches." From there we cut to a paper fisherman eating tuna salad in his kitchen, smiling at the camera. The little cutouts kind of looked like an episode of *South Park*, only done by an actual fourteen-year-old.

"Tongola Tuna—the tastier tuna!" My voiceover ended, and I winced. I'd never sounded so psyched about anything in my life than that can of tuna.

A couple kids in class clapped.

"Great job, Parvin! The stop-motion was effective, as were the selling points. Brava!" Mr. Clarke smiled. For once, I smiled back at him.

Mr. Clarke turned to another student just as Sir passed me a note. What next? A dirty game of tic-tac-toe? I unfolded it.

Will you go to Homecoming with me? —SIR. Jesus Louisus . . . Et tu, Sir? Et tu?

I took a second to think about how I would respond, knowing he was staring at me as I wrote down each word.

Sorry, I'm already going with someone. I passed Sir the note back.

He nodded, then wrote a follow-up message. *Who?*

I smiled at him and mouthed, *It's a secret*.

. . .

LUNCH
12:00 P.M.

Mrs. Song packed my favorite meal for lunch today. Ruth had probably told her what happened, because she'd sent Ruth to school with kimchi jjigae, or kimchi stew, to give me. It was spicy and sour and just what I needed.

"Thanks, Ruth." She passed me a spoon. Naomi was eating lunch in the courtyard with us today and gave me a sad smile.

"Sorry to hear about what happened," she said. She wore

a **VISIT MARS** shirt and those round glasses that made her look like a cool college student.

"Thanks."

Fabián sauntered up, sporting a jacket with enamel pins and tight black jeans. He kissed my cheek.

"Sorry about your aunt, P," he said, sitting next to me.

"At least she wasn't detained too long, or shipped off somewhere she didn't know," I whispered back.

Fabián's brown eyes flickered for a second. "That's right. Your aunt's safe." He wrapped an arm around me, and I rested my head on his shoulder. We were going to get through this. The rest of freshman year was going to be a cakewalk compared to all the challenges we'd already been through.

Ruth took a bite of stew. "So, what is everyone wearing to Homecoming this weekend?"

"Wait, is your mom letting you go?" Fabián asked.

"She says I can't have a date, but I'm still allowed to go."

"So, we're going to meet each other there," Naomi said, turning to Ruth. I could tell she was squeezing Ruth's hand under the table.

"Ugh, get a room." Fabián sighed.

"You two are seriously too cute," I said. It felt good to see Ruth back to her hopeful self.

"What about you, Parvin? Do you have a dress?" Ruth asked.

I sipped some more kimchi jjigae, chewing a piece of spicy cabbage. "Not yet." Ameh Sara was supposed to help me shop for a dress in person, but I went online and pulled a bunch of choices to send to her instead. "It's not like I have to match my outfit with my date's." Though that technically wasn't true. I was rolling up to Homecoming with someone, and I roughly knew what kind of color I should get to match their outfit. They just didn't know it yet.

Fabián perked up. "So, you're not going with Matty?" he asked.

I swiveled back to him. "How did you know he asked me?"

Fabián shrugged. "He asked me if everything was okay at rehearsal when you missed school yesterday. I told him what happened, and he said he'd asked you."

Ruth squealed. "Wait, Operation Matty Fumero was a success?!"

I nodded. It didn't feel like that much of an accomplishment at this point.

"Hold up—you had a plan for Matty to ask you to Homecoming—and he asked you?" Naomi said, her light brown eyes shocked.

"It wasn't that hard," I said miserably into my soup.

Naomi raised her eyebrows. "That is some serious self-actualization! Tell me all your secrets." As if Naomi "4.3 GPA" Johnson needed tips from *me*.

"But you're not going with Matty," Fabián clarified.

I nodded.

"So he's solo," Fabián stated, as if just adding it up.

"I guess?" I replied. "Why do you care? I thought you were thinking of going to Homecoming with Austin?"

"Do you even like Matty anymore?" Fabián wheedled.

I shrugged. "Nah."

"Excellent," he said. Suddenly he got up, his lunch half finished.

"Where are you going?" Ruth asked.

Fabián smiled. "I have some business to take care of."

"Like what? You don't even have a bank account yet!" I retorted. Which was true—all the money from his influencer gigs went straight to his parents.

Fabián just gave me a sly grin and walked away, whistling.

. . .

AFTER CLASS
3:00 P.M.

I'd never seen Amir at school unless we were meeting at the bleachers. James K. Polk High was just too big to randomly run into people unless you memorized their class schedule. But I knew he was leaving English at the end of the day.

I waited for him outside his classroom, and he looked surprised to see me.

"Hey, Amir, can we talk?" I asked as his class spilled into the hallway.

"What's up?"

"Let's go someplace quiet," I said, pushing the door open to head outside. I sat down on the low brick wall, scooching over so he could sit next to me.

"This isn't going to be a fun conversation, is it?" Amir sighed.

I winced. I'd thought a lot about Amir this week. And Matty. And Wesley. And how I had been relying on guys to build my self-esteem. But that wasn't how self-esteem worked. Only you could decide how high or low an opinion you held of yourself.

"The truth is," I began, awkwardly kicking the wall

beneath me, "I like you, too. But I'm not sure I'm ready for a relationship right now, and I think I need to be boy-free for a while."

I exhaled. I got it out all in one go—like I'd practiced in the mirror last night—and it had paid off. Even though it was fun to just blurt things out, it also felt good to think things through before you said them sometimes. I wasn't Loud Parvin right now, but I wasn't Quiet Parvin, either. I was someone more thoughtful. Someone who was trying to be better.

I couldn't just brush off my feelings anymore or bury them deep down. I had to give them space and share them clearly if I wanted people to get to know the real me. The Real Parvin.

The fact was, I felt closer to Amir than anyone I'd ever had a crush on. But I'd jumped from Wesley to Matty to Amir so fast, it was hard to even remember what life was like before I let boys rule my brain. I was still scared of doing something wrong with Amir, or getting hurt again.

He ran his hands through his hair, the curls flopping back into his eyes. "I don't understand. You like me, but you don't want to go out with me?"

I shook my head. "It's not just that. There's stuff I need to work on. Like being a better friend. And a better me, actually. Because I've been pretty crappy to myself lately."

Amir sighed. "So, you're saying you just want to be friends?"

I nodded, my face set. "That's what I want."

Amir held out his hand. I shook it.

"For the record, I still want to be friends, too." Amir

tried to smile, but faltered. God, he was so cute. "But I think it might be best if we change Farsi partners for a while."

"That makes sense." My heart tanked. I'd finally gotten the hang of Farsi school, thanks to Amir's help. I didn't know how it would be without him as my study buddy.

"Also, I forgot to tell you—we have to write our own poem for Sunday's class. Aghayeh Khosrowshahi says you don't have to do it if you don't want to, since . . . well . . ."

"Thanks for letting me know."

Amir nodded and stayed there, our legs kicking back and forth against the brick wall.

"The student journal starts up next week," Amir said into the silence. "Finally."

"That's so great!" I knew Amir had worked really hard to make that happen. Now he'd get to show his parents what he could do.

"Yeah," he said. "We still need more content, though. It's tough starting without a full club roster."

"Well, let me know if you need any help with it," I offered. I doubted he'd take me up on it, though. Writing was not my strong suit.

"Actually, do you think you could write an article for the first issue?"

"About what?" I asked, flabbergasted. "Like a restaurant review or something?"

Amir laughed. "No, like . . . a piece about immigration?"

I thought for a minute. I hadn't really considered sharing our family's story beyond telling my friends. But then I thought of how we were in the museum yesterday, surrounded by people who had no idea what had happened to

Ameh Sara. People should know. They needed to know how people were treated at our borders.

"Okay," I said. "Deal." It was my turn to hold my hand out. Amir shook it.

. . .

HOME
7:00 P.M.

Mom was actually making dinner tonight. I think it was lasagna. Or some kind of pasta served in a casserole dish. It was best not to look too closely.

"What's the occasion?" I asked, pulling a piece of melted cheese from the top of the pan. Mom shooed me away from the kitchen island.

"Actually, we have company tonight."

My eyes narrowed. "Who?"

And then, the doorbell rang. "Salaam, bitches!" I heard someone exclaim in the hallway, letting themselves in.

"Hanna!" Mom chided.

Wait, Hanna? From Farsi school?

"Sorry, Mrs. Mohammadi. 'Sup, Parvin," Hanna said, waltzing into our kitchen with a makeup case in each hand.

"Hey," I said. What was she doing here? Hanna was a senior in the next county over. Was she teaching my mom Farsi basics or something?

"Your ameh enlisted my help," Hanna explained. "Our mamans knew each other, back in Iran."

"Oh," I replied. That was cool. What did that have to do with her being here?

"I'm gonna show you how to be a badass Persian bitch," Hanna said, slamming the makeup cases on the kitchen counter.

"Hanna!" Mom scolded again.

"Er, I mean, zan," Hanna said, using the word for *woman*.

"Really?" I asked. Hanna was the coolest Iranian American I knew. Her eyeliner was like a master class in application. I couldn't believe she was going to teach me that stuff.

"Really, dustam."

Hanna just called me her friend.

I had a friend date.

"Why don't you girls head upstairs, and I'll bring up dinner when it's ready, okay?" Mom said, winking at me.

"What is that? Deep-dish pizza?" Hanna asked, looking suspiciously at dinner.

"It's lasagna!" Mom sighed, exasperated.

Hanna nodded, following me up the stairs to my room.

"I don't trust any dinner that doesn't involve polow," she whispered to me.

"You eat rice with every meal?" I asked, shocked. What kind of parent had time to cook Iranian rice every night?

She put her arm around me. "Oh, Parvin jaan, I have so much to teach you."

. . .

MY ROOM
LATER

Hanna put her makeup cases on my desk and pivoted toward me, her eyes narrowing as she inspected my face. I inched back a little farther on my bed. Hanna was not messing around.

"Okay, we don't have a lot of time since it's a school night, but your ameh said it was an emergency. Let's start with the basics. What's your skincare regimen?"

"Um, I have face wash?" I shrugged. "And I put on moisturizer?"

I handed Hanna the moisturizer I used. She inspected it.

"Where's the SPF? Do you not wear sunscreen?" She looked horrified.

I shrugged. "I've never gotten sunburned. Mom says I don't need it."

"*What?*" Hanna cried. "Just because you're brown doesn't mean you can't get skin cancer!"

She looked distraught. We were only five minutes into this impromptu womanhood lesson and I'd already failed it.

"My mom thinks I'm fine. She burns way more easily."

Hanna sat down next to me on the bed. "Parvin, your mom's skin tone is literally marshmallow. It's different for her, okay? But you still need to wear SPF."

I never knew SPF was so important. Dad just slathered olive oil onto himself whenever he was worried about getting crispy at the beach, saying, "That's what we did in the Caspian."

Hanna got up and started riffling through her kit. "Here's some sunscreen you can use until we can go to the store," she said, tossing me a small jar. "Now show me the box your ameh gave you."

I got the box out from under my bed and handed it to Hanna for inspection. While she went through it, I took the opportunity to stare at her. Her dark brown skin was so clear, her curls shiny and defined without any frizz. Would I ever look that flawless?

Hanna got out a clear bottle.

"Oooh, this is an Iranian brand. I haven't seen this before!" she said, opening up the package. Instantly, my room smelled of rosewater, and I wondered what Amir was doing right now. Probably writing some incredible article for the school journal.

"What is it?" I asked, looking at the golden-tipped bottle.

"It's for ingrown hairs," Hanna said, handing it to me. "Sara said you had a pretty big one. Let's see it."

I sighed and edged up my tie-dyed skirt to my thigh. There was the ingrown hair, so big it almost looked like a cyst at this point. It didn't hurt if I didn't mess with it, but it was still purple and pus-filled.

"Oof, that looks intense"—Hanna winced—"I'm gonna get it out, okay?"

I nodded. Hanna washed her hands, then pinched her thumbs around the bump and began to squeeze. The pain shot up my leg. It hurt so much my eyes began to water.

"Breathe," she ordered. I took a deep breath, and it hurt a little less. I felt something give in my thigh, and Hanna held up the ingrown hair triumphantly: a kernel of hard skin with a thread of hair inside. It was absolutely disgusting, and also so, so satisfying to have it taken out of my body.

"See? The hair had folded in on itself. You need to exfoliate more often to prevent them."

She took the bottle Sara had mailed and dabbed some of the liquid onto a cotton ball, placing it where the ingrown hair had been.

She pressed down. "This kills the bad bacteria and prevents it from happening in the same spot again," Hanna explained. I nodded, flinching at the stinging sensation. I wished I'd remembered to write all this down. She began looking at my arms for some reason, and then my face.

"Parvin, what have you been doing to yourself? You have razor burns all over your arms. And some bruising on your eyebrows. Have you been overplucking?"

"Huh?" I asked. Hanna led me to my bathroom and pointed in the mirror.

"See? Those little purple and red flecks you get on your eyebrows are bruises. You've been messing with them too much."

I leaned toward the mirror and saw what Hanna was talking about—there were small pinpricks of bruised skin where I'd been shoving my tweezers every day, back when I was trying to copy hairless leading ladies.

"And these red marks on your arms mean you've been shaving too much. See how dry and irritated your skin is?"

She pointed to the little red bumps on my arms. Even though I'd stopped shaving my arms after my confrontation with Wesley, I could still see the razor burn. I looked away, not sure what to say.

"You know body hair isn't gross, right?" Hanna said, turning me from the mirror so that I faced her. "You don't have to do this stuff if you don't want to, or if it doesn't feel good."

"I know, I know." I sighed. "It's just . . . easier," I finished softly.

What would people say if I rolled up to school with my hairy arms? Or a full unibrow? Never mind how horrified people like Wesley and Teighan would be. The whole school would probably be weirded out.

Hanna nodded, her curls bouncing. "I used to think that, too. But body hair is normal in other parts of the world. It's only in countries like the US that people spend so much time getting rid of it. Did you know that in Iran, a unibrow was a sign of beauty?"

"Really?" I couldn't believe it. Did that mean I was naturally beautiful?

"Yep, the old Qajar dynasty has paintings of women with unibrows." She held up her phone with a photo of a classical illustration featuring a woman with one thick eyebrow across her forehead. "I've stopped plucking my eyebrows, so you can kind of see mine growing back in." Hanna pointed to her forehead, and sure enough, I could see the black fuzz that met in the middle of her eyebrows. I hadn't even noticed it. It actually looked, well, kind of cool.

"Just think about it, okay?" Hanna said, patting my back. She turned to the box of Sara's stuff while I mulled over what she said. I'd always thought body hair was something you got rid of, but I never knew there were cultures that thought it was beautiful, or something to be desired.

"And you already know how to use this, right?" Hanna held up a bottle full of what looked like oil.

"Like . . . for cooking?" I shrugged. I didn't know how to use oil, much less cook with it.

Hanna's eyes went wide. "No, Parvin! This is for your hair. To make your curls less frizzy."

I stared at her blankly. "Do I comb it in?"

Hanna gasped. "Parvin! You have curly hair! You *never* brush it dry. *EVER*."

Hanna took away the hair oil and said, "This is more serious than I thought. Homecoming is this weekend, right? I'll come over beforehand and help you get ready."

"But I—" I started.

"Oh, don't worry, I'll help you pick a dress," Hanna said, packing up her things.

"But what about—"

"It's fine, our school's Homecoming already happened." Hanna waved me away.

"So—" I said, trying hard to get a word in edgewise. Hanna cut me off again, cupping my chin in her hand and staring straight into my eyes.

"Parvin, worrying is bad for your face. Now I'm going to go before your mom tries to make me eat that thing for dinner. I will see you Saturday."

She sauntered out of my room and closed the door with a snap. I flopped back onto my bed, clutching my new bottles of beauty product.

I had a lot to learn.

Saturday

HOME
5:45 P.M.

I didn't have much time before I had to leave tonight, but I knew Ameh Sara would want to see how I looked. She picked up on the first ring.

"Parvin joon, you look amazing!"

I grinned, walking backward in my bedroom so she could see my full outfit for Homecoming. Hanna had helped me pick a dress that was a cross between orange and salmon, and it made my tan skin glow.

"Thanks, Ameh."

"I knew Hanna would do a great job. Look at you!"

I twirled. I couldn't help it. I felt like a vibrant, radiant orb of shiny clothing and pretty skin. Even trying not to smile was a struggle, that's how giddy I was.

"I wish you could be here, Ameh," I said, my little bubble of happiness deflating a bit. I still couldn't believe my aunt wasn't going to be able to see me off for one of the biggest dances of my life. It wasn't fair, and I wasn't sure I'd ever be able to forgive this country for taking her away from me.

"I wish I could be there, too, joonam." Even through the computer screen, her eyes looked wet. I had to remind myself not to cry or I'd ruin my makeup.

"Do you have a date to the dance?" she asked. I swallowed.

"Sort of?" I replied.

Sara didn't say anything, she just chewed on the ends of the laces that ran through her sweatshirt's hood.

"I ruined it, Ameh. I thought . . . I thought I had to be someone different to get a date. And I ignored the people who already liked me the way I am."

Sara took the laces out of her mouth and moved closer to the computer screen.

"Oh, ameh! You are so great the way you are. I wish I could be there to tell you that in person. But you are enough, okay? You don't need to be anything else."

I tipped my eyes up. This mascara was not waterproof.

"Thanks, Ameh. I needed to hear that," I sniffed.

She smiled. "Just be yourself. I know people always say that, but only you get to decide what that means."

I smiled back, my eyes still watery.

"I will," I promised.

"Parvin! Time to go!" Mom called up the stairs.

"I still need to set your makeup!" Hanna shouted after her. She was downstairs with my parents, sipping chai.

"Go, go!" Ameh Sara shooed me away from the computer.

"I'll call you tomorrow after Farsi class, okay?"

"Okay, azizam." Sara waved and hung up.

I took one last look in the mirror and headed downstairs.

. . .

FRONT PORCH
6:00 P.M.

"Stand back and close your eyes," Hanna commanded from our porch swing. She got out a big bottle of makeup-setting spray, and I closed my eyes just before she doused me with it.

"Now your makeup won't move all night!" She grinned. I tried to grin back, but my face was frozen in place from the spray.

The limo pulled up. It had been Mom's idea to rent one. I gave her a big hug, trying not to smudge my makeup.

"I love you, Mom."

She squeezed me back. "I love you, too, sweetie. But let me grab a photo before you leave! You look so beautiful. Mahmoud! We're taking photos!"

"Yeah, I need a photo for the 'after' picture," Hanna piped up. I didn't even realize Hanna had taken a "before" photo. Soon, Mom, Dad, Hanna, and I were all assembled on our porch, and I couldn't remember the last time our house felt so loud.

Dad got out his nerdy Polaroid camera and snapped

some photos while Mom went in with her smartphone. Meanwhile, Hanna got photos from every angle, instructing me to put my arm on my hip and turn slightly toward the camera to set off the pinks and oranges in my dress.

"Guys! I'm gonna be late," I whined. Hanna shooed me toward the car before Mom could start her my-little-girl-is-all-grown-up speech. Meanwhile, Dad opened the door for me to get into the limo, as if I were a princess or something on my way to a ball.

Here goes nothing.

. . .

LATER

The limo pulled up in front of Ruth's house and honked.

"Can you open the sunroof?" I called to the driver. I stuck my head through and waved at Mrs. Song, who was peeking out the window.

"Parvin, what's going on? I thought we were meeting at school!" Ruth shouted, appearing in the doorway. She looked stunning in her pink tulle dress, and she had her hair up in two buns on the top of her head. I held up the corsage I'd gotten her, made of white roses with a sparkly pink band.

"Get in, loser," I shouted. "I'm taking you to Homecoming!"

Ruth squealed. "Let me get my purse!"

Mrs. Song appeared in the doorway, smiling.

"Annyeonghaseyo, Parvin!"

"Annyeonghaseyo, Mrs. Song. Thanks for helping me with the surprise." I'd texted Mrs. Song from the museum asking if I could take Ruth to Homecoming as a friend, even though Mrs. Song was scary. Thank goodness she'd said yes. Hanna had helped me find a dress that matched Ruth's, and I brought my makeup kit so I could give her a full Homecoming look in the limo.

"Is anyone else in the limo with you?" Mrs. Song walked toward the car suspiciously, probably thinking I'd squirreled Naomi away somewhere.

"No, ma'am," I replied. "But we're picking up Fabián on the way." He'd been cagey when I asked him whether he had a date, so I'd gotten him a boutonniere, along with some special eyeliner, just in case.

She nodded. "But you're meeting Naomi at the dance, right?"

"Er . . . ," I replied, not sure what to say. I stood there awkwardly in the sunroof, staring down at Mrs. Song.

She opened the limo door, and I popped my head back into the car. Mrs. Song sat down next to me. She wore one of those intimidating all-white cashmere sweaters that was probably dry-clean only. "Just make sure Ruth doesn't get hurt, okay? I don't want things getting too serious before she has to take her exams. Will you do that for me?"

I nodded. "I will." Though I was pretty sure Ruth had already decided where she and Naomi would be honeymooning and what they'd name their children.

"Good!" Mrs. Song clapped her hands. "Because if she does get hurt, I'll tell your parents and you'll be grounded forever."

"What?" I cried.

"Just kidding." Mrs. Song cackled as she exited the limo. But I didn't think she was joking.

Ruth reappeared with her purse, and Mrs. Song insisted

on taking a billion photos of her bright pink outfit. Ruth ran to the limo as soon as she finished the photo shoot.

"Wait!" Mrs. Song shouted. "I need a photo with both of you!"

"Come on, Ruthie," I said, gesturing to the sunroof. We both popped up, and she wrapped her arm around me as Mrs. Song snapped photos of us on her phone, the two of us grinning like idiots in our first-ever limo ride.

"Bye, Oma!" Ruth shouted. We ducked back inside the limo as the driver started the car. "I can't believe you rented a limo!"

"I wanted my friends to have a good Homecoming," I said. I placed the corsage around her wrist.

"You mean *best friends*," Ruth corrected. Then we were off, heading to Fabián's so we could arrive in style.

. . .

HOMECOMING
7:00 P.M.

Fabián, Ruth, and I looked like we were in a music video, that's how awesome our outfits were. Hanna had helped me wash my hair properly (with sulfate-free shampoo), moisturize (with facial oil and SPF), and do my makeup (with warm colors that flattered my skin tone). Basically, I looked Instagram-famous.

Fabián went all out on his outfit. Ruth had helped him embroider a black mariachi jacket with silver thread, and I gave him an excellent smoky eye in the limo. His red charro tie matched impeccably with his red Chuck Taylors, and his boutonniere of black roses was the perfect accessory.

The limo dropped us off at the main doors, and we got out as classmates stared. Did they think we were sophomores, or even juniors? I grinned at Fabián and Ruth, and they both grinned back. It was nice to be the center of attention, even if some people thought it was too loud or too showy or too obnoxious. I had given my friends the Homecoming entrance they deserved, even without Ameh Sara's help.

We strolled into the gym, and Ruth gasped. The entire space had been absolutely transformed.

"Don't get too excited"—Fabián rolled his eyes at the decorations—"these are the set pieces from *Twelfth Night* with balloons."

Still. It was impressive to see wooden trees hung with gold streamers in every corner.

"Ruth!" a voice cried out. Naomi floated over in a vision of light blue, her locs twisted into a complicated updo studded with tiny pearls. Her brown skin glowed, either from her expertly applied highlighter or from sheer joy.

"Naomi!" Ruth squealed. "You look incredible!" They stepped onto the dance floor, and Ruth looked blissed out in Naomi's arms. It made me glad I was able to help give her the fairy-tale entrance she'd always wanted. As Naomi and Ruth slow-danced, staring into each other's eyes, I realized that it wouldn't be just me, Fabián, and Ruth anymore. Our little circle was growing.

"They look so happy," I said to Fabián.

"Yeah," he said. "Wanna dance?"

"Please don't make me do a death drop."

Fabián laughed. "I won't."

We swayed on the floor, and my orangey-pink dress next to Fabián's dark outfit made us look like the perfect

Halloween duo. I could tell Fabián was holding back, his feet itching to do more complicated steps, but he kept it simple for me.

"So, you turned Emerson Cheng down," Fabián said.

"Yep."

"And Sir Thompson."

"How did you know?" I asked.

"And Matty Fumero," Fabián continued, ignoring me.

"Where is this going, Fabián?" I asked.

"And Amir Shirazi," he finished, looking at me.

I bit my lip. "I'm just not ready."

Fabián nodded, twirling me out of nowhere.

"Hey!"

He laughed. "Sometimes love just happens to you, Parvin," Fabián said, suddenly turning serious. My eyes narrowed. I could count on one hand the amount of times Fabián Castor had been serious, including our big fight. "You can't really control who you like, you know? Or who likes you back."

I nodded. Truer words had never been trued. This time last year I would have begged for a boy to like me, *any* boy. But now I knew that you couldn't just like someone because you decided you wanted to. And that you couldn't control who you liked, either.

"May I cut in?"

Matty appeared over my shoulder. He wore a charcoal-gray suit with high trousers that ended at his ankle, along with some cool suspenders. His hair flopped over his eye, and he flicked it away, smiling at both of us.

"Oh . . . um . . ." I floundered. It had felt like Fabián and I were having a Big Talk, and I wasn't sure I wanted it to end yet.

"Remember how I said you couldn't control who you liked?" Fabián said anxiously.

I nodded. "Yeah. So?"

Fabián gulped. Gulped! "Well . . . um . . ."

And then Matty took Fabián's hand. Matty wasn't asking if he could dance with me—he was asking if he could dance with Fabián!

"Oh!" I started. "Oh, sorry, I didn't understand . . ." I could feel my face turn bright red. I stepped aside, letting Matty take my place.

"Sorry, Parvin," Fabián said, grimacing. "This wasn't how I wanted to tell you." He glared at Matty, and Matty gave me an apologetic shrug. Dang. They were both glowing as much as Naomi and Ruth were. I guess they really liked each other.

"No, no, this is great," I said, mustering a smile.

"You sure?" Fabián asked, his eyes searching mine. "Matty, could you give us a minute?"

"Of course." Matty nodded, heading back to some kids I recognized from band.

"Listen," Fabián said, looking uncomfortable. "I wanted to tell you I really liked him earlier, but then you weren't at school on Monday, and the next day when you said you turned him down, you didn't seem that upset about it . . . and I just kind of went for it."

I grabbed Fabián's hands as the song changed, and we switched to an awkward shuffle. I glanced back at Matty on the edge of the dance floor, laughing at one of his friends' jokes. Did I even really know him? Did he have siblings? What was his favorite candy? Why did he play the trumpet?

I sighed, turning back to Fabián. "Honestly, I think I liked the idea of Matty more than Matty himself. I was trying to get over Wesley, and Matty was a good distraction." Bringing up Wesley's name didn't hurt anymore. It felt good saying it out loud and not feeling ashamed.

Fabián pulled me closer. "I'm sorry I didn't mention Matty earlier," he said into my cheek. "Though, to be fair, I've been crushing on him since day one."

I nuzzled him back. "I wish you'd told me you were going to ask him. But I'm happy you're with someone you really like."

Fabián pulled back and smiled. "God, he's handsome, isn't he?"

I laughed. "He seriously is."

"And you're sure you're all right? I don't have to dance with him if you're not okay with it."

"I'm positive. You two make a cute couple."

He kissed me on the cheek. "Thanks, P. I'm definitely going to make him do a death drop."

. . .

HOMECOMING
8:00 P.M.

I thought everything would be different this year, but here I was, sitting on the bleachers at a school dance, next to the soda table once again.

Maybe high school wasn't so different from middle school after all.

Sir had already asked me twice if I wanted a Shirley Temple. They weren't being served in the gym. Where would he have even gotten that drink? From a cooler in his locker? The mind reels.

I'd resolved to just watch beauty tutorials on my phone and not make eye contact with anyone the rest of the night. I'd used my selfie camera twice to make sure my curls weren't frizzing, but thankfully the oil Ameh Sara sent me was working. I spied Wesley and Teighan in the corner of the gym, the two of them awkwardly trying to move to a fast song. I doubted he'd even noticed me here. Why had I tried so hard to impress him? It all felt so stupid now.

I had hoped that my plan of rolling up to Homecoming with my friends and not some boy meant that we'd be spending the whole night together, but it looked like everyone had already moved on.

This had been the longest week ever, and I was so ready for it to be over.

"Is this seat taken?"

I turned around. There, sitting down next to me, was Jake Gyllenhaal from the movie *Prince of Persia*. Except this time, the prince was actually Persian.

"*Amir?*" I asked.

He waggled his eyebrows, doing his best Aghayeh Khosrowshahi impression. "Salaam!"

I laughed, still taking him in. His curly hair wasn't covering his face anymore; he'd slicked it back in a way that showed off his huge brown eyes and thick lashes. His black suit fit him perfectly, paired with a thin paisley tie.

He looked, if possible, ten times cuter.

"I . . . um . . . hi." I gulped. Had I really made out with this Iranian Adonis? It didn't seem possible.

"You look nice," Amir said, smiling.

"You . . . too," I yelped. Be strong, Parvin. Be strong.

Now was the moment to be True Parvin, the kind of girl who didn't let boys define her self-worth, no matter how handsome they were.

"Wanna dance?" Amir asked, holding out his hand. I felt butterflies swirl in my stomach, the kind that felt good and didn't cause indigestion.

"Yes," I said with every bone in my body.

. . .

HOMECOMING
LATER

Amir and I danced so much I kicked off the fancy heels Hanna had let me borrow. How did women wear those things all day? My makeup, however, hadn't budged.

"Listen," Amir shouted over the music on the dance floor. "I brought some chia seeds with me. What if we put them in the punch, then tell everyone it's contaminated? I know how much you like pranks."

My face lit up. This *was* a good prank. "We could tell everyone it's frog spawn from the bio department. They'll be so grossed out!"

"Exactly!" Amir cried. A lot of Iranian iced drinks have chia, which is a little black seed the size of a sesame that makes all the liquid surrounding it plump up into a jelly. It's supposed to be really good for you, but it definitely looks like frog spawn.

I watched as Amir "ladled" himself a cup of punch at the soda table while secretly adding the seeds. He gave me a covert thumbs-up as he dropped them in. I swooned. Even though Wesley and I had done a dozen pranks before, in that moment, I realized *I'd* been the one to come up with them all. I'd never had someone else suggest their own scheme. Amir was even more wonderful than I'd realized.

I couldn't remember the last time I'd had this much fun. I thought it would be weird, each of us all paired off with a different person, but when Amir and I had joined the group, it felt like our crew was finally complete. Just then, someone approached the punch bowl. Amir winked at me from across the gym.

"What's he doing?" Ruth asked. We watched as Amir pointed frantically at the punch bowl, planting the frog-spawn rumor with some sophomore. The sophomore looked horrified at the bright pink drink that was now plumping up with chia seeds.

"He's pulling a pretty good prank."

"Oh, Parvin." Ruth shook her head, but she smiled. "Wanna dance?"

But Naomi cut in. "Nice try, Ruth, it's my turn to dance with Parvin."

Ruth beamed at Naomi, her eyes about to pop out of her head with little hearts. Naomi took me onto the dance floor right as another fast song came on, and we jumped like crazy, our hair bouncing up and down as we sang every word. I peeked over Naomi's shoulder and saw Fabián dancing with Amir, and Ruth dancing with Matty. I was smiling so hard my face hurt.

"Come on," Naomi said during the chorus, and she led us over to the rest of the gang where we formed a circle, all of us shouting the lyrics.

This was what I had hoped Homecoming would be like. This was what I had dreamed of.

After that song, the DJ switched to a slower one, probably to make sure nobody fainted from jumping up and down so much.

Amir walked over, suddenly looking shy, and I could see everyone coupling up around us. I squinted past a balloon tower and even saw Yessenia López dancing with Emerson Cheng, who had some sparklers in his back pocket.

That made sense.

"May I?" Amir asked. I nodded, and he put his arm around my waist. We shuffled back and forth.

"Did you finish your Farsi homework?" he asked, trying to make small talk.

"Yeah, I did, actually." I had finished it earlier this week instead of leaving it to the last minute, for once.

I rested my head against his chest. What was I doing? I thought I hadn't wanted to date Amir, but here we were, dancing together. The truth was, I had no idea what I wanted. I thought I had, like wanting Matty Fumero to like me, or for Wesley to be my boyfriend. But right now, I had no clue.

Amir placed his chin on the top of my head, and I smiled to myself.

Sorry, Principal Saulk, but maybe it was okay that I didn't know what I wanted.

Maybe that was the best place to start.

Before I could get *too* thoughtful, though, the fire alarm went off.

"CHENG!" Fabián roared.

Sunday

FARSI SCHOOL
11:00 A.M.

Hanna looked at the pictures I took from last night before the fire department came. "See how your dress complements your skin's undertones?" She pointed to the photo. "It's supposed to make you look warm, not wash you out. That's how you know it's working."

I think Hanna was proud of the look she'd made for me.

"Next week I'll teach you how to deal with oily skin, okay?" she offered.

"Yes, please." I nodded gratefully. My face had gotten shiny from dancing so much last night.

Just then, Amir walked into the Farsi classroom, his hair still styled from Homecoming. Hanna raised a perfectly shaped eyebrow at me and turned back to her poem.

"Hey," Amir said, sitting down next to me. I was glad he wanted to stay Farsi partners, after all.

"Hey," I said, and smiled.

"All right! Today we will be reading our poems," Aghayeh Khosrowshahi announced from the front of the class. He had a thermos of black tea sitting next to him, and I could tell from the way he bounced on his toes that it was probably already empty.

"Who wants to go first?" he asked, his eyes roving the classroom. For the first time in Farsi class, I raised my hand.

"Parvin joon!" he exclaimed. "Befarmain," he said, gesturing. I stood up at my desk and cleared my throat, the words in Farsi tumbling out.

من فکر می‌کنم هر ستاره‌ای برای خودش
یک اندازه درخشش و روشنایی دارد،
چرا که آن‌ها
در دنیای خودشان روشن‌ترینند.
و همین برایشان کافی است، همین روشنایی.

The classroom clapped, whether out of pity for what had happened last week or in support of my poem, it was hard to tell. But I think everyone was glad to see me actually volunteering in class for once.

I sat back down. Hanna mouthed, *Good job,* to me. Amir gave my hand a squeeze.

Even though I wasn't wearing makeup, I knew I was glowing.

I looked down at my desk, where I had the translated version of my poem to hand in to Aghayeh Khosrowshahi. I was so amazed by those little sentences. After everything that had happened, after all the ups and downs I'd had this school year, it felt like a talisman that would keep me strong.

I was proud of how hard I'd worked on it. And I was proud of what had happened when I tried to be my true self and took the job of being Parvin seriously. I read the poem again, the English version echoing in my head.

I think that every star
Shines a different amount,
Because to them
They are the brightest thing in their world.
To them, they are enough. Their shine is enough.

AUTHOR'S NOTE

ON JANUARY 27, 2017, the Muslim Ban was signed into law via executive order. I remember traveling to Denver International Airport the next day to protest, joining hundreds of other Coloradans as we stood in support of an Iranian family who was being unjustly detained despite having a legal visa. A call for Farsi translators went out, saying the family was having trouble communicating with the DHS and CBP agents. I remember the feeling of knowing my Farsi was not good enough to help that poor family, and I drove home stewing in feelings of anger, fear, and shame.

I write this on the day the Muslim Ban was rescinded. But we will never forget the families that were torn apart, the students who couldn't attend the universities that accepted them, and the hate and vitriol the United States was sanctioned to spew.

ACKNOWLEDGMENTS

THIS BOOK WOULD not have been possible without my agent, Jim McCarthy. I am so grateful for your lightning-fast responses, hand-holding, and negotiating on my behalf. You and the team at Dystel, Goderich, and Bourret are simply The Best.

Huge thank-you to my editor, Stacey Barney. You have made this such a stronger (and funnier!) book. I'm so grateful you took a chance on *Parvin*.

Big thanks to Caitlin Tutterow, who I would walk through fire with, or a Zoom call about Farsi translation (same thing), anytime.

Thank you to my publisher Jennifer Klonsky at G. P. Putnam's Sons Books for Young Readers for supporting my weird little book. Khayley mamnoon to Samira Iravani for such a gorgeous cover and to Jasmine Moshiri for not only modeling but taking her own photos in the middle of a pandemic.

To Kate Heidinger, the very first person to set eyes on this manuscript, you truly are ride or die. I would go to Costco and buy you Hot Cheetos in bulk anytime. Back when this book was just a forty-thousand-word lump of Google Docs, I hired the incredible Kate Racculia to help me polish my manuscript and get an agent. It worked! You can hire her at kateracculia.com.

Thank you to Romy Natalia Goldberg, Viniyanka Prasad, Axie Oh, Ben Dwork, and Tina Ehsanipour, the best critique partners a girl could ever ask for. Massive thank-you to Brenna Yovanoff for reading *Parvin* and walking me through the entire publication process. Gracias a mi primo Andrés Proaño Mattioli y mi cuate Pablo Aron. Thank you, Kit Song, for the excellent soybean joke.

Thanks to the team at Penguin for making this such a wonderful experience. Cindy Howle, Anne Heausler, Chandra Wohleber, Ariela Rudy Zaltzman, and Yekta Khaghani: I am so grateful. There is nothing more satisfying than reading your copyeditor's comments and seeing the reluctant "lol" peppered in there along with the reminder that you don't, in fact, speak English properly. I still have no idea how commas work.

Thank you to Felicity Vallence, James Akinaka, Shannon Spann, Kara Brammer, Lathea Mondesir, and Suki Boynton. I could not be in better hands. And speaking of hands, thank you, Natalie Vimont, for fixing mine when they didn't work anymore.

Enormous thank-you to my mother for always supporting me and for teaching me to be such an enthusiastic reader. My father helped me write the poem at the end in Farsi—merci, Baba. The biggest thank-you of all goes to my husband for encouraging me to pursue my writing career and helping me get this far.

To the people reading this: thank you for giving this book a chance. All my life I was told I could never be a writer. The fact that you stuck with me this far means the world.

Lastly, thank you to my daughter. I wrote this book before you were even conceived, and the dedication long before that. It's looking like your dad's genes have won the war, so here we are, three generations of mothers and daughters who look nothing like each other. May this book be a mirror in times of loneliness and a testament to why you will always be enough. I love you so much.